The Defence

The Defence

A novel

VLADIMIR NABOKOV

*Translated by Michael Scammell
in collaboration with the author*

Weidenfeld and Nicolson
5 Winsley Street London W1

The original Russian text of this novel first appeared in book form under the title *Zashchita Luzhina* (Berlin, 1930). The present version appeared originally in *The New Yorker*.

Reprinted 1969

SBN 297 17996 9

Printed in Great Britain by
Lowe & Brydone (Printers) Ltd., London

To Véra

FOREWORD

THE Russian title of this novel is *Zashchita Luzhina*, which means 'the Luzhin defense' and refers to a chess defense supposedly invented by my creature, Grandmaster Luzhin: the name rhymes with 'illusion' if pronounced thickly enough to deepen the 'u' into 'oo'. I began writing it in the spring of 1929, at Le Boulou – a small spa in the Pyrenees Orientales where I was hunting butterflies – and finished it the same year in Berlin. I remember with special limpidity a sloping slab of rock, in the ulex- and ilex-clad hills, where the main thematic idea of the book first came to me. Some curious additional information might be given if I took myself more seriously.

Zaschchita Luzhina under my penname, 'V. Sirin,' ran in the émigré Russian quarterly *Sovremennye Zapiski* (Paris) and immediately afterwards was brought out in book form by the émigré publishing house Slovo (Berlin, 1930). That paper-bound edition, 234 pp., 21 by 4 cm., jacket a solid dull black with gilt lettering, is now rare and may grow even rarer.

Poor Luzhin has had to wait thirty-five years for an English-language edition. True, there was a promising flurry in the late thirties when an American publisher showed interest in it, but he turned out to belong to the type of publisher who dreams of becoming a male muse to his author, and our brief conjunction ended abruptly upon his suggesting I replace chess by music and make Luzhin a demented violinist.

Rereading this novel today, replaying the moves of its plot. I feel rather like Anderssen fondly recalling his sacrifice of both Rooks to the unfortunate and noble Kieseritsky – who is doomed to accept it over and over again through an infinity of textbooks, with a question mark for monument. My story was difficult to compose, but I greatly enjoyed taking advantage of this or that image and scene to introduce a fatal pattern into Luzhin's life and to endow the description of a garden, a journey, a sequence of humdrum events, with the semblance of a game of skill, and, especially in the final chapters, with that of a regular chess attack demolishing the innermost elements of the poor fellow's sanity. In this connection, I would like to spare the time and effort of hack reviewers – and, generally, persons who move their lips when reading and cannot be expected to tackle a dialogueless novel when so much can be gleaned from its foreword – by drawing their attention to the first appearance of the frosted-window theme (associated with Luzhin's suicide, or rather suimate) as early as Chapter Eleven, or to the pathetic way my morose grandmaster remembers his professional journeys not in terms of sunburst luggage labels and magic-lantern shots but in terms of the tiles in different hotel bathrooms and corridor toilets – that floor with the white and blue squares where he found and scanned from his throne imaginary continuations of the match game in progress; or a teasingly asymmetrical, commercially called 'agate', pattern with a knight move of three harlequin colors interrupting here and there the neutral tint of the otherwise regularly checkered linoleum between Rodin's 'Thinker' and the door; or certain large glossy-black and yellow rectangles whose H-file was painfully cut off by the ocher vertical of the hot-water pipe; or that palatial water closet on whose lovely marble flags he recognized, intact, the shadowy figurations of the exact position he had brooded upon, chin on fist, one night many years ago. But the chess effects I planted are distinguishable not only in these separate scenes; their concatenation can be found in the basic structure of this attractive novel. Thus toward the end of Chapter Four an unexpected move is made by me in a corner of the board, sixteen years elapse in the course of one paragraph, and Luzhin, suddenly promoted to seedy manhood and transferred to a German resort, is discovered at a garden table, pointing out with his cane a remembered hotel window (not the last glass square in his life) and talking to somebody (a woman, if we judge by the handbag on the iron table) whom we do not meet till Chapter Six. The retrospective theme begun in Chapter Four shades now into the image of Luzhin's late father, whose own past is taken up in Chapter Five when he, in his turn, is perceived recalling his son's early chess career and stylizing it in his mind so as to make of it a sentimental tale for the young. We switch back to the Kurhaus in Chapter Six and find Luzhin still fiddling with the handbag and still addressing his blurry companion whereupon she unblurs, takes it away from him, mentions Luzhin senior's death, and becomes a distinct part of the design. The entire sequence of moves in these three control chapters reminds one – or should remind one – of a certain type of chess problem where the point is not merely the finding of a mate in so many moves, but what is termed 'retrograde analysis,' the solver being required to prove from a back-cast study of the diagram position that Black's last move *could not* have been castling or *must* have been the capture of a white Pawn *en passant*.

It is unnecessary to enlarge, in this elementary Foreword, on the more complex aspects of my chessmen and lines of play. But the following must be said. Of all my Russian books, *The Defense* contains and diffuses the greatest 'warmth' – which may seem odd seeing how supremely abstract chess is supposed to be. In point of fact, Luzhin has been found lovable even by those who understand nothing about chess and/or detest all my other books. He is uncouth, unwashed, uncomely – but as my gentle young lady (a dear girl in her own right) so quickly notices, there is something in him that transcends both the coarsenesss of his gray flesh and the sterility of his recondite genius.

In the Prefaces I have been writing of late for the English-language editions of my Russian novels (and there are more to come) I have made it a rule to address a few words of encouragement to the Viennese delegation. The present Foreword shall not be an exception. Analysts and analyzed will enjoy, I hope, certain details of the treatment Luzhin is subjected to after his breakdown (such as the curative insinuation that a chess player sees Mom in his Queen and Pop in his opponent's King), and the little Freudian who mistakes a Pixlok set for the key to a novel will no doubt continue to identify my characters with his comic-book notion of my parents, sweethearts and serial selves. For the benefit of such sleuths I may as well confess that I gave Luzhin my French governess, my pocket chess set, my sweet temper, and the stone of the peach I plucked in my own walled garden.

VLADIMIR NABOKOV

Montreux
Dec. 15, 1963

CHAPTER ONE

WHAT struck him most was the fact that from Monday on he would be Luzhin. His father – the real Luzhin, the elderly Luzhin, the writer of books – left the nursery with a smile, rubbing his hands (already smeared for the night with transparent cold cream), and with his suede-slippered evening gait padded back to his bedroom. His wife lay in bed. She half raised herself and said: 'Well, how did it go?' He removed his gray dressing gown and replied: 'We managed. Took it calmly. *Ouf* . . . that's a real weight off my shoulders.' 'How nice . . .' said his wife, slowly drawing the silk blanket over her. 'Thank goodness, thank goodness . . .'

It was indeed a relief. The whole summer – a swift country summer consisting in the main of three smells: lilac, new-mown hay, and dry leaves – the whole summer they had debated the question of when and how to tell him, and they had kept putting it off so that it dragged on until the end of August. They had moved around him in apprehensively narrowing circles, but he had only to raise his head and his father would already be rapping with feigned interest on the barometer dial, where the hand always stood at storm, while his mother would sail away somewhere into the depths of the house, leaving all the doors open and forgetting the long, messy bunch of bluebells on the lid of the paino. The stout French governess who used to read *The Count of Monte Cristo* aloud to him (and interrupt her reading in order to exclaim feelingly 'poor, poor Dantè!') proposed to the parents that she herself take the bull by the horns, though this bull inspired mortal fear in her. Poor, poor Dantès did not arouse any sympathy in him, and observing her educational sigh he merely slitted his eyes and rived his drawing paper with an eraser, as he tried to portray

11

her protuberant bust as horribly as possible.

Many years later, in an unexpected year of lucidity and enchantment, it was with swooning delight that he recalled these hours of reading on the veranda, buoyed up by the sough of the garden. The recollection was saturated with sunshine and the sweet, inky taste of the sticks of licorice, bits of which she used to hack off with blows of her penknife and persuade him to hold under his tongue. And the tacks he had once placed on the wickerwork seat destined, with crisp, crackling sounds, to receive her obese croup were in retrospect equivalent with the sunshine and the sounds of the garden, and the mosquito fastening onto his skinned knee and blissfully raising its rubescent abdomen. A ten-year-old boy knows his knees well, in detail – the itchy swelling that had been scrabbled till it bled, the white traces of fingernails on the suntanned skin, and all those scratches which are the appended signatures of sand grains, pebbles and sharp twigs. The mosquito would fly away, evading his slap; the governess would request him not to fidget; in a frenzy of concentration, baring his uneven teeth – which a dentist in St. Petersburg had braced with platinum wire – and bending his head with its heliced crown, he scratched and scraped at the bitten place with all five fingers – and slowly, with growing horror, the governess stretched toward the open drawing book, toward the unbelievable caricature.

'No, I'd better tell him myself,' replied Luzhin senior uncertainly to her suggestion. 'I'll tell him later, let him write his dictations in peace. "Being born in this world is hardly to be borne,"' Luzhin senior dictated steadily, strolling back and forth about the schoolroom. 'Being born in this world is hardly to be borne.' And his son wrote, practically lying on the table and baring his teeth in their metallic scaffolding, and simply left blanks for the words 'born' and 'borne'. Arithmetic went better; there was mysterious sweetness in the fact that a long number, arrived at with difficulty, would at the decisive moment, after many adventures, be divided by nineteen without any remainder.

He was afraid, Luzhin senior, that when his son learned why the founders of Russia, the completely featureless Sineus and Truvor, were necessary, as well as the table of Russian words taking the letter 'yat'' and the principal rivers of Russia, the child would go into the same tantrum as had happened two years before, when slowly and heavily, to the sound of creaking stairs, crackling floor-boards and shifting trunks, filling the whole house with her presence, the French governess had first appeared. But nothing of the kind occurred now; he listened calmly; and when his father, trying to pick out the most interesting and attractive details, said among other things that he would be called by his surname as grown-ups are called, the son blushed, began to blink, threw himself supine on his pillow, opening his mouth and rolling his head ('Don't squirm like that,' said his father apprehensively, noting his confusion and expecting tears), but did not break into tears and instead buried his face in the pillow, making bursting sounds with his lips into it, and suddenly rising – crumpled, warm, with glistening eyes – he asked rapidly whether at home, too, they would call him Luzhin.

And now, on this dull, tense day, on the way to the station to catch the St. Petersburg train, Luzhin senior, sitting next to his wife in the open carriage, looked at his son and was ready to smile immediately if the latter should turn his stubbornly averted face toward him, and wondered what had caused the boy suddenly to become so 'stiffish,' as his wife expressed it. He sat opposite them on the front seat, wrapped in a dark woollen tweed cloak, wearing a sailor cap which was set askew but which no one on earth would have dared to straighten now, and looked aside at the thick birch trunks spinning past along a ditch that was full of their leaves.

'Aren't you cold?' asked his mother when the road turned toward the river and a gust of wind set up a downy ripple in the gray bird's wing of her hat. 'Yes, I am,' said her son, looking at the river. His mother with a mewing sound was about to reach out and arrange his cloak, but noticing the look in his eye she swiftly snatched her hand back and merely indicated with a twiddle of her fingers in mid-air: 'Close it up, close it tighter.' The boy did not stir. Pursing her lips to unstick her *voilette* from her mouth – a constant gesture, almost a tic – she looked at her husband with a silent request for support. He was also wearing a woolen cloak; his hands encased in thick gloves rested on a plaid traveling rug which sloped down gently to form a valley and then slightly rose again, as far as the waist of little Luzhin. 'Luzhin', said his father with forced jollity, 'eh, Luzhin?' and tenderly nudged his son with his leg beneath the rug. Luzhin withdrew his knees. Here come the peasant log cabins, their roofs thickly overgrown with bright moss, here comes the familiar old signpost with its half-erased inscription (the name of the village and the number of its 'souls') and here comes the village well, with its bucket, black mud and white-legged peasant women. Beyond the village the horses climbed the hill at a walk and behind them, below, appeared the second carriage on which, sitting squeezed together, came the governess and the housekeeper, who hated one another. The driver smacked his lips and the horses again broke into a trot. In the colorless sky a crow flew slowly over the stubble.

The station was about a mile and a half from the manor, at a point where the road, after passing smoothly and resonantly through a fir wood, cut across the St. Petersburg highway and flowed farther, across the rails, beneath a barrier and into the unknown. 'If you like you can work the puppets,' said Luzhin senior ingratiatingly when his son jumped out of the carriage and fixed his eyes on the ground, moving his neck which the wool of his cloak irritated. He silently took the proffered ten-kopeck coin. The governess and the housekeeper crawled ponderously out of the second carriage, one to the right and the other to the left. Father took off his gloves. Mother, disengaging her veil, kept an eye on the barrel-chested porter who was gathering up their traveling rugs. A sudden wind raised the horses' manes and dilated the driver's crimson sleeves.

Finding himself alone on the station platform, Luzhin

14

walked toward the glass case where five little dolls with pendent bare legs awaited the impact of a coin in order to come to life and revolve; but today their expectation was in vain for the machine turned out to be broken and the coin was wasted. Luzhin waited a while and then turned and walked to the edge of the tracks. To the right a small girl sat on an enormous bale eating a green apple, her elbow propped in her palm. To the left stood a man in gaiters with a riding stick in his hand, looking at the distant fringe of the forest, whence in a few minutes would appear the train's harbinger – a puff of white smoke. In front of him, on the other side of the tracks, beside a tawny, second-class car without wheels that had taken root in the ground and turned into a permanent human dwelling, a peasant was chopping firewood. Suddenly all this was obscured by a mist of tears, his eyelids burned, it was impossible to bear what was about to happen – Father with a fan of tickets in his hands, Mother counting their baggage with her eyes, the train rushing in, the porter placing the steps against the car platform to make it easier to mount. He looked around. The little girl was eating her apple; the man in gaiters was staring into the distance; everything was calm. As if on a stroll he walked to the end of the station platform and then began to move very fast; he ran down some stairs, and there was a beaten footpath, the stationmaster's garden, a fence, a wicket gate, fir trees – then a small ravine and immediately after that a dense wood.

At first he ran straight through the wood, brushing against swishing ferns and slipping on reddish lily-of-the-valley leaves – and his cap hung at the back of his neck, held only by its elastic, his knees were hot in the woolen stockings already donned for city wear, he cried while running, lisping childish curses when a twig caught him across the forehead – and finally he came to a halt and, panting, squatted down on his haunches so that the cloak covered his legs.

Only today, on the day of their annual move from country to city, on a day which in itself was never sweet, when the house was full of drafts and you envied so much the gardener who was not going anywhere, only today did he realize the full horror of the change that his father had spoken of. Former autumn returns to the city now seemed happiness. His daily morning walks with the governess – always along the same streets, along the Nevsky and back home, by way of the Embankment, would never be repeated. Happy walks. Sometimes she had suggested to him they begin with the Embankment, but he had always refused – not so much because he had liked the habitual from earliest childhood as because he was unbearably afraid of the cannon at the Peter and Paul Fortress, of the huge thunderlike percussion that made the windowpanes in the houses rattle and was capable of bursting one's eardrum – and he always contrived (by means of imperceptible maneuvers) to be on the Nevsky at twelve o'clock, as far as possible from the cannon – whose shot, if he had changed the order of his walk, would have overtaken him right by the Winter Palace. Finished also were his agreeable after lunch musings on the sofa, beneath the tiger rug, and at the stroke of two, his milk in a silver cup, giving it such a precious taste, and at the stroke of three, a turn in the open landau. In exchange for all this came something new, unknown and therefore hideous, an impossible, unacceptable world where there would be five lessons from nine to three and a crowd of boys still more frightening than those who just recently, on a July day, here in the country, right on the bridge, had surrounded him, aimed tin pistols at him and fired at him sticklike projectiles whose rubber suction cups had perfidiously been pulled off.

The wood was still and damp. Having cried his fill, he played for a while with a beetle nervously moving its feelers, and then had quite a time crushing it beneath a stone as he tried to repeat the initial, juicy scrunch. Presently he noticed that it had begun to drizzle. Then he got up from the ground, found a familiar footpath and, stumbling over roots, started to run with vague vengeful thoughts of getting back to the manor: he would hide there, he

16

would spend the winter there, subsisting on cheese and jam from the pantry. The footpath meandered for ten minutes or so through the wood, descended to the river, which was all covered with circles from the raindrops, and five minutes later there hove into sight the sawmill, its footbridge where you sank in up to the ankles in sawdust, and the path upward, and then – through the bare lilac bushes – the house. He crept along the wall, saw that the drawing room window was open, climbed up by the drainpipe onto the green, peeling cornice and rolled over the windowsill. Once inside the drawing room, he stopped and listened. A daguerreotype of his maternal grandfather – black sidewhiskers, violin in hand – stared down at him, but then completely vanished, dissolving in the glass, as soon as he regarded the portrait from one side – a melancholy amusement that he never omitted when he entered the drawing room. Having thought for a moment and moved his upper lip, which caused the platinum wire on his front teeth to travel freely up and down, he cautiously opened the door, wincing at the sound of the vibrant echo which had too hastily occupied the house upon the departure of its owners, and then darted along the corridor and thence up the stairs into the attic. The attic was a special one, with a small window through which one could look down at the staircase, at the brown gleam of its balustrade that curved gracefully lower down and vanished in the penumbra. The house was absolutely quiet. A little later, from downstairs, from his father's study, came the muffled ring of a telephone. The ringing continued with intervals for quite a while. Then again there was silence.

He settled himself on a box. Next to it was a similar case, but open and with books in it. A lady's bicycle, the green net of its rear wheel torn, stood on its head in the corner, between an unplaned board propped against the wall and an enormous trunk. After a few minutes Luzhin grew bored, as when one's throat is wrapped in flannel and one is forbidden to go out. He touched the gray dusty books in the open box, leaving black imprints on them.

Besides books there was a shuttlecock with one feather, a large photograph (of a military band), a cracked chess-board, and some other not very interesting things.

In this way an hour went by. Suddenly he heard the noise of voices and the whine of the front door. Taking a cautious look through the little window he saw below his father, who like a young boy ran up the stairs and then, before reaching the landing, descended swiftly again, throwing his knees out on either side. The voices below were now clear: the butler's, the coachman's, the watch-man's. A minute later the staircase again came to life; this time his mother came quickly up it, hitching up her skirt, but she also stopped short of the landing, leaning, instead, over the balustrade, and then swiftly, with arms spread out, she went down again. Finally, after another minute had passed, they all went up in a posse – his father's bald head glistened, the bird on mother's hat swayed like a duck on a troubled pond, and the butler's gray crew cut bobbed up and down; at the rear, leaning at every moment over the balustrade, came the coachman, the watchman, and for some reason the milkmaid Akulina, and finally a black-bearded peasant from the water mill, future in-habitant of future nightmares. It was he, as the strongest, who carried Luzhin down from the attic to the carriage.

CHAPTER TWO

LUZHIN senior, the Luzhin who wrote books, often thought of how his son would turn out. Through his books (and they all, except for a forgotten novel called *Fumes*, were written for boys, youths and high school students and came in sturdy colorful covers) there constantly flitted the image of a fair-haired lad, 'headstrong,' 'brooding,' who later turned into a violinist or a painter, without losing his moral beauty in the process. The barely perceptible peculiarity that distinguished his son from all those children who, in his opinion, were destined to become completely unremarkable people (given that such people exist) he interpreted as the secret stir of talent, and baring firmly in mind the fact that his deceased father-in-law had been a composer (albeit a somewhat arid one and susceptible, in his mature years, to the doubtful splendors of virtuosity), he more than once, in a pleasant dream resembling a lithograph, descended with a candle at night to the drawing room where a *Wünderkind*, dressed in a white nightshirt that came down to his heels, would be playing on an enormous, black piano.

It seemed to him that everybody ought to see how exceptional his son was; it seemed to him that strangers, perhaps, could make better sense of it than he himself. The school he had selected for his son was particularly famous for the attention it paid to the so-called 'inner' life of its pupils, and for its humaneness, thoughtfulness, and friendly insight. Tradition had it that during the early part of its existence the teachers had played with the boys during the long recess: the physics master, looking over his shoulder, would squeeze a lump of snow into a ball; the mathematics master would get a hard little ball in the ribs as he made a run in *lapta* (Russian baseball); and even the headmaster himself would be there, cheering the game on with jolly ejaculations. Such games in common no longer took place, but the idyllic fame had remained. His son's class master was the Russian literature teacher, a good acquaintance of Luzhin the writer and incidentally not a bad lyric poet who had put out a collection of imitations of Anacreon. 'Drop in,' he had said on the day when Luzhin first brought his son to school. 'Any Thursday around twelve.' Luzhin dropped in. The stairs were deserted and quiet. Passing through the hall to the staff room he heard a muffled, multivocal roar of laughter coming from Class Two. In the ensuing silence, his steps rang out with a stressed sonority on the yellow parquetry of the long hall. In the staff room at a large table covered with baize (which reminded one of examinations), the teacher sat writing a letter.

Since the time of his son's entrance to the school he had not spoken to the teacher and now, visiting him a month later, he was full of titillating expectation, of a certain anxiety and timidity – of all those feelings he had once experienced as a youth in his university uniform when he went to see the editor of a literary review to whom he had shortly before sent his first story. And now, just as then, instead of the words of delighted amazement he had vaguely expected (as when you wake up in a strange town, expecting, with your eyes still shut, an extraordinary, blazing morning), instead of all those words which he himself would so willingly have provided, had it not been for the hope that nonetheless they would eventually come – he heard chilly and dull phrases that proved the teacher understood his son even less than he did. On the subject of any kind of hidden talent not a single word was uttered. Inclining his pale bearded face with two pink grooves on either side of the nose, from which he carefully removed his tenacious pince-nez, and rubbing his eyes with his palm, the teacher began to speak first, saying that the boy might do better than he did, that the boy seemed not to get on with his companions, that the boy did not run about much during the recess period. . . . 'The boy undoubtedly has ability,' said the teacher, concluding his eye-rubbing, 'but we notice a certain listlessness.' At this moment a bell was generated somewhere downstairs, and then bounded upstairs and passed unbearably shrilly throughout the whole building. After this there were two or three seconds of the most complete silence – and suddenly everything came to life and burst into noise; desk lids banged and the hall filled with talking and the stamp of feet. 'The long recess,' said the teacher. 'If you like we'll go down to the yard, and you can watch the boys at play.'

These descended the stone stairs swiftly, hugging the balustrade and sliding the soles of their sandals over the step rims well polished by use. Downstairs amid the crowded darkness of coat racks they changed their shoes; some of them sat on the broad window sills, grunting as they hastily tied their shoelaces. Suddenly he caught sight of his son, who, all hunched up, was disgustedly taking his boots from a cloth bag. A hurrying, tow-haired boy bumped into him and, moving aside, Luzhin suddenly caught sight of his father. The latter smiled at him, holding his tall astrakhan *shapka* and implanting the necessary furrow on top with the edge of one hand. Luzhin narrowed his eyes and turned away as if he had not seen his father. Squatting on the floor with his back to his father, he busied himself with his boots; those who had already managed to change stepped over him and after every push he hunched himself up still more as if hiding in a dark nook. When at last he went out – wearing a long gray overcoat and a little astrakhan cap (which was constantly being tipped off by one and the same burly boy), his father was already standing at the gate at the other end of the yard and looking expectantly in his direction. Next to Luzhin senior stood the literature teacher and when the large gray rubber ball the boys used for soccer happened to roll up to his feet, the literature teacher, instinctively continuing that enchanting tradition, made as if he wanted to kick it, but only shifted awkwardly from foot to foot and almost lost one of his galoshes, and laughed with great good humor. The father supported him by the

21

elbow, and Luzhin junior, grasping the opportunity, returned to the vestibule, where all was now quiet and where the janitor, concealed by clothes racks, was heard yawning blissfully. Through the glass of the door, between the cast-iron rays of the star-shaped grille, he saw his father suddenly remove his glove, quickly take leave of the teacher and disappear through the gate. Only then did he creep out again, and, carefully skirting the players, make his way left to where firewood was stacked under the archway. There, raising his collar, he sat down on a pile of logs.

In this way he sat through approximately two hundred and fifty long intermissions, until the year that he was taken abroad. Sometimes the teacher would suddenly appear from around a corner. 'Why are you always sitting in a heap, Luzhin? You should run about a bit with the other boys.' Luzhin would get up from the woodpile, trying to find a point equidistant from those three of his classmates who were especially fierce at this hour, shy away from the ball propelled by someone's resounding kick and, having reassured himself that the teacher was far off, would return to the woodpile. He had chosen this spot on the very first day, on that dark day when he had discovered such hatred and derisive curiosity around him that his eyes had automatically filled with a burning mist, and everything he looked at – out of the accursed necessity of looking at something – was subject to intricate, optical metamorphoses. The page with criss-cross blue lines grew blurry; the white numbers on the blackboard alternately contracted and broadened; the arithmetic teacher's voice, as if steadily receding, would get more and more hollow and incomprehensible, and his desk neighbor, an insidious brute with down on his cheeks, would say with quiet satisfaction: 'Now he's going to cry.' But Luzhin never once cried, not even in the lavatory when they made a concerted effort to thrust his head into the low bowl with yellow bubbles in it. 'Gentlemen,' the teacher had said at one of the first lessons, 'your new comrade is the son of a writer. Whom, if you haven't

22

read him, you should proceed to read.' And in large letters he wrote on the board, pressing so hard that the chalk was pulverized crunchingly beneath his fingers: TONY'S ADVENTURES, SILVESTROV AND CO. PUBLISHERS. During two or three months after that his classmates called him Tony. With a mysterious air the downy-cheeked brute brought the book to class and during the lesson stealthily showed it to the others, casting significant glances at his victim – and when the lesson was over began to read aloud from the middle, purposely mangling the words. Petrishchev, who was looking over his shoulder, wanted to hold back a page and it tore. Krebs gabbled: 'My dad says he's a very second-rate writer.' Gromov shouted: 'Let Tony read to us aloud ' 'Better to give everybody a piece each,' said the clown of the class with gusto, and took possession of the handsome red and gold book after a stormy struggle. Pages were scattered over the whole classroom. One of them had a picture on it – a bright-eyed schoolboy on a street corner feeding his luncheon to a scruffy dog. The following day Luzhin found this picture neatly tacked on to the underside of his desk lid.

Soon, however, they left him in peace; only his nickname flared up from time to time, but since he stubbornly refused to answer it that too finally died down. They stopped taking any notice of Luzhin and did not speak to him, and even the sole quiet boy in the class (the sort there is in every class, just as there are invariably a fat boy, a strong boy and a wit) steered clear of him, afraid of sharing his despicable condition. This same quiet boy, who six years later, in the beginning of World War One, received the St. George Cross for an extremely dangerous reconnaisance and later lost an arm in the civil war, when trying to recall (in the twenties of the present century) what Luzhin had been like in school, could not visualize him otherwise than from the rear, either sitting in front of him in class with protruding ears, or else receding to one end of the hall as far away as possible from the hubbub, or else departing for home in a sleigh cab – hands in pockets, a large piebald satchel on his back, snow falling. ... He tried to run ahead and look at Luzhin's face, but that special snow of oblivion, abundant and soundless snow, covered his recollection with an opaque white mist. And the former quiet boy, now a restless émigré, said as he looked at a picture in the newspaper: 'Imagine, I just can't remember his face. . . . Just can't remember. . .'

But Luzhin senior, peering through the window around four o'clock, would see the approaching sleigh and his son's face like a pale spot. The boy usually came straight to his study, kissed the air as he touched his father's cheek with his and immediately turned away. 'Wait,' his father would say, 'wait. Tell me how it was today. Were you called to the blackboard ?'

He would look greedily at his son, who turned his face away, and would want to take him by the shoulders, shake him and kiss him soundly on his pale cheek, on the eyes and on his tender concave temple. From anemic little Luzhin that first school winter came a touching smell of garlic as a result of the arsenic injections prescribed by the doctor. His platinum band had been removed, but he continued to bare his teeth and curl his upper lip out of habit. He wore a gray Norfolk jacket with a strap at the back, and knickerbockers with buttons below the knee. He would stand by the desk, balancing on one leg, and his father did not dare to do anything against his impenetrable sullenness. Little Luzhin would go away, trailing his satchel over the carpet; Luzhin senior would lean his elbow on the desk, where he was writing one of his usual stories in blue exercise books (a whim which, perhaps, some future biographer would appreciate), and listen to the monologue in the neighboring dining room, to his wife's voice persuading the silence to drink a cup of cocoa. A frightening silence, thought Luzhin senior. He's not well, he has a painful inner life of some sort. . . . Perhaps he shouldn't have been sent to school But on the other hand he has to get used to being with other lads. . . . An enigma, an enigma. . . .

'Well. take some cake, then,' the voice behind the wall would continue sorrowfully, and again silence. But sometimes something horrible occurred: suddenly, for no apparent reason at all, another voice would reply, strident and hoarse, and the door would slam as if shut by a hurricane. Then Luzhin senior would jump up and make for the dining room, holding his pen like a dart. With trembling hands his wife would be setting aright an overturned cup and saucer and trying to see if there were any cracks. 'I was asking him about school,' she would say, not looking at her husband. 'He didn't want to answer and then – like a madman ...' They would both listen. The French governess had left that autumn for Paris and now nobody knew what he did there in his room. The wallpaper there was white, and higher up was a blue band on which were drawn gray geese and ginger puppies. A goose advanced on a pup and so on thirty-eight times around the entire room. An étagère supported a globe and a stuffed squirrel, bought once on Palm Sunday at the Catkin Fair. A green clockwork locomotive peeped out from beneath the flounces of an armchair. It was a nice bright room. Gay wallpaper, gay objects.

There were also books. Books written by his father, with red and gold embossed bindings and a handwritten inscription on the first page: *I earnestly hope that my son will always treat animals and people the same way as Tony*, and a big exclamation mark Or: *I wrote this book thinking of your future, my son*. These inscriptions inspired in him a vague feeling of shame for his father, and the books themselves were as boring as Korolenko's *The Blind Musician* or Goncharov's *The Frigate Pallas*. A large volume of Pushkin with a picture of a thick-lipped, curly-haired boy on it was never opened. On the other hand there were two books, both given him by his aunt, with which he had fallen in love for his whole life, holding them in his memory as if under a magnifying glass, and experiencing them so intensely that twenty years later, when he read them over again, he saw only a dryish paraphrase, an abridged edition, as if they had been outdistanced by the unrepeatable, immortal image that he had retained. But it was not a thirst for distant peregrinations that forced him to follow on the heels of Phileas Fogg, nor was it a boyish inclination for mysterious adventures that drew him to that house in Baker Street, where the lanky detective with the hawk profile, having given himself an injection of cocaine, would dreamily play the violin. Only much later did he clarify in his own mind what it was that had thrilled him so about these two books; it was that exact and relentlessly unfolding pattern: Phileas, the dummy in the top hat, wending his complex elegant way with its justifiable sacrifices, now on an elephant bought for a million, now on a ship of which half has to be burned for fuel; and Sherlock endowing logic with the glamour of a daydream, Sherlock composing a monograph on the ash of all known sorts of cigars and with this ash as with a talisman progressing through a crystal labyrinth of possible deductions to the one radiant conclusion. The conjuror whom his parents engaged to perform on Christmas day somehow managed to blend in himself briefly both Fogg and Holmes, and the strange pleasure which Luzhin experienced on that day obliterated all the unpleasantness that accompanied the performance. Since requests – cautious infrequent requests – to 'invite your school friends' never led to anything, Luzhin senior, confident that it would be both enjoyable and useful, got in touch with two acquaintances whose children attended the same school and he also invited the children of a distant relative, two quiet, flabby little boys and a pale girl with a thick braid of black hair. All the boys invited wore sailor suits and smelled of hair oil. Two of them little Luzhin recognized with horror as Bersenev and Rosen from Class Three, who at school were always dressed sloppily and behaved violently. 'Well, here we are,' said Luzhin senior, joyfully holding his son by the shoulder (the shoulder slowly sliding out from under his hand). 'Now I'll leave you alone. Get to know one another and play for a while – and later you'll be called, we have a surprise for you.' Half an hour later he went to call them. In the room there was silence. The little girl was sitting in a corner and leafing through the supplement to the review

26

Niva (*The Cornfield*), looking for pictures. Bersenev and Rosen were selfconsciously sitting on the sofa, both very red and shiny with pomade. The flabby nephews wandered around the room examining without interest the English woodcuts on the walls, the globe, the squirrel and a long since broken pedometer lying on a table. Luzhin himself, also wearing a sailor suit, with a whistle on a white cord on his chest, was sitting on a hard chair by the window, glowering and biting his thumbnail. But the conjuror made up for everything and even when on the following day Bersenev and Rosen, by this time again their real disgusting selves, came up to him in the school hall and bowed low, afterwards breaking into vulgar guffaws of laughter and quickly departing, arm in arm and swaying from side to side – even then this mockery was unable to break the spell. Upon his sullen request – whatever he said nowadays his brows came painfully together – his mother brought him from the Bazaar a large box painted a mahogany color and a book of tricks with a bemedaled gentleman in evening dress on the cover lifting a rabbit by its ears. Inside the box were smaller boxes with false bottoms, a wand covered with starry paper, a pack of crude cards where the picture cards were half jacks or half kings and half sheep in uniforms, a folding top hat with compartments, a rope with two wooden gadgets at the ends whose function was unclear. And there also were coquettish little envelopes containing powders for tinting water blue, red and green. The book was much more entertaining, and Luzhin had no difficulty in learning several card tricks which he spent hours showing to himself before the mirror. He found a mysterious pleasure, a vague promise of still unfathomed delights, in the crafty and accurate way a trick would come out, but still there was something missing, he could not grasp that secret which the conjuror had evidently mastered in order to be able to pluck a ruble out of the air or extract the seven of clubs, tacitly chosen by the audience, from the ear of an embarrassed Rosen. The complicated accessories described in the book irritated him. The secret for which he

27

strove was simplicity, harmonious simplicity, which can amaze one far more than the most intricate magic.

In the written report on his progress that was sent at Christmas, in this extremely detailed report where under the rubric of *General Remarks* they spoke at length, pleonastically, of the lethargy, apathy, sleepiness and sluggishness and where marks were replaced by epithets, there turned out to be one 'unsatisfactory' in Russian language and several 'barely satisfactorys' – among other things in mathematics. However, it was just at this time that he had become extraordinarily engrossed in a collection of problems entitled 'Merry Mathematics,' in the fantastical misbehavior of numbers and the wayward frolics of geometric lines, in everything that the schoolbook lacked. He experienced both bliss and horror in contemplating the way an inclined line, rotating spokelike, slid upwards along another, vertical one – in an example illustrating the mysteries of parallelism. The vertical one as infinite, like all lines, and the inclined one, also infinite, sliding along it and rising ever higher as its angle decreased, was doomed to eternal motion, for it was impossible for it to slip off, and the point of their intersection, together with his soul, glided upwards along an endless path. But with the aid of a ruler he forced them to unlock: he simply redrew them, parallel to one another, and this gave him the feeling that out there, in infinity, where he had forced the inclined line to jump off, an unthinkable catastrophe had taken place, an inexplicable miracle, and he lingered long in those heavens where earthly lines go out of their mind.

For a while he found an illusory relief in jigsaw puzzles. At first they were simple childish ones, consisting of large pieces cut out with rounded teeth at the edges, like petit-beurre cookies, which interlocked so tenaciously that it was possible to lift whole sections of the puzzle without breaking them. But that year there came from England the fad of jigsaw puzzles invented for adults – 'poozels' as they called them at the best toyshop in Petersburg – which were cut out with extraordinary ingenuity: pieces of all shapes, from a simple disk (part of a future blue sky) to the most intricate forms, rich in corners, capes, isthmuses, cunning projections, which did not allow you to tell where they were supposed to fit – whether they were to fill up the piebald hide of a cow, already almost completed, or whether this dark border on a green background was the shadow of the crook of a shepherd whose ear and part of whose head were plainly visible on a more outspoken piece. And when a cow's haunch gradually appeared on the left, and on the right, against some foliage, a hand with a shepherd's pipe, and when the empty space above became built up with heavenly blue, and the blue disk fitted smoothly into the sky Luzhin felt wonderfully stirred by the precise combinations of these vari-colored pieces that formed at the last moment an intelligible picture. Some of these brain-twisters were very expensive and consisted of several thousand pieces; they were brought by his young aunt, a gay, tender, red-haired aunt – and he would spend hours bent over a card table in the drawing room, measuring with his eyes each projection before trying if it would fit into this or that gap and attempting to determine by scarcely perceptible signs the essence of the picture in advance. From the next room, full of the noise of guests, his aunt would plead: 'For goodness' sake, don't lose any of the pieces!' Sometimes his father would come in, look at the puzzle and stretch out a hand tableward, saying: 'Look, this undoubtedly goes in here,' and then Luzhin without looking round would mutter: 'Rubbish, rubbish, don't interfere,' and his father would cautiously apply his lips to the tufted top of his son's head and depart – past the gilded chairs, past the vast mirror, past the reproduction of Phryne Taking Her Bath, past the piano – a large silent piano shod with thick glass and caparisoned with a brocaded cloth.

CHAPTER THREE

ONLY in April, during the Easter holidays, did that inevitable day come for Luzhin when the whole world suddenly went dark, as if someone had thrown a switch, and in the darkness only one thing remained brilliantly lit, a newborn wonder, a dazzling islet on which his whole life was destined to be concentrated. The happiness onto which he fastened came to stay; that April day froze forever, while somewhere else the movement of seasons, the city spring, the country summer, continued in a different plane – dim currents which barely affected him.

It began innocently. On the anniversary of his father-in-law's death, Luzhin senior organized a musical evening in his apartment. He himself had little understanding of music; he nourished a secret, shameful passion for *La Traviata* and at concerts listened to the piano only at the beginning, after which he contented himself with watching the pianist's hands reflected in the black varnish. But willy-nilly he had to organize that musical evening at which works of his late father-in-law would be played: as it was the newspapers had been silent for too long – the oblivion was complete, leaden, hopeless – and his wife kept repeating with a tremulous smile that it was all intrigue, intrigue, intrigue, that even during his lifetime others had envied her father's genius and that now they wanted to suppress his posthumous fame. Wearing a black, open-necked dress and a superb diamond dog collar, with a permanent expression of drowsy amiability on her puffy white face, she received the guests quietly, without exclaiming, whispering to each a few rapid, soft-sounding words; but inwardly she was beset by shyness and kept looking about for her husband, who was moving back and forth with mincing steps, his starched shirtfront swelling cuirasslike out of his waistcoat – a genial, discreet gentleman in the first timid throes of literary venerability. 'Stark naked again,' sighed the editor of an art magazine, taking a passing look at Phryne, who was particularly vivid as a result of the intensified light. At this point young Luzhin cropped up under his feet and had his head stroked. The boy recoiled. 'How huge he's grown,' said a woman's voice from behind. He hid behind someone's tails. 'No, I beg your pardon,' thundered out above his head: 'Such demands must not be made on our press.' Not at all huge but on the contrary very small for his years, he wandered among the guests trying to find a quiet spot. Sometimes somebody caught him by the shoulder and asked idiotic questions. The drawing room looked especially crowded because of the gilded chairs which had been placed in rows. Someone carefully came through the door carrying a music stand.

By imperceptible stages Luzhin made his way to his father's study, where it was dark, and settled on a divan in the corner. From the distant drawing room, through two rooms, came the tender wail of a violin.

He listened sleepily, clasping his knees and looking at a chink of lacy light between the loosely closed curtains, through which a gas-lamp from the street shone lilac-tinged white. From time to time a faint glimmer sped over the ceiling in a mysterious arc and a gleaming dot showed on the desk – he did not know what: perhaps one facet of a paperweight in the guise of a heavy crystal egg or a reflection in the glass of a desk photograph. He had almost dozed off when suddenly he started at the ringing of a telephone on the desk, and it became immediately clear that the gleaming dot was on the telephone support. The butler came in from the dining room, turned on in passing a light which illuminated only the desk, placed the receiver to his ear, and without noticing Luzhin went out again, having carefully laid the receiver on the leather-bound blotter. A minute later he returned accompanying a gentleman who as soon as he entered the circle of light picked up the receiver from the desk and with his other hand groped for the back of the desk chair. The servant closed the door behind him, cutting off the distant ripple of music. 'Hello,' said the gentleman. Luzhin looked at him out of the darkness, fearing to move and embarrassed by the fact that a complete stranger was reclining so comfortably at his father's desk. 'No, I've already played,' he said looking upwards, while his white restless hand fidgeted with something on the desk. A cab clip-clopped hollowly over the wooden pavement. 'I think so,' said the gentleman. Luzhin could see his profile – an ivory nose, black hair, a bushy eyebrow. 'Frankly, I don't know why you are calling me here,' he said quietly, continuing to fiddle with something on the desk. 'If it was only to check up ... You silly,' he laughed and commenced to swing one foot in its patent leather shoe regularly back and forth. Then he placed the receiver very skillfully between his ear and his shoulder and replying intermittently with 'yes' and 'no' and 'perhaps,' used both hands to pick up the object he had been playing with on the desk. It was a polished box that had been presented to his father a few days before. Luzhin junior had still not had a chance to look inside and now he watched the gentleman's hands with curiosity. But the latter did not open the box immediately. 'Me too,' he said. 'Many times, many times. Good night, little girl.' Having hung up the receiver he sighed and opened the box. However, he turned in such a way that Luzhin could see nothing from behind his black shoulder. Luzhin moved cautiously, but a cushion slid onto the floor and the gentleman quickly looked round. 'What are you doing here?' he asked, spying Luzhin in the dark corner. 'My, my, how bad it is to eavesdrop!' Luzhin remained silent. 'What's your name?' asked the gentleman amiably. Luzhin slid off the divan and came closer. A number of carved figures lay closely packed in the box. 'Excellent chessmen,' said the gentleman. 'Does Papa play?' 'I don't know,' said Luzhin. 'And do you play yourself?' Luzhin shook his head. 'That's a pity. You should learn. At ten I was already a good player. How old are you?'

Carefully the door was opened. Luzhin senior came in –

on tiptoe. He had been prepared to find the violinist still talking on the telephone and had thought to whisper very tactfully: 'Continue, continue, but when you finish the audience would very much like to hear something more.' 'Continue, continue,' he said mechanically and was brought up short upon seeing his son. 'No, no, I've already finished,' replied the violinist, getting up. 'Excellent chessmen. Do you play?' 'Indifferently,' said Luzhin senior. ('What are you doing here? You too come and listen to the music ...') 'What a game, what a game,' said the violinist, tenderly closing the box. 'Combinations like melodies. You know, I can simply *hear* the moves.' 'In my opinion one needs great mathematical skill for chess,' said Luzhin senior. 'And in that respect I ... They are awaiting you, Maestro.' 'I would rather have a game,' laughed the violinist, as he left the room. 'The game of the gods. Infinite possibilities.' 'A very ancient invention,' said Luzhin senior and looked around at his son: 'What's the matter? Come with us!' But before reaching the drawing room Luzhin contrived to tarry in the dining room where the table was laid with refreshments. There he took a plateful of sandwiches and carried it away to his room. He ate while he undressed and then ate in bed. He had already put the light out when his mother looked in and bent over him, the diamonds around her neck glinting in the half-light. He pretended to be asleep. She went away and was a long, long time – so as not to make a noise – closing the door.

He woke up next day with a feeling of incomprehensible excitement. The April morning was bright and windy and the wooden street pavements had a violent sheen; above the street near Palace Arch an enormous red-blue-white flag swelled elastically, the sky showing through it in three different tints: mauve, indigo and pale blue. As always on holidays he went for a walk with his father, but these were not the former walks of his childhood; the midday cannon no longer frightened him and father's conversation was unbearable, for finding a pretext in last night's concert, he kept hinting that it would be a good idea to take up music. For lunch there was the remains of the paschal cream cheese (now a squat little cone with a grayish shading on its round summit) and a still untouched Easter cake. His aunt, the same sweet copper-haired aunt, second cousin to his mother, was gay in the extreme, threw cake crumbs across the table and related that for twenty-five rubles Latham was going to give her a ride in his 'Antoinette' monoplane, which, by the way, was unable to leave the ground for the fifth day, while Voisin on the contrary kept circling the aerodrome like clockwork, and moreover so low that when he banked over the stands one could even see the cotton wool in the pilot's ears. Luzhin for some reason remembered that morning and that lunch with unusual brightness, the way you remember the day preceding a long journey. His father said it would be a good idea after lunch to drive to the Islands beyond the Neva, where the clearings were carpeted with anemones, and while he was speaking, the young aunt landed a crumb right in Father's mouth. His mother remained silent. Suddenly after the second course she got up, trying to conceal her face twitching with restrained tears and repeating under her breath 'It's nothing, nothing, it'll pass in a moment,' hastily left the dining room. Father threw his napkin on the table and followed her. Luzhin never discovered exactly what had happened, but passing along the corridor with his aunt he heard subdued sobs from his mother's room and his father's voice remonstrating and loudly repeating the phrase 'imagining things.'

'Let's go away somewhere,' whispered his aunt in an embarrassed and nervous manner, and they entered the study where a band of sunbeams, in which spun tiny particles of dust, was focused on an overstuffed armchair. She lit a cigarette and folds of smoke started to sway, soft and transparent, in the sunbeams. This was the only person in whose presence he did not feel constrained, and now it was especially pleasant: a strange silence in the house and a kind of expectation of something. 'Well, let's play some game,' said his aunt hurriedly and took him by the neck from behind. 'What a thin little neck you have, one can clasp it with one hand. . . .' 'Do you know how to play chess?' asked Luzhin

34

stealthily, and freeing his head he rubbed his cheek against the delightful bright blue silk of her sleeve. 'A game of Snap would be better,' she said absentmindedly. A door banged somewhere. She winced and turned her face in the direction of the noise, listening. 'No, I want to play chess,' said Luzhin. 'It's complicated, my dear, you can't learn it in an instant.' He went to the desk and found the box, which was standing behind a desk photograph. His aunt got up to take an ashtray, ruminatively crooning in conclusion of some thought of hers: 'That would be terrible, that would be terrible . . .' 'Here,' said Luzhin and put the box down on a low, inlaid Turkish table. 'You need the board as well,' she said. 'And you know, it would be better for me to teach you checkers, it's simpler.' 'No, chess,' said Luzhin and unrolled an oilcloth board.

'First let's place the pieces correctly,' began his aunt with a sigh. 'White here, black over there. King and Queen next to each other. These here are the Officers. These are the Horses. And these, at each corner, are the cannons. Now . . .' Suddenly she froze, holding a piece in mid-air and looking at the door. 'Wait,' she said anxiously. 'I think I left my handkerchief in the dining room. I'll be right back.' She opened the door but returned immediately. 'Let it go,' she said and again sat down. 'No, don't set them out without me, you'll do it the wrong way. This is called a Pawn. Now watch how they all move. The Horse gallops, of course.' Luzhin sat on the carpet with his shoulder against her knee and watched her hand with its thin platinum bracelet picking up the chessmen and putting them down. 'The Queen is the most mobile,' he said with satisfaction and adjusted the piece with his finger, since it was standing not quite in the center of the square. 'And this is how one piece eats another,' said his aunt. 'As if pushing it out and taking its place. The Pawns do this obliquely. When you can take the King but he can move out of the way, it's called check; and when he's got nowhere to go it's mate. So your object is to take my King and I have to take yours. You see how long it all takes to explain. Perhaps we can play another time, eh?' 'No, now,' said Luzhin and suddenly kissed her hand. 'That

35

was sweet of you,' said his aunt softly, 'I never expected such tenderness . . . You are a nice little boy after all.' 'Please let's play,' said Luzhin, and moving in a kneeling position on the carpet, reached the low table. But at that moment she got up from her seat so abruptly that she brushed the board with her skirt and knocked off several pieces. In the doorway stood his father.

'Go to your room,' he said, glancing briefly at his son. Luzhin, who was being sent out of a room for the first time in his life, remained as he was on his knees out of sheer astonishment. 'Did you hear?' said his father, Luzhin flushed and began to look for the fallen pieces on the carpet. 'Hurry up,' said his father in a thunderous voice such as he had never used before. His aunt hastily began to put the pieces any which way into their box. Her hands trembled. One Pawn just would not go in. 'Now take it, take it,' she said. He slowly rolled up the oilcloth board and, his face darkened by a sense of deep injury, took the box. He was unable to close the door behind him since both hands were full. His father took a swift stride and slammed the door so hard that Luzhin dropped the board, which immediately unfolded; he had to put the box down and roll up the thing again. Behind the door of the study there was at first silence, then the creak of an armchair under his father's weight, and then his aunt's breathless interrogative whisper. Luzhin reflected disgustedly that today everyone had gone mad and went to his room. There he immediately set out the pieces as his aunt had shown him and considered them for a long time, trying to figure something out; after which he put them away very neatly in their box. From that day the chess set remained with him and it was a long time before his father noticed its absence. From that day there was in his room a fascinating and mysterious toy, the use of which he had still not learned. From that day his aunt never again came to visit them.

A week or so later, an empty gap occurred between the first and third lesson: the geography teacher had caught a cold. When five minutes had passed after the bell and still no one had come in, there ensued such a premonition of happiness that it seemed the heart would not hold out should the glass door nonetheless now open and the geography teacher, as was his habit, come dashing almost at a run into the room. Only Luzhin was indifferent. Bent low over his desk, he was sharpening a pencil, trying to make the point as sharp as a pin. An excited din swelled around him. Our bliss, it seemed, was bound to be realized. Sometimes however there were unbearable disappointments: in place of the sick teacher the predatory little mathematics teacher would come creeping into the room, and, having closed the door soundlessly, would begin to select pieces of chalk from the ledge beneath the blackboard with an evil smile on his face. But a full ten minutes elapsed and no one appeared. The din grew louder. From an excess of happiness somebody banged a desk lid. The class tutor sprang up out of nowhere. 'Absolute quiet,' he said. 'I want absolute quiet. Valentin Ivanovich is sick. Occupy yourselves with something. But there must be absolute quiet.' He went away. Large fluffy clouds shone outside the window; something gurgled and dripped; sparrows chirped. Blissful hour, bewitching hour. Luzhin apathetically began to sharpen yet another pencil. Gromov was telling some story in a hoarse voice, pronouncing strange obscene words with gusto. Petrishchev begged everyone to explain to him how we know that they are equal to two right-angled ones. And suddenly, behind him, Luzhin distinctly heard a special sound, wooden and rattly, that caused him to grow hot and his heart to skip a beat. Cautiously he turned around. Krebs and the only quiet boy in the class were nimbly setting out light little chessmen on a six-inch board. The board was on the desk bench between them. They sat extremely uncomfortably, sideways. Luzhin, forgetting to finish sharpening his pencil, went up to them. The players took no notice of him. The quiet boy, when trying many years later to remember his schoolmate Luzhin, never recalled that casual chess game, played during an empty hour. Mixing up dates he extracted from the past a vague impression of Luzhin's once winning a school match, something itched in his memory, but he could not get at it.

'There goes the Tower,' said Krebs. Luzhin followed his hand, thinking with a tremor of momentary panic that his aunt had not told him the names of all the pieces. But 'tower' turned out to be a synonym for 'cannon'. 'I didn't see you could take, that's all,' said the other. 'All right, take your move back,' said Krebs.

With gnawing envy and irritating frustration Luzhin watched the game, striving to perceive those harmonious patterns the musician had spoken of and feeling vaguely that in some way or other he understood the game better than these two, although he was completely ignorant of how it should be conducted, why this was good and that bad, and what one should do to penetrate the opposite King's camp without losses. And there was one kind of move that pleased him very much, amusing in its sleekness: Kreb's King slid up to the piece he called a Tower, and the Tower jumped over the King. Then he saw the other King come out from behind its Pawns (one had been knocked out, like a tooth) and begin to step distractedly back and forth. 'Check,' said Krebs, 'check' (and the stung King leaped to one side); 'you can't go here and you can't go here either. Check, I'm taking your Queen, check.' At this point he lost a piece himself and began insisting he should replay his move. The class bully filliped Luzhin on the back of the head and simultaneously with his other hand knocked the board onto the floor. For the second time in his life Luzhin noticed how unstable a thing chess was.

And the following morning, while still lying in bed, he made an unprecedented decision. He usually went to school in a cab and always made a careful study of the cab's number, dividing it up in a special way in order the better to store it away in his memory and extract it thence whole should he require it. But today he did not go as far as school and forgot in his excitement to memorize the number; fearfully glancing around he got out at Karavannaya Street and by a circular route, avoiding the region of the school, reached Sergievskaya Street. On the way he happened to run into the geography teacher, who with enormous strides, a briefcase under his arm, was rushing in the direction of the school blowing his nose and expectorating phlegm as he went, Luzhin turned aside so abruptly that a mysterious object rattled heavily in his satchel. Only when the teacher, like a blind wind, had swept past him did Luzhin become aware that he was standing before a hairdresser's window and that the frizzled heads of three waxen ladies with pink nostrils were staring directly at him. He took a deep breath and swiftly walked along the wet sidewalk, unconsciously trying to adjust his steps so that his heel always landed on a join between two paving slabs. But the slabs were all of different widths and this hampered his walk. Then he stepped down onto the pavement in order to escape temptation and sloshed on in the mud along the edge of the sidewalk. Finally he caught sight of the house he wanted, plum-coloured, with naked old men straining to hold up a balcony, and stained glass in the front door. He turned in at the gate past a spurstone showing the white marks of pigeons, stole across an inner court where two individuals with rolled-up sleeves were washing a dazzling carriage, went up a staircase and rang the bell. 'She's still asleep,' said the maid, looking at him with surprise. 'Wait here, won't you? I'll let Madam know in a while.' Luzhin shrugged off his satchel in businesslike fashion and laid it beside him on the table, which also bore a porcelain inkwell, a blotting case embroidered with beads, and an unfamiliar picture of his father (a book in one hand, a finger of the other pressed to his temple), and from nothing better to do he commenced to count the different hues in the carpet. He had been in this room only once before, last Christmas – when, on his father's advice, he had taken his aunt a large box of chocolates, half of which he had himself eaten and the remainder of which he had rearranged so that it would not be noticed. Up until just recently his aunt had been at their place every day, but now she had stopped coming and there was something in the air, some elusive interdiction, that prevented him from asking about it at home. Having counted up to nine different shades he shifted his gaze to a silk screen embroidered with rushes and storks. He had just begun to wonder whether similar storks were on the other side as well when at last his aunt came – her hair not yet done and wearing a kind of flowery kimono with sleeves like wings. 'Where did you spring from?' she exclaimed. 'And what about schoool? Oh what a funny boy you are. . . .'

Two hours later he again emerged onto the street. His satchel, now empty, was so light that it bounced on his shoulder blades. He had to pass time somehow until the usual hour of return. He wandered into Tavricheski Park and the emptiness in his satchel gradually began to annoy him. In the first place the thing he had left as a precaution with his aunt might somehow get lost before next time, and in the second place it would have come in handy at home during the evenings. He resolved to act differently in future.

'Family circumstances,' he replied the next day when the teacher casually inquired why he had not been in school. On Thursday he left school early and missed three days in a row, explaining afterwards that he had had a sore throat. On Wednesday he had a relapse. On Saturday he was late for the first lesson even though he had left home earlier than usual. On Sunday he amazed his mother by announcing that he had been invited to a friend's house – and he was away five hours. On Wednesday school broke up early (it was one of those wonderful blue dusty days at the very end of April when the end of the school term is already imminent and such indolence overcomes one), but he did not get home until much later than usual. And then there was a whole week of absence – a rapturous intoxicating week. The teacher telephoned his home to find out what was the matter with him. His father answered the phone.

When Luzhin returned home around four o'clock in the afternoon his father's face was gray, his eyes bulging, while his mother gasped as if deprived of her tongue and then began to laugh unnaturally and hysterically, with wails and cries. After a moment's confusion Father led him without a word into his study and there, with arms folded across his chest, requested an explanation. Luzhin, holding the heavy and precious satchel under his arm, stared at the floor, wondering whether his aunt was capable of betrayal. 'Kindly give me an explanation,' repeated his father. She was incapable of betrayal and in any case how could she know he had been caught? 'You refuse?' asked his father. Besides, she somehow seemed even to like his truancy. 'Now listen,' said his father conciliatorily, 'let's talk as friends.' Luzhin sighed and sat on the arm of a chair, continuing to look at the floor. 'As friends,' repeated his father still more soothingly. 'So now it turns out you have missed school several times. So *now* I would like to know where you have been and what you have been doing. I can even understand that, for instance, the weather is fine and one gets the urge to go for walks.' 'Yes, I get the urge,' said Luzhin indifferently, growing bored. His father wanted to know where exactly he had gone for a walk and whether his need of walks was long-standing. Then he reminded him that every man has his duty as citizen, as family man, as soldier, and also as schoolboy. Luzhin yawned. 'Go to your room!' said his father hopelessly and when his son had left he stood for a long time in the middle of his study and looked at the door in blank horror. His wife, who had been listening from the next room, came in, sat on the edge of the divan and again burst into tears. 'He cheats,' she kept repeating, 'just as you cheat. I'm surrounded by cheats.' He merely shrugged his shoulders and thought how sad life was, how difficult to do one's duty, not to meet anymore, not to telephone, not to go where he was irresistibly drawn ... and now this trouble with his son ... this oddity, this stubbornness ... A sad state of affairs, a very sad state. ...

CHAPTER FOUR

IN Grandfather's former study, which even on the hottest days was the dampest room in their country house no matter how much they opened the windows that looked straight out on grim dark fir trees, whose foliage was so thick and intricate that it was impossible to say where one tree ended and another began – in this uninhabited room where a bronze boy with violin stood on the bare desk – there was an unlocked bookcase containing the thick volumes of an extinct illustrated magazine. Luzhin would swiftly leaf through them until he reached the page where between a poem by Korinfski, crowned with a harp-shaped vignette, and the miscellany section containing information about shifting swamps, American eccentrics and the length of the human intestine, there was the woodcut of a chessboard. Not a single picture could arrest Luzhin's hand as it leafed through the volumes – neither the celebrated Niagara Falls nor starving Indian children (potbellied little skeletons) nor an attempted assassination of the King of Spain. The life of the world passed by with a hasty rustle, and suddenly stopped – the treasured diagram, problems, openings, entire games.

At the beginning of the summer holiday he had sorely missed his aunt and the old gentleman with the bunch of flowers – especially that fragrant old man smelling at times of violets and at times of lilies of the valley, depending upon what flowers he had brought to Luzhin's aunt. Usually he would arrive just right – a few minutes after Luzhin's aunt had glanced at her watch and left the house. 'Never mind, let's wait a while,' the old man would say, removing the damp paper from his bouquet, and Luzhin would draw up an armchair for him to the table where the chessmen had already been set out. The appearance of the old gentleman with the flowers had provided him with a way out of a rather awkward situation. After three or four truancies from school it became apparent that his aunt had really no aptitude for chess. As the game proceeded, her pieces would conglomerate in an unseemly jumble, out of which there would suddenly dash an exposed helpless King. But the old gentleman played divinely. The first time his aunt, pulling on her gloves, had said rapidly, 'Unfortunately I must leave but you stay on and play chess with my nephew, thank you for the wonderful lilies of the valley,' the first time the old man had sat down and sighed: 'It's a long time since I touched . . . now, young man – left or right ?' – this first time when after a few moves Luzhin's ears were burning and there was nowhere to advance, it seemed to Luzhin he was playing a completely different game from the one his aunt had taught him. The board was bathed in fragrance. The old man called the Officer a Bishop and the Tower, a Rook, and whenever he made a move that was fatal for his opponent he would immediately take it back, and as if disclosing the mechanism of an expensive instrument he would show the way his opponent should have played in order to avert disaster. He won the first fifteen games without the slightest effort, not pondering his moves for a moment, but during the sixteenth game he suddenly began to think and won with difficulty, while on the last day, the day he drove up with a whole bush of lilac for which no place could be found, and the boy's aunt darted about on tiptoe in her bedroom and then, presumably, left by the back door – on this last day, after a long exciting struggle during which the old man revealed a capacity for breathing hard through the nose – Luzhin perceived something, something was set free within him, something cleared up, and the mental myopia that had been painfully beclouding his chess vision disappeared. 'Well, well, it's a draw' said the old man. He moved his Queen back and forth a few times the way you move the lever of a broken machine and repeated: 'A draw. Perpetual check.' Luzhin also tried the lever to see if it would work, wiggled it, wiggled it, and then sat still, staring stiffly at the board. 'You'll go far,' said the old man. 'You'll go far if you continue on the same lines. Tremendous progress!

43

Never saw anything like it before. .... Yes, you'll go very, very far. ...'

It was this old man who explained to Luzhin the simple method of notation in chess, and Luzhin, replaying the games given in the magazine, soon discovered in himself a quality he had once envied when his father used to tell somebody at table that he personally was unable to understand how his father-in-law could read a score for hours and hear in his mind all the movements of the music as he ran his eye over the notes, now smiling, now frowning, and sometimes turning back like a reader checking a detail in a novel – a name, the time of the year. 'It must be a great pleasure,' his father had said, 'to assimilate music in its natural state.' It was a similar pleasure that Luzhin himself now began to experience as he skimmed fluently over the letters and numbers representing moves. At first he learned to replay the immortal games that remained from former tournaments – he would rapidly glance over the notes of chess and silently move the pieces on his board. Now and then this or that move, provided in the text with an exclamation or a question mark (depending upon whether it had been beautifully or wretchedly played), would be followed by several series of moves in parentheses, since that remarkable move branched out like a river and every branch had to be traced to its conclusion before one returned to the main channel. These possible continuations that explained the essence of blunder or foresight Luzhin gradually ceased to reconstruct actually on the board and contented himself with perceiving their melody mentally through the sequence of symbols and signs. Similarly he was able to 'read' a game already perused once without using the board at all; and this was all the more pleasant in that he did not have to fiddle about with chessmen while constantly listening for someone coming; the door, it is true, was locked, and he would open it unwillingly, after the brass handle had been jiggled many times – and Luzhin senior, coming to see what his son was doing in that damp uninhabited room, would find his son restless and sullen with red ears; on the desk lay the bound volumes of the magazine and Luzhin

44

senior would be seized by the suspicion that his son might have been looking for pictures of naked women. 'Why do you lock yourself up?' he would ask (and little Luzhin would draw his head into his shoulders and with hideous clarity imagine his father looking under the sofa and finding the chess set). 'The air in here's really icy. And what's so interesting about these old magazines? Let's go and see if there are any red mushrooms under the fir trees.'

Yes, they were there, those edible red boletes. Green needles adhered to their delicately brick-colored caps and sometimes a blade of grass would leave on one of them a long narrow trace. Their undersides might be holey, and occasionally a yellow slug would be sitting there – and Luzhin senior would use his pocketknife to clean moss and soil from the thick speckled-gray root of each mushroom before placing it in the basket. His son followed behind him at a few paces' distance, with his hands behind his back like a little old man, and not only did he not look for mushrooms but even refused to admire those his father, with little quacks of pleasure, unearthed himself. And sometimes, plump and pale in a dreary white dress that did not become her, Mrs. Luzhin would appear at the end of the avenue and hurry toward them, passing alternately through sunlight and shadow, and the dry leaves that never cease to occur in northern woods, would rustle beneath the slightly skewed high heels of her white slippers. One July day, she slipped on the veranda steps and sprained her foot, and for a long time afterwards she lay in bed – either in her darkened bedroom or on the veranda – wearing a pink negligee, her face heavily powdered, and there would always be a small silver bowl with *boules-de-gomme* – balls of hard candy standing on a little table beside her. The foot was soon better but she continued to recline as if having made up her mind that this was to be her lot, that this precisely was her destiny in life. Summer was unusually hot, the mosquitoes gave no peace, all day long the shrieks of peasant girls bathing could be heard from the river, and on one such oppressive and voluptuous day, early in the morning before the gadflies had yet begun to torment the black horse daubed with pungent

45

ointment, Luzhin senior stepped into the calash and was taken to the station to spend the day in town. 'At least be reasonable it's essential for me to see Silvestrov,' he had said to his wife the night before, pacing about the bedroom in his mouse-colored dressing gown. 'Really, how queer you are. Can't you see this is important? I myself would prefer not to go.' But his wife continued to lie with her face thrust into the pillow, and her fat helpless back shook with sobs. Nonetheless, in the morning he left – and his son standing in the garden saw the top part of the coachman and his father's hat skim along the serrated line of young firs that fenced off the garden from the road.

That day Luzhin junior was in low spirits. All the games in the old magazine had been studied, all the problems solved, and he was forced to play with himself, but this ended inevitably in an exchange of all the pieces and a dull draw. And it was unbearably hot. The veranda cast a black triangular shadow on the bright sand. The avenue was paved with sunflecks, and these spots, if you slitted your eyes, took on the aspect of regular light and dark squares. An intense latticelike shadow lay flat beneath a garden bench. The urns that stood on stone pedestals at the four corners of the terrace threatened one another across their diagonals. Swallows soared: their flight recalled the motion of scissors swiftly cutting out some design. Not knowing what to do with himself he wandered down the footpath by the river, and from the opposite bank came ecstatic squeals and glimpses of naked bodies. He stole behind a tree trunk and with beating heart peered at these flashes of white. A bird rustled in the branches, and taking fright he quickly left the river and went back. He had lunch alone with the housekeeper, taciturn sallow-faced old woman who always gave off a slight smell of coffee. Afterwards, lolling on the drawing room couch, he drowsily listened to all manner of slight sounds, to an oriole's cry in the garden, to the buzzing of a bumblebee that had flown in the window, to the tinkle of dishes on a tray being carried down from his mother's bedroom – and these limpid sounds were strangely transformed in his reverie and assumed the

46

shape of bright intricate patterns on a dark background; and in trying to unravel them he fell asleep. He was wakened by the steps of the maid dispatched by his mother. ... It was dim and cheerless in the bedroom; his mother drew him to her but he braced himself and turned away so stubbornly that she had to let him go. 'Come, tell me something,' she said softly. He shrugged his shoulders and picked at his knee with one finger. 'Don't you want to tell me anything?' she asked still more softly. He looked at the bedside table, put a *boule-de-gomme* in his mouth and began to suck – he took a second, a third, another and another until his mouth was full of sweet-thudding and bumping balls. 'Take some more, take as many as you wish,' she murmured, and stretching one hand from under the bedclothes she tried to touch him, to stroke him. 'You haven't got tanned at all this year,' she said after a pause. 'But perhaps I simply can't see, the light here is so dead, everything looks blue. Raise the Venetian blinds, please. Or no, wait, stay. Later.' Having sucked his *boules-de-gomme* to the end he inquired if he could leave. She asked him what he would do now and would he not like to drive to the station and meet his father off the seven o'clock train? 'Let me go,' he said. 'It smells of medicine in here.'

He tried to slide down the stairs the way they did at school – they way he himself never did it there; but the steps were too high. Beneath the staircase, in a cupboard that had still not been thoroughly explored, he looked for magazines. He dug out one and found a checkers section in it, diagrams of stupid clumsy round blobs on their boards, but there were no chess. As he rummaged on, he kept coming across a bothersome herbarium album with dried edelweiss and purple leaves in it and with inscriptions in pale violet ink, in a childish, thin-spun hand that was so different from his mother's present handwriting: *Davos 1885; Gatchina 1886*. Wrathfully he began to tear out the leaves and flowers, sneezing from the fine dust as he squatted on his haunches amid the scattered books. Then it got so dark beneath the stairs that the pages of the magazine he was again leafing through began to merge into a gray blur and

47

sometimes a small picture would trick him, because it looked like a chess problem in the diffuse darkness. He thrust the books back anyhow into the drawers and wandered into the drawing room, thinking listlessly that it must be well past seven o'clock since the butler was lighting the kerosene lamps. Leaning on a cane and holding on to the banisters, his mother in mauve peignoir came heavily down the stairs, a frightened look on her face. 'I don't understand why your father isn't here yet,' she said, and moving with difficulty she went out onto the veranda and began to peer down the road between the fir trunks that the setting sun banded with bright copper.

He came only around ten, said he had missed the train, had been extremely busy, had dined with his publisher – no no soup, thank you. He laughed and spoke very loudly and ate noisily, and Luzhin was struck by the feeling that his father was looking at him all the time as if staggered by his presence. Dinner graded into late evening tea. Mother, her elbow propped on the table, silently slitted her eyes at her plate of raspberries, and the gayer her husband's stories became the narrower her eyes grew. Then she got up and quietly left and it seemed to Luzhin that all this had happened once before. He remained alone on the veranda with his father and was afraid to raise his head, feeling that strange searching stare on him the whole time.

'How have you been passing the time?' asked his father suddenly. 'What have you been doing?' 'Nothing,' replied Luzhin. 'And what are you planning to do now?' asked Luzhin senior in the same tone of forced jollity, imitating his son's manner of using the formal plural for 'you'. 'Do you want to go to bed or do you want to sit here with me?' Luzhin killed a mosquito and very cautiously stole a glance upwards and sideways at his father. There was a crumb on his father's beard and an unpleasantly mocking expression gleamed in his eyes. 'Do you know what?' his father said and the crumb jumped off. 'Do you know what? Let's play some game. For instance, how about me teaching you chess?'

He saw his son slowly blush and taking pity on him immediately added: 'Or cabala – there is a pack of cards over there in the table drawer.' 'But no chess set, we have no chess set,' said Luzhin huskily and again stole a cautious look at his father. 'The good ones remained in town,' said his father placidly, 'but I think there are some old ones in the attic. Let's go take a look.'

And indeed, by the light of the lamp that his father held aloft, among all sorts of rubbish in a case Luzhin found a chessboard, and again he had the feeling that all this had happened before – that open case with a nail sticking out of its side, those dust-powdered books, that wooden chess-board with a crack down the middle. A small box with a sliding lid also came to light; it contained puny chessmen. And the whole time he was looking for the chess set and then carrying it down to the veranda, Luzhin tried to figure out whether it was by accident his father had mentioned chess or whether he had noticed something – and the most obvious explanation did not occur to him, just as sometimes in solving a problem its key turns out to be a move that seemed barred, impossible, excluded quite naturally from the range of possible moves.

And now when the board had been placed on the illuminated table between the lamp and the raspberries, and its dust wiped off with a bit of newspaper, his father's face was no longer mocking, and Luzhin, forgetting his fear, forgetting his secret, felt permeated all at once with proud excitement at the thought that he could, if he wanted dis-play his art. His father began to set out the pieces. One of the Pawns was replaced by an absurd purple-colored affair in the shape of a tiny bottle; in place of one Rook there was a checker; the Knights were headless and the one horse's head that remained after the box had been emptied (leaving a small die and a red counter) turned out not to fit any of them. When everything had been set out, Luzhin suddenly made up his mind and muttered: 'I already can play a little.' 'Who taught you?' asked his father without lifting his head. 'I learned it at school,' replied Luzhin. 'Some of the boys could play.' 'Oh! Fine,' said his father, and added (quoting Pushkin's doomed duelist): 'Let's start, if you are willing.'

He has played chess since his youth, but only seldom and sloppily, with haphazard opponents – on serene evenings aboard a Volga steamer, in the foreign sanatorium where his brother was dying years ago, here, in the country, with the village doctor, an unsociable man who periodically ceased calling on them – and all these chance games, full of oversights and sterile meditations, were for him little more than a moment of relaxation or simply a means of decently preserving silence in the company of a person with whom conversation kept petering out – brief, uncomplicated games, remarkable neither for ambition nor inspiration, which he always began in the same way, paying little attention to his adversary's moves. Although he made no fuss about losing, he secretly considered himself to be not at all a bad player, and told himself that if ever he lost it was through absentmindedness, good nature or a desire to enliven the game with daring sallies, and he considered that with a little application it was possible, without theoretic knowledge, to refute any gambit out of the textbook. His son's passion for chess had so astounded him, seemed so unexpected – and at the same time so fateful and inescapable – so strange and awesome was it to sit on this bright veranda amid the black summer night, across from this boy whose tensed forehead seemed to expand and swell as soon as he bent over the pieces – all this was so strange and awesome that Luzhin senior was incapable of thinking of the game, and while he feigned concentration, his attention wandered from vague recollections of his illicit day in St. Petersburg, that left a residue of shame it was better not to investigate, to the casual, easy gestures with which his son moved this or that piece. The game had lasted but a few minutes when his son said: 'If you do this it's mate and if you do that you lose your Queen,' and he, confused, took his move back and began to think properly, inclining his head first to the left and then to the right, slowly stretching out his fingers toward the Queen and quickly snatching them away again, as if burned, while in the meantime his son calmly, and with uncharacteristic tidiness, put the taken pieces into their box. Finally Luzhin senior made his move whereupon there started a devastation of his positions, and then he laughed unnaturally and knocked his King over in sign of surrender. In this way he lost three games and realized that should he play ten more the result would be just the same, and yet he was unable to stop. At the very beginning of the fourth game Luzhin pushed back the piece moved by his father and with a shake of his head said in a confident unchildlike voice: 'The worst reply. Chigorin suggests taking the Pawn.' And when with incomprehensible, hopeless speed he had lost this game as well, Luzhin senior again laughed, and with trembling hand began to pour milk into a cut-glass tumbler, on the bottom of which lay a raspberry core, which now floated to the surface and circled, unwilling to be extracted. His son put away the board, and the box on a wicker table in the corner and having blurted a phlegmatic 'good night' softly closed the door behind him.

'Oh well, I should have expected something like this,' said Luzhin senior, wiping the tips of his fingers with a handkerchief. 'He's not just amusing himself with chess, he's performing a sacred rite.'

A fat-bodied, fluffy moth with glowing eyes fell on the table after colliding with the lamp. A breeze stirred lightly through the garden. The clock in the drawing room started to chime daintily and struck twelve.

'Nonsense,' he said, 'stupid imagination. Many youngsters are excellent chess players. Nothing surprising in that. The whole affair is getting on my nerves, that's all. Bad of her – she shouldn't have encouraged him. Well, no matter. . . .'

He thought drearily that in a moment he would have to lie, to remonstrate, to soothe, and it was midnight already . . .

'I want to sleep,' he said, but remained sitting in the armchair.

And early next morning in the darkest and mossiest corner of the dense coppice behind the garden little Luzhin buried his father's precious box of chessmen, assuming this to be the simplest way of avoiding any kind of complications, for now there were other chessmen that he could use openly. His father, unable to suppress his interest in the matter, went off to see the gloomy country doctor, who was a far better chess player than he, and in the evening after dinner, laughing and rubbing his hands, doing his best to ignore the fact that all this was wrong – but why wrong he could not say – he sat his son down with the doctor at the wicker table on the veranda, himself set out the pieces (apologizing for the purple thingum), sat down beside the players and began avidly following the game. Twitching his bushy eyebrows and tormenting his fleshy nose with a large hairy fist, the doctor thought long over every move and from time to time would lean back in his chair as if able to see better from a distance, and make big eyes, and then lurch heavily forward, his hands braced against his knees. He lost – and grunted so loudly that his wicker armchair creaked in response. 'But look, look!' exclaimed Luzhin senior. 'You should go this way and everything is saved – you even have the better position.' 'Don't you see I'm in check?' growled the doctor in a bass voice and began to set out the pieces anew. And when Luzhin senior went out into the dark garden to accompany the doctor as far as the footpath with its border of glowworms leading down to the bridge, he heard the words he had so thirsted to hear once, but now these words weighed heavy upon him – he would rather not have heard them at all.

The doctor started coming every night and since he was really a first-rate player he derived enormous pleasure from these incessant defeats. He brought Luzhin a chess hand-book, advising him, however, not too get too carried away by it, not to tire himself, and to read in the open air. He spoke about the grand masters he had had the occasion to see, about a recent tournament and also about the past of chess, about a somewhat doubtful rajah and about the great Philidor, who was also an accomplished musician. At times, grinning gloomily, he would bring what he termed 'a sugar-plum' – an ingenious problem cut out of some periodical. Luzhin would pore over it a while, find finally the solution and with an extraordinary expression on his face and rad-iant bliss in his eyes would exclaim, burring his r's: 'How glorious, how glorious!' But the notion of composing problems himself did not entice him. He dimly felt that they would be a pointless waste of the militant, charging, bright force he sensed within him whenever the doctor, with strokes of his hairy finger, removed his King farther and farther, and finally, nodded his head and sat there quite still, looking at the board, while Luzhin senior, who was always present, always craving a miracle – his son's defeat – and was both frightened and overjoyed when his son won (and suffered from this complicated mixture of feelings), would seize a Knight or a Rook, crying that everything was not lost and would himself sometimes play to the end a hopelessly compromised game.

And thus it began. Between this sequence of evenings on the veranda and the day when Luzhin's photograph appeared in a St. Petersburg magazine it was as if nothing had been, neither the country autumn drizzling on the asters, nor the journey back to town, nor the return to school. The photograph appeared on an October day soon after his first unforgettable performance in a chess club. And everything else that took place between the return to town and the photograph – two months after all – was so blurry and so mixed up that later, in recalling this time, Luzhin was unable to say exactly when, for instance, that social evening had taken place at school – where in a corner, almost unnoticed by his schoolfellows, he had quietly beaten the geography teacher, a well-known amateur – or when on his father's invitation a gray-haired Jew came to dinner, a senile chess genius who had been victorious in all the cities of the world but now lived in idleness and poverty, purblind, with a sick heart, having lost forever his fire, his grip, his luck. . . . But one thing Luzhin remembered quite clearly – the fear he experienced in school, the fear they would learn of his gift and ridicule him – and consequently, guided by this infallible recollection, he judged that after the game played at the social evening he must not have gone to school any more, for remembering all the shudders of his childhood he was unable to imagine the horrible sensation he would have experienced upon entering the classroom on the following morning and meeting those inquisitive, all-knowing eyes. He remembered, on the other hand, that after his picture appeared he refused to go to school and it was impossible to untangle in his memory the knot in which the social evening and the photograph were joined, it was impossible to say which came first and which second. It was his father who brought him the magazine, and the photograph was one taken the previous year, in the country: a tree in the garden and he next to it, a pattern of foliage on his forehead, a sullen expression on his slightly inclined face, and those narrow white shorts that always used to come unbuttoned in front. Instead of the joy expected by his father, he expressed nothing – but he did feel a secret joy: now this would put an end to school. They pleaded with him during the course of a week. His mother, of course, cried. His father threatened to take away his new chess set – enormous pieces on a morocco board. And suddenly – everything was decided of itself. He ran away from home – in his autumn coat, since his winter one had been hidden after one unsuccessful attempt to run away – and not knowing where to go (a stinging snow was falling and settling on the cornices, and the wind would blow it off, endlessly reenacting this miniature blizzard), he wandered finally to his aunt's place, not having seen her since spring. He met her as she was leaving. She was wearing a black hat and holding flowers wrapped in a paper, on her way to a funeral. 'Your old partner is dead,' she said. 'Come with me.' Angry at not being allowed to warm himself, angry at the snow falling, and at the sentimental tears shining behind his aunt's veil, he turned sharply and walked away, and after walking about for an hour set off home. He did not remember the actual return – and even more curiously, was never sure whether things had happened thus or differently; perhaps his memory later added much that was taken from his delirium – for he was delirious for a whole week, and since he was extremely delicate and high-strung, the doctors presumed he would not pull through. It was not the first time he had been ill and when later reconstructing the sensation of this particular illness, he involuntarily recalled others.

54

of which his childhood had been full: he remembered especially the time when he was quite small, playing all alone, and wrapping himself up in the tiger rug, to represent, rather forlornly, a king – it was nicest of all to represent a king since the imaginary mantle protected him against the chills of fever, and he wanted to postpone for as long as possible that inevitable moment when they would feel his forehead, take his temperature and then bundle him into bed. Actually, there had been nothing quite comparable to his October chess-permeated illness. The gray-haired Jew who used to beat Chigorin, the corpse of his aunt's admirer muffled in flowers, the sly, gay countenance of his father bringing a magazine, and the geography teacher petrified with the suddenness of the mate, and the tobacco-smoke-filled room at the chess club where he was closely surrounded by a crowd of university students, and the clean-shaven face of the musician holding for some reason the telephone receiver like a violin, between shoulder and cheek – all this participated in his delirium and took on the semblance of a kind of monstrous game on a spectral, wobbly, and endlessly disintegrating board.

Upon his recovery, a taller and thinner boy, he was taken abroad, at first to the Adriatic coast where he lay on the garden terrace in the sun and played games in his head, which nobody could forbid him, and then to a German resort where his father took him for walks along footpaths fenced off with the twisted beech railings. Sixteen years later when he revisited this resort he recognized the bearded earthenware dwarfs between the flower beds, and the garden paths of colored gravel before the hotel that had grown bigger and handsomer, and also the dark damp wood on the hill and the motley daubs of oil paint (each hue marking the direction of a given walk) with which a beech trunk or a rock would be equipped at an intersection, so that the stroller should not lose his way. The same paperweights bearing emerald-blue views touched up with mother-of-pearl beneath convex glass were on sale in the shops near the spring and no doubt the same orchestra on the stand in the park was playing potpourris of opera, and the same maples were casting their lively shade over small tables where people drank coffee and ate wedge-shaped slices of apple tart with whipped cream.

'Look, do you see those windows?' he said, pointing with his cane at the wing of the hotel. 'It was there we had that pretty little tournament. Some of the most respectable German players took part. I was a boy of fourteen. Third prize, yes, third prize.

He replaced both hands on the crook of his thick cane with that sad, slightly old-mannish gesture that was natural to him now, and bent his head as if listening to distant music.

'What? Put on my hat? The sun is scorching, you say? I'd say it is ineffective. Why should you fuss about it? We are sitting in the shade.'

Nevertheless he took the straw hat extended to him across the little table, drummed on the bottom where there was a blurred dark spot over the hatmaker's name, and donned it with a wry smile – wry in the precise sense: his right cheek and the corner of his mouth went up slightly, exposing bad, tobacco-stained teeth; he had no other smile. And one would never have said that he was only beginning his fourth decade: from the wings of his nose there descended two deep, flabby furrows, his shoulders were bent; in the whole of his body one remarked an unhealthy heaviness; and when he rose abruptly, with raised elbow defending himself from a wasp, one saw he was rather stout – nothing in the little Luzhin had foreshadowed this lazy, unhealthy fleshiness. 'But why does it pester me?' he cried in a thin, querulous voice, continuing to lift his elbow and endeavoring with his other hand to get out his handkerchief. The wasp, having described one last circle, flew away, and he followed it with his eyes for a long time, mechanically shaking out his handkerchief; then he set his metal chair more firmly on the gravel picked up his fallen cane and sat down again, breathing heavily.

'Why are you laughing? Wasps are extremely unpleasant insects.' Frowning, he looked down at the table. Beside his cigarette case lay a handbag, semicircular, made of black

56

silk. He reached out for it absently and began to click the lock.

'Shuts badly,' he said without looking up. 'One fine day you'll spill everything out.'

He sighed, laid the handbag aside and added in the same tone of voice: 'Yes, the most respectable German players. And one Austrian. My late papa was unlucky. He hoped there would be no real interest in chess here and we landed right in a tournament.'

Things had been rebuilt and jumbled, the wing of the house now looked different. They had lived over there, on the second floor. It had been decided to stay until the end of the year and then return to Russia – and the ghost of school, which his father dared not mention, again loomed into view. His mother went back much earlier, at the beginning of summer. She said she was insanely homesick for the Russian countryside, and that protracted 'insanely' with such a plaintive, aching middle syllable was practically the sole intonation of hers that Luzhin retained in his memory. She left reluctantly, however, not really knowing whether to go or stay. It was already some time since she had begun to experience a strange feeling of estrangement from her son, as if he had drifted away somewhere, and the one she loved was not this grown-up boy, not the chess prodigy that the newspapers were writing about, but that little warm insupportable child who at the slightest pro-vocation would throw himself flat on the floor, screaming and drumming his feet. And everything was so sad and so unnecessary – that sparse un-Russian lilac in the station garden, those tulip-shaped lamps in the sleeping car of the Nord Express, and those sinking sensations in the chest, a feeling of suffocation, perhaps angina pectoris and perhaps, as her husband said, simply nerves. She went away and did not write; his father grew gayer and moved to a smaller room; and then one July day when little Luzhin was on his way home from another hotel – in which lived one of those morose elderly men who were his playmates – accidentally, in the bright low sun, he caught sight of his father by the wooden railings of a hillside path. His father was with a

57

lady, and since that lady was certainly his young red-haired aunt from St. Petersburg, he was very surprised and somehow ashamed and he did not say anything to his father. Early one morning a few days after this he heard his father swiftly approach his room along the corridor, apparently laughing loudly. The door was burst open and his father entered holding out a slip of paper as if thrusting it away. Tears rolled down his cheeks and along his nose as if he had splashed his face with water and he kept repeating with sobs and gasps: 'What's this? What's this? It's a mistake, they've got it wrong' – and continued to thrust away the telegram.

CHAPTER FIVE

HE played in St. Petersburg, Moscow, Nizhny Novgorod, Kiev, Odessa. There appeared a certain Valentinov, a cross between tutor and manager. Luzhin senior wore a black armband – mourning for his wife – and told provincial journalists that he would never have made such a thorough survey of his native land had he not had a prodigy for a son.

He battled at tournaments with the best Russian players. He often took on a score of amateurs. Sometimes he played blind. Luzhin senior, many years later (in the years when his every contribution to émigré newspapers seemed to him to be his swan song – and goodness knows how many of these swan songs there were, full of lyricism and misprints) planned to write a novella about precisely such a chess-playing small boy, who was taken from city to city by his father (foster father in the novella). He began to write it in 1928 – after returning home from a meeting of the Union of Émigré Writers, at which he had been the only one to turn up. The idea of the book came to him unexpectedly and vividly, as he was sitting and waiting in the conference room of a Berlin coffeehouse. As usual he had come very early, expressed surprise that the tables had not been placed together, told the waiter to do this immediately and ordered tea and a pony of brandy. The room was clean and brightly lit, with a still life on the wall representing plump peaches around a watermelon minus one wedge. A clean tablecloth ballooned gently and settled over the connected tables. He put a lump of sugar in his tea and watching the bubbles rise, warmed his bloodless, always cold hands on the glass. Nearby in the bar a violin and piano were playing selections from *La Traviata* – and the sweet music, the brandy, the whiteness of the clean tablecloth – all this made old Luzhin so sad, and this sadness was so pleasant, that he was loath to move: so he just sat there, one elbow propped on the table, a finger pressed to his temple – a gaunt, red-eyed old man wearing a knitted waistcoat under his brown jacket. The music played, the empty room was flooded with light, the wound of the watermelon glowed scarlet – and nobody seemed to be coming to the meeting. Several times he looked at his watch, but then the tea and the music bemisted him so mellowly that he forgot about time. He sat quietly thinking about this and that – about a typewriter he had acquired second-hand, about the Marinsky Theater, about the son who so rarely came to Berlin. And then he suddenly realized that he had been sitting there for an hour, that the tablecloth was still just as bare and white. . . . And in this luminous solitude that seemed to him almost mystical, sitting at a table prepared for a meeting that did not take place, he forthwith decided that after a long absence literary inspiration had revisited him.

Time to do a little summing up, he thought and looked round the empty room – tablecloth, blue wallpaper, still life – the way one looks at a room where a famous man was born. And old Luzhin mentally invited his future biographer (who as one came nearer to him in time became paradoxically more and more insubstantial, more and more remote) to take a good close look at this chance room where the novella *The Gambit* had been evolved. He drank the rest of his tea in one gulp, donned his coat and hat, learned from the waiter that today was Tuesday and not Wednesday, smiled not without a certain satisfaction over his own absentmindedness and immediately upon returning home removed the black metal cover from his typewriter.

The most vivid thing standing before his eyes was the following recollection (slightly retouched by a writer's imagination): a bright hall, two rows of tables, chessboards on the tables. A person sits at each table and at the back of each sitter spectators stand in a cluster, craning their necks. And now down the aisle between the tables, looking at no one, hurries a small boy – dressed like the Tsarevich in an elegant white sailor suit. He stops in turn at each board and quickly makes a move or else lapses briefly in thought, inclining his golden-brown head. An onlooker knowing nothing about simultaneous chess would be utterly baffled at the sight of these elderly men in black sitting gloomily behind boards that bristle thickly wth curiously cut manikins, while a nimble, smartly dressed lad whose presence here is inexplicable walks lightly from table to table in the strange, tense silence, the only one to move among these petrified people. . . .

The writer Luzhin did not himself notice the stylized nature of his recollection. Nor did he notice that he had endowed his son with the features of a musical rather than a chess-playing prodigy, the result being both sickly and angelic – eyes strangely veiled, curly hair, and a transparent pallor. But now he was faced with certain difficulties: this image of his son, purged of all alien matter and carried to the limits of tenderness, had to be surrounded with some sort of habitus. One thing he decided for sure – he would not let this child grow up, would not transform him into that taciturn person who sometimes called upon him in Berlin, replied to questions monosyllabically, sat there with his eyes half closed, and then went away leaving an envelope with money in it on the windowsill.

'He will die young,' he said aloud, pacing restlessly about the room and around the open typewriter, whose keys were all watching him with their pupils of reflected light. 'Yes, he will die young, his death will be logical and very moving. He will die in bed while playing his last game.' He was so taken with this thought that he regretted the impossibility of beginning the writing of the book from the end. But as a matter of fact, why was it impossible? One could try. . . . He started to guide his thought backwards – from this touching and so distinct death back to his hero's vague origin, but presently he thought better of it and sat down at his desk to ponder anew.

His son's gift had developed in full only after the war when the *Wunderkind* turned into the maestro. In 1914, on the very eve of that war which so hindered his memories from ministering to a neat literary plot, he had again gone abroad with his son, and Valentinov went too. Little Luzhin was invited to play in Vienna, Budapest and Rome. The fame of the Russian boy who had already beaten one or two of those players whose names appear in chess textbooks was growing so fast that his own modest literary fame was also being incidentally alluded to in foreign newspapers. All three of them were in Switzerland when the Austrian archduke was killed. Out of quite casual considerations (the notion that the mountain air was good for his son . . . Valentinov's remark that Russia now had no time for chess, while his son was kept alive solely by chess . . . the thought that the war would not last for long) he had returned to St. Petersburg alone. After a few months he could stand it no longer and sent for his son. In a bizarre, orotund letter that was somehow matched by its roundabout journey, Valentinov informed him that his son did not wish to come. Luzhin wrote again and the reply, just as orotund and polite, came not from Tarasp but from Naples. He began to loathe Valentinov. There were days of extraordinary anguish. There were absurd complications with the transfer of money. However, Valentinov proposed in one of his next letters to assume all the costs of the boy's maintenance himself – they would settle up later. Time passed. In the unexpected role of war correspondent he found himself in the Caucasus. Days of anguish and keen hatred for Valentinov (who wrote, however, diligently) were followed by days of mental peace derived from the feeling that life abroad was good for his son – better than it would have been in Russia (which was precisely what Valentinov affirmed).

Now, a decade and a half later, these war years turned out to be an exasperating obstacle; they seemed an encroachment upon creative freedom, for in every book describing the gradual development of a given human personality one had somehow to mention the war, and even the hero's dying in his youth could not provide a way out of this situation. There were characters and circumstances surrounding his son's image that unfortunately were conceivable only against the background of the war and which could not have existed without this background. With the revolution it was even worse. The general opinion was that it had influenced the course of every Russian's life; an author could not have his hero go through it without getting scorched, and to dodge it was impossible. This amounted to a genuine violation of the writer's free will. Actually, how could the revolution affect his son? On the long-awaited day in the fall of nineteen hundred and seventeen Valentinov appeared, just as cheerful, loud and magnificently dressed as before, and behind him was a pudgy young man with a rudimentary mustache. There was a moment of sorrow, embarrassment and strange disillusionment. The son hardly spoke and kept glancing askance at the window ('He's afraid there might be some shooting,' explained Valentinov in a low voice). All this resembled a bad dream at first – but one gets used to everything. Valentinov continued to assert that whatever was owed him could be settled 'among friends' later. It turned out that he had important secret business affairs and money tucked away in all the banks of allied Europe. Young Luzhin began to frequent an eminently quiet chess club that had trustfully blossomed forth at the very height of civil chaos, and in spring, together with Valentinov, he disappeared – once more abroad. After this came recollections that were purely personal, unbidden recollections, of no use to him – starvation, arrest, and so forth, and suddenly – legal exile, blessed expulsion, the clean yellow deck, the Baltic breeze, the discussion with Professor Vasilenko over the immortality of the soul.

Out of all this, out of all this crude mish-mash that stuck to the pen and tumbled out of every corner of his memory, degrading every recollection and blocking the way for free thought, he was unavoidably compelled to extract – carefully and piece by piece – and admit whole to his book – Valentinov. A man of undoubted talent, as he was characterized by those who were about to say something nasty about him; an odd fellow, a Jack-of-all trades, an indispensable man for the organization of amateur shows, engineer, superb mathematician, chess and checkers enthusiast, and 'the amusingest gentleman,' in the words of his own recommendation. He had wonderful brown eyes and an extraordinarily attractive laugh. On his index finger he wore a death's head ring and he gave one to understand that there had been duels in his life. At one time he had taught calisthentics in little Luzhin's school, and pupils and teachers alike had been much impressed by the fact that a mysterious lady used to come for him in a limousine. He invented in passing an amazing metallic pavement that was tried in St. Petersburg on the Nevsky, near Kazan Cathedral. He had composed several clever chess problems and was the first exponent of the so-called 'Russian' theme. He was twenty-eight the year war was declared and suffered from no illness. The anemic word 'deserter' somehow did not suit this cheerful, sturdy, agile man; no other word, however, can be found for it. What he did abroad during the war remained unknown.

And so Luzhin the writer decided to utilize him in full; thanks to his presence any story acquired extraordinary liveliness, a smack of adventure. But the most important part still remained to be invented. Everything he had up to now was the coloration – warm and vivid, no doubt, but floating in separate spots; he had still to find a definite design, a sharp line. For the first time the writer Luzhin had involuntarily begun with the colors.

And the brighter these colors became in his mind the harder it was to sit down at the typewriter. A month went by, another, the summer began, and still he continued to clothe his yet invisible theme in the most festive hues. Sometimes it seemed to him that the book was already written and he clearly saw the set-up type; the galley proof scrolls with red hieroglyphs in the margin, and then the advance copy, so fresh and crisp to the touch; and beyond that was a marvelous mist, delectable rewards for all his failures, for all the fickleness of fame. He visited his numerous acquaintances and lengthily, with great gusto, spoke of his coming book. One émigré newspaper printed a note to the effect that after a long silence he was working on a new tale. And this note, which he himself had written and sent in, he excitedly read over three times and then cut out and placed in his wallet. He began to appear with greater frequency at literary evenings, and he supposed that everyone must be looking at him with curiosity and respect. Once, on a treacherous summer day, he went to a suburban wood, got soaked in a sudden downpour while vainly looking for boletes, and the following day took to his bed. He ailed briefly and lonesomely, and his end was not pacific. The board of the Union of Émigré Writers honored his memory with a minute of silence.

CHAPTER SIX

'EVERYTHING will be spilled, that's certain,' said Luzhin, again taking possession of the handbag.

She quickly stretched forth her hand and moved her handbag farther away, banging it down on the table as if thereby to underline the interdiction. 'You always have to fiddle with something,' she said amicably.

Luzhin looked at his hand, splaying the fingers and then closing them up again. The nails, tawny with nicotine, had ragged cuticles around them; fat little furrows ran across the finger joints, and a few hairs grew lower down. He placed his hand on the table next to her hand, milky-pale and soft to look at, with short, neatly trimmed nails.

'I regret not having known your father,' she said after a pause. 'He must have been very kind, very earnest and very fond of you.'

Luzhin was silent.

'Tell me some more – how was your life here? Were you really a little boy once, running and romping about?'

He replaced both hands on his cane, and from the expression on his face, from the sleepy lowering of his heavy lids and from his slightly open mouth, looking as if he were about to yawn, she concluded that he had grown bored, that he was tired of reminiscing. And anyway, he reminisced coldly; she was puzzled that having lost his father only a month ago, he was now able to look dry-eyed at the hotel where they had lived together during his boyhood. But even in this indifference, in his clumsy words and in the cumbrous stirrings of his soul, that seemed to be drowsily turning over and falling asleep again, she fancied she saw something pathetic, a charm that was difficult to define but one that she had felt in him from the first day of their acquaintance. And how mysterious it was that despite the evident tepidity of his relationship with his father, he had chosen precisely this resort and precisely this hotel, as if expecting to receive from these once-seen objects and landscapes the tingle he was unable to experience without outside assistance. And he had arrived magnificently, on a gray and green day in a drizzling rain, wearing a disgraceful, black, shaggy hat and huge rubbers; and looking through the window at his figure as he clambered ponderously out of the hotel bus, she had felt that this unknown newcomer was someone quite special, unlike any other resident at the resort. That same evening she learned who he was. Everybody in the restaurant looked at this stout, gloomy man who ate greedily and sloppily and sometimes became lost in thought, one finger stroking the tablecloth. She did not play chess, took no interest in chess tournaments, but somehow or other his name was familiar to her, it had unconsciously imprinted itself in her memory, though she was unable to recall when she had first heard it. A German manufacturer who was a long time sufferer from constipation and liked to talk about it, a man with a one-track mind, but who was good-natured and pleasant and dressed with some taste, suddenly forgot his constipation and, in the gallery where they were drinking the curative water, informed her of several amazing facts about the gloomy gentleman who now, having exchanged his shaggy fedora for an old boater, was standing before a small display window let into one of the columns and examining some handcrafted knickknacks that were being exhibited for sale. 'Your fellow countryman,' said the manufacturer, indicating him with a jerk of the eyebrow, 'is a famous chess player. He has come from Paris for the tournament that will be held in Berlin in two months' time. If he wins he'll challenge the world champion. His father recently died. It's all here in the newspaper.'

She wanted to make his acquaintance, talk Russian – so attractive did he seem to her with his uncouthness, his gloominess and his low turndown collar which for some reason made him look like a musician – and she was pleased that he did not take any notice of her and seek an excuse to talk to her, as did all the other single men in the hotel.

She was not particularly pretty, there was something lacking in her small regular features, as if the last decisive jog that would have made her beautiful – leaving her features the same but endowing them with an ineffable significance – had not been given them by nature. But she was twenty-five, her fashionably bobbed hair was neat and lovely and she had one turn of the head which betrayed a hint of possible harmony, a promise of real beauty that at the last moment remained unfulfilled. She wore extremely simple and extremely well-cut dresses that left her arms and neck bare, as if she were flaunting a little their tender freshness. She was rich – her father had lost a fortune in Russia and made another in Germany. Her mother was due soon at the resort and since the advent of Luzhin the thought of her fussy arrival had become unpleasant.

She made his acquaintance on the third day after his arrival, made it the way they do in old novels or in motion pictures: she drops a handkerchief and he picks it up – with the sole difference that they interchanged roles. Luzhin was walking along a path in front of her and in succession shed: a large checked handkerchief that was unusually dirty and had all sorts of pocket debris sticking to it; then a broken and crushed cigarette minus half of its contents; a nut; and a French franc. She gathered up only the handkerchief and the coin and walked on, slowly catching up with him and curiously awaiting some new loss. With the cane he carried in his right hand, Luzhin touched in passing every tree trunk and every bench, while groping in his pocket with his left, until finally he stopped, turned out his coat pocket, shed another coin, and started to examine the large hole in the lining. 'Right through,' he said in German, taking the handkerchief from her hand ('This also,' she said in Russian). 'Poor material,' he continued without looking up, neither switching to Russian nor showing any surprise, as if the return of his things had been quite natural. 'Oh, don't put them back there,' she said with a sudden peal of laughter. Only then did he lift his head and glance morosely at her. His puffy gray face with its badly shaven, razor-nicked cheeks acquired a strange expression of bewilderment. He had wonderful eyes: they were narrow, even slightly slanting, and as if sprinkled with dust under their drooping lids; but through that fluffy dust there showed a moist bluish gleam containing something insane and attractive. 'Don't drop them again,' she said and walked away, feeling his glance on her back. That evening as she entered the restaurant she could not help smiling at him from afar and he responded with the same gloomy, crooked half-smile he sometimes bestowed on the hotel cat as it slipped noiselessly along the floor from one table to another. And on the following day, in the hotel garden, among the grottoes, fountains and earthenware dwarfs, he went up to her and began in his deep and melancholy voice to thank her for the handkerchief and the coin (and from that time, dimly and almost unconsciously, he constantly watched to see whether she would drop anything – as if trying to reestablish some secret symmetry). 'Don't mention it, don't mention it,' she replied and added many similar words – the poor relations of real words – and how many there are of them, these little throw-away words that are spoken hurriedly and temporarily fill the void. Employing such words and feeling their petty vapidity, she asked him if he liked the resort, was he there for long and took the waters. Then, fully aware of the stupidity of the question but incapable of stopping herself, she asked how long he had been playing chess. He gave no answer and turned away and she felt so embarrassed that she began to reel off a list of all the meteorological indications for yesterday, today and tomorrow. He continued silent and she also fell silent, and then she began to rummage in her handbag, searching agonizingly for a topic and finding only a broken comb. Suddenly he turned his face to her and said: 'Eighteen years, three months and four days.' For her this was an exquisite relief, and furthermore she was somehow flattered by the elaborate circumstantiality of his reply. Subsequently, however, she began to grow a little annoyed that he in his turn never asked any questions, taking her, as it were, for granted.

An artist, a great artist, she frequently thought, contemplating his heavy profile, his corpulent hunched body, the

69

dark lock of hair clinging to his always moist forehead. And perhaps it was precisely because she knew nothing at all about chess that chess for her was not simply a parlor game or a pleasant pastime, but a mysterious art equal to all the recognized arts. She had never been in close contact with such people – there was no one to compare him with except those inspired eccentrics, musicians and poets whose image one knows as clearly and as vaguely as that of a Roman Emperor, an inquisitor or a comedy miser. Her memory contained a modest dimly lit gallery with a sequence of all the people who had in any way caught her fancy. Here were her school reminiscences – the girls' school in St. Petersburg, with an unusual bit of ivy on its frontage that ran along a short, dusty, tramless street, and the geography teacher – who also taught in a boys' school – a large-eyed man with a very white forehead and tousled hair, suffering – they said – from tuberculosis; once a guest – they said – of the Dalai Lama; in love – they said – with one of the upper-form girls, a niece of the white-haired, blue-eyed headmistress, whose tidy little office was so cozy with its blue wallpaper and white Dutch stove. And it was precisely on a blue background, surrounded by blue air, that the geography teacher had remained in her memory: he would dash noisily into the classroom in his usual impulsive manner and then melt away and vanish, yielding his place to another person, who also seemed to her unlike all the rest. The appearance of this person was preceded by lengthy admonitions on the part of the headmistress not to laugh, not on any account to laugh. This was the first year of the Soviet regime; out of forty pupils in the class only seventeen remained, and every day they met the teachers with the question 'Will there be lessons today?' and the latter invariably replied: 'We still haven't received final instructions.' The headmistress ordered there to be no giggles when the man came from the Commissariat for Popular Education, whatever he might say and however he might behave himself. And he came and took up his abode in her memory as an extraordinarily amusing person, a visitor from a different, absurd world. He was lame but very lively

70

and squirmy, with quick, flickering eyes. The girls were crowded in the hushed hall, and he walked back and forth in front of them, limping briskly and turning with simian agility. And as he limped past them, nimbly dragging his foot on its double heel and with his right hand, cutting the air up into regular slices, or else smoothing it out like cloth, he spoke swiftly and at length about the lectures in sociology he would be giving and about an imminent merger with a boys' school – and restrained laughter made one's jaws ache and caused spasms in one's throat. And later in Finland, which had remained in her heart as something more Russian than Russia, perhaps because the wooden villa and the fir trees and the white boat on the lake, black with the reflected conifers, were especially Russian, being treasured as something forbidden on the far side of the frontier. In this Finland which was still vacation land, still part of St. Petersburg life, she saw several times from afar a celebrated writer, a very pale man with a very conspicuous goatee who kept glancing up at the sky, which enemy airplanes had begun to haunt. And he remained in some strange manner beside the Russian officer who subsequently lost an arm in the Crimea during the civil war – a most shy and retiring boy with whom she used to play tennis in summer and ski in winter – and with this snowy recollection there would float up once more against a background of night the celebrated writer's villa, in which he later died, and the cleared path and snowdrifts illumined by electric light, phantasmal stripes on the dark snow. These men with their various occupations, each of whom tinted her recollection his own particular color (blue geographer, khaki commissar, the writers' black overcoat and a youth all in white lobbing a fir cone with his tennis racket) were followed by glinting and dissolving images: émigré life in Berlin, charity balls, monarchist meetings and lots of identical people – all this was still so close that her memory was unable to focus properly and sort out what was valuable and what rubbish, and moreover there was no time now to sort it out, too much space had been taken up by this taciturn, fabulous, enigmatical man, the most attractive of all

71

the men she had known. His very art and all the manifestations and signs of this art were mysterious. She quickly learned that in the evenings after supper he worked until late at night. But this work was beyond the powers of her imagination, since there was nothing to link it to, neither an easel nor a piano, and it was just such a definite emblem of art that her thoughts reached out for. His room was on the first floor and men with cigars strolling in the darkness of the garden sometimes glimpsed his lamp and his inclined face. Somebody told her finally that he sat at an empty chessboard. She wanted to look for herself and one night, soon after their first conversation, she made her way along the footpath between the oleander bushes to his window. But feeling a sudden awkwardness she went straight by without looking and came out into the avenue, where she could hear music coming from the kursaal, and then, unable to master her curiosity, she went back again to the window, but this time deliberately making the gravel creak so as to convince herself she was not spying. His window was open, the blind unlowered, and in the bright depth of the room she saw him take off his jacket, tense his neck muscles and yawn. And in the slow, massive motion of his shoulder, the image of which continued to heave and turn before her eyes as she hastily walked away in the darkness toward the illuminated terrace of the hotel, she fancied the presence of a mighty fatigue after undivulged but surely miraculous labors.

Luzhin was indeed tired. Lately he had been playing too frequently and too unsystematically; he was particularly fatigued by playing blind, a rather well-paid performance that he willingly gave. He found therein deep enjoyment: one did not have to deal with visible, audible, palpable pieces whose quaint shape and wooden materiality always disturbed him and always seemed to him but the crude, mortal shell of exquisite, invisible chess forces. When playing blind he was able to sense these diverse forces in their original purity. He saw then neither the Knight's carved mane nor the glossy heads of the Pawns – but he felt quite clearly that this or that imaginary square was occupied by a definite, concentrated force, so that he envisioned the movement of a piece as a discharge, a shock, a stroke of lightning – and the whole chess field quivered with tension, and over this tension he was sovereign, here gathering in and there releasing electric power. Thus he played against fifteen, twenty, thirty opponents and of course the sheer number of boards told – since it affected the actual playing time – but this physical weariness was nothing compared to the mental fatigue – retribution for the stress and rapture involved in the game itself, which he conducted in a celestial dimension, where his tools were incorporeal quantities. He also found a certain solace in these blind games and the victories they afforded him, for in recent years he had been having no luck at international tournaments; a ghostly barrier had arisen that kept preventing him from coming first. Valentinov had happened to foretell this in the past, shortly before they parted. 'Shine while you can,' he had said after that unforgettable tournament in London, the first after the war, when the twenty-year-old Russian player came out the victor. 'While you can,' repeated Valentinov slyly, 'because you won't be a boy prodigy much longer.' And this was very important for Valentinov. He was interested in Luzhin only inasmuch as he remained a freak, an odd phenomenon, somewhat deformed but enchanting, like a dachshund's crooked legs. During the whole time that he lived with Luzhin he unremittingly encouraged and developed his gift, not bothering for a second about Luzhin as a person, whom, it seemed, not only Valentinov but life itself had overlooked. He showed him to wealthy people as an amusing monster, acquired useful contacts through him, and organized innumerable tournaments, and only when he began to suspect that the prodigy was turning simply into a young chess player did he bring him back to his father in Russia, and afterwards, like a kind of valuable, he took him away again when he thought that perhaps he had made a mistake, that the freak still had a year or two of life left in him. When even this span had run out he made a gift to Luzhin of some money, the way one does to a mistress one has tired of, and disappeared, finding fresh amusement in the movie business, that mysterious astrological business where they read scripts and look for stars. And having departed to the sphere of jaunty, quick-talking, self-important con-men with their patter about the philosophy of the screen, the tastes of the masses and the intimacy of the movie camera, and with pretty good incomes at the same time, he dropped out of Luzhin's world, which for Luzhin was a relief, that odd kind of relief you get in resolving an unhappy love affair. He had become attached to Valentinov immediately – as early as the days of his chess tours in Russia – and later he regarded him the way a son might a frivolous, coldish, elusive father to whom one could never say how much one loved him. Valentinov was interested in him only as a chess player. At times he had about him something of the trainer who hovers about an athlete establishing a definite regime with merciless severity. Thus Valentinov asserted that it was all right for a chess player to smoke (since there was in both chess and smoking a touch of the East) but not in any circumstances to drink, and during their life together in the dining rooms of large hotels, enormous hotels deserted in wartime, in chance restaurants, in Swiss inns and in Italian *trattorie*, he invariably ordered mineral water for young Luzhin. The food he chose for him was light so that his brain could function freely, but for some reason (perhaps also because of a hazy connection with 'the East') he encouraged Luzhin a great deal in his passion for sweets. Finally he had a peculiar theory that the development of Luzhin's gift for chess was connected with the development of the sexual urge, that with him chess represented a special deflection of this urge, and fearing lest Luzhin should squander his precious power in releasing by natural means the beneficial inner tension, he kept him at a distance from women and rejoiced over his chaste moroseness. There was something degrading in all this; Luzhin, recalling that time, was surprised to note that not a single, kind, humane word had passed between him and Valentinov. Nevertheless when, three years after their final departure from Russia, that land which had grown so unpleasant, Valentinov had vanished, he experienced a feeling of emptiness, a lack of support, and then he acknowledged the inevitability of what had happened, sighed, turned around and again was lost in thought over the chessboard. After the war, tournaments began to increase. He played in Manchester, where the decrepit champion of England forced a draw after a two-day struggle; in Amsterdam, where he lost the deciding game because he exceeded the time limit and his opponent, with an excited grunt, banged down the stop of Luzhin's clock; in Rome, where Turati triumphantly unleashed his celebrated debut; and in many other cities which for him were all identical – hotel, taxi, a hall in a café or club. These cities, these regular rows of blurry lamps marching past and suddenly advancing and encircling a stone horse in a square, were as much a habitual and unnecessary integument as the wooden pieces and the black and white board, and he accepted this external life as something inevitable but completely uninteresting. Similarly, in his way of dressing and in the manner of his everyday life, he was prompted by extremely dim motives, stopping to think about nothing, rarely changing his linen, automatically winding his watch at night, shaving with the same safety blade until it ceased to cut altogether, and feeding haphazardly and plainly. From some kind of melancholy inertia he continued to order at dinner the same mineral water, which effervesced slightly in his sinuses and evoked a tickling sensation in the corners of his eyes, like tears for the vanished Valentinov. Only rarely did he notice his own existence, when for example lack of breath – the revenge of a heavy body – forced him to halt with open mouth on a staircase, or when he had toothache, or when at a late hour during his chess cogitations an outstretched hand shaking a matchbox failed to evoke in it the rattle of matches, and the cigarette that seemed to have been thrust unnoticed into his mouth by someone else suddenly grew and asserted itself, solid, soulless, and static, and his whole life became concentrated in the single desire to smoke, although goodness knows how many cigarettes had already been unconsciously consumed.

In general, life around him was so opaque and demanded so little effort of him that it sometimes seemed someone – a mysterious, invisible manager – continued to take him from tournament to tournament; but occasionally there were odd moments, such quietness all around, and when you looked out into the corridor – shoes, shoes, shoes, standing at all the doors, and in your ears the roar of loneliness. When his father was still alive Luzhin used to think with a sinking feeling about his arrival in Berlin, about the necessity of seeing his father, helping him, talking to him – and this cheerful-looking old man in his knitted waistcoat, clapping him clumsily on the shoulder, was intolerable to him, like a shameful recollection that you try to throw off, screwing up your eyes and moaning through your teeth. He did not come from Paris for his father's funeral, fearing, above all, corpses, coffins, wreaths and the responsibility connected with all this – but he came later, set off for the cemetery, tramped around in the rain among the graves in mud-caked rubbers, failed to find his father's grave and behind some trees caught sight of a man who was probably the caretaker, but a strange feeling of inertia and shyness prevented him from inquiring; he raised his collar and plodded back over a patch of waste ground toward the waiting taxi. His father's death did not interrupt his work. He was getting ready for the Berlin tournament with the definite idea of finding the best defense against the complex opening of the Italian Turati who was the most awesome of the future participants in the tournament. This player, a representative of the latest fashions in chess, opened the game by moving up on the flanks, leaving the middle of the board unoccupied by Pawns but exercising a most dangerous influence on the center from the sides. Scorning the cozy safety of castling he strove to create the most unexpected and whimsical interrelations between his men. Luzhin had already met him once and lost, and this defeat particularly rankled because Turati, by temperament, by his style of play and by his proclivity for fantastic arrayals, was a player with a kindred mentality to his own, only Turati had gone farther. Luzhin's game, which in his early youth had so astounded the experts with its unprecedented boldness and disregard for the basic, as it seemed, rules of chess, now appeared just a little old-fashioned compared with the glittering extremism of Turati. Luzhin's present plight was that of a writer or composer who, having assimilated the latest things in art at the beginning of his active career and caused a temporary sensation with the originality of his devices, all at once notices that a change has imperceptibly taken place around him, that others, sprung from goodness knows where, have left him behind in the very devices where he recently led the way, and then he feels himself robbed, sees only ungrateful imitators in the bold artists who have overtaken him, and seldom understands that he himself is to blame, he who has petrified in his art which was once new but has not advanced since then.

Looking back over eighteen and more years of chess Luzhin saw an accumulation of victories at the beginning and then a strange lull, bursts of victories here and there but in general – irritating and hopeless draws, thanks to which he imperceptibly earned the reputation of a cautious, impenetrable prosaic player. And this was strange. The bolder his imagination, the livelier his invention during his secret work between matches, the more oppressive became his feeling of helplessness when the contest began and the more timidly and circumspectly he played. Having long ago entered the ranks of international grandmasters, extremely well known, cited in all chess textbooks, a candidate among five or six others for the title of world champion, he owed this flattering reputation to his early performances, which had left around him a kind of indistinct light, the halo of the chosen, a haze of glory. His father's death presented itself to him as a landmark by which to measure the road he had traveled. And looking back he saw with something of a shudder how slowly he had been going of late, and having seen it he plunged with gloomy passion into new calculations, inventing and already vaguely sensing the harmony of the moves he needed: a dazzling defense. He had been unwell that night in a Berlin hotel after his trip to

77

the cemetery; palpitations of the heart and queer thoughts, and a feeling that his brain had gone numb and been varnished over. The doctor he saw in the morning advised him to take a rest, to go to some quiet place '... where there is greenery all around,' said the doctor. And Luzhin, canceling a promised display of blind chess, went away to the obvious place, which had immediately loomed before him when the doctor referred to greenery; in fact, he felt dimly grateful to an obliging memory that indicated the necessary resort so aptly, took all the trouble on itself and put him into a ready-made, ready-waiting hotel.

He did feel better amid this green scenery that was moderately beautiful and transmitted a feeling of security and tranquillity. And suddenly, as in a fairground booth when a painted paper screen is burst starwise, admitting a smiling human face, there appeared from no one knew where a person who was so unexpected and so familiar, and who spoke with a voice that seemed to have been sounding mutely all his life and now had suddenly burst through the usual murk. Trying to unravel in his mind this impression of something very familiar he recalled quite irrelevantly but with stunning clarity the face of a bare-shouldered, black-stockinged young prostitute, standing in a lighted doorway in a dark side street in a nameless town. And in some ridiculous way it seemed to him that this was she, that she had come now, primly dressed and somewhat less pretty, as if she had washed off some bewitching makeup but because of this had become more accessible. This was his first impression when he saw her, when he noticed with surprise that he was actually talking to her. It irked him a little that she was not quite as good-looking as she might have been, judging by odd dreamy signs strewn about in his past. He reconciled himself to this and gradually began to forget her vague prototypes, and then he felt reassured and proud that here talking to him, spending her time with him and smiling at him, was a real live person. And that day on the garden terrace, where bright yellow wasps kept settling on the iron tables and moving their lowered antennae – that day when he started to speak of how he had once

78

lived in this hotel as a small boy – Luzhin began with a series of quiet moves, the meaning of which he himself only vaguely sensed, his own peculiar declaration of love. 'Go on, tell me more,' she repeated, despite having noticed how morosely and dully he had fallen silent.

He sat leaning on his cane and thinking that with a Knight's move of this lime tree standing on a sunlit slope one could take that telegraph pole over there, and simultaneously he tried to remember what exactly he had just been talking about. A waiter with a dozen empty beer mugs hanging from his crook'd fingers ran along the wing of the building, and Luzhin remembered with relief that he had been speaking about the tournament that once took place in that very wing. He grew agitated and hot, and the band of his hat constricted his temples, and this agitation was not quite comprehensible yet. 'Let's go,' he said. 'I'll show you. It must be empty there now. And cool.' Stepping heavily and trailing his cane which grated along the gravel and bounced against the doorstep, he entered the door first. How ill-bred he is, she reflected and caught herself shaking her head, and then accused herself of introducing a slightly false note – his manners had nothing at all to do with ill-breeding. 'Here, I think it's this way,' said Luzhin and pushed a side door. A fire was burning, a fat man in white was shouting something and a tower of plates ran past on human legs. 'No, farther,' said Luzhin and walked along the corridor. He opened another door and almost fell: steps going down, and some shrubs at the bottom, and a pile of rubbish, and an apprehensive hen, jerkily walking away. 'I made a mistake,' said Luzhin, 'it's probably here to the right.' He removed his hat, feeling burning beads of sweat gather on his brow. Oh, how clear was the image of that cool, empty, spacious hall and how difficult it was to find it! 'Let's try this door here,' he said. The door proved to be locked. He pressed the handle down several times. 'Who's there?' a hoarse voice said abruptly, and a bed creaked. 'Mistake, mistake,' muttered Luzhin and went farther; then he looked back and stopped: he was alone. 'Where is she?' he said aloud, shuffling his feet as he turned this way and that. Corridor. Window

79

giving on garden. Gadget on wall, with numbered pigeon-holes. A bell whirred. In one of the pigeonholes a number popped up awry. He was bemused and troubled, as if he had lost his way in a bad dream – and he quickly walked back, repeating under his breath: 'Queer jokes, queer jokes.' He came out unexpectedly into the garden, and there two characters were sitting on a bench and looking at him curiously. Suddenly he heard laughter overhead and raised his face. She was standing on the little balcony of her room and laughing, her elbows propped on the railings, her palms pressed against her cheeks, and shaking her head with sly reproachfulness. She looked at his ample face, the hat on the back of his head, and waited to see what he would do now. 'I couldn't keep up with you,' she cried, straightening up and opening her arms in some kind of explanatory gesture. Luzhin lowered his head and entered the building. She supposed that in a moment he would knock on her door and she decided not to let him in and say the room was untidy. But he did not knock. When she went down to supper he was not in the dining room. He's taken offense, she decided and went to bed earlier than usual. In the morning she went out for a walk and looked to see if he was waiting in the garden, reading his newspaper on a bench as usual. He was not in the garden, he was not in the gallery, and she went for a walk without him. When he did not appear for dinner and his table was taken by an ancient couple who had long had their eye on it, she asked in the office if Mr. Luzhin was sick. 'Mr. Luzhin left this morning for Berlin,' replied the girl.

An hour later his baggage returned to the hotel. The janitor and a bellboy, with matter-of-fact indifference, carried in the bags which that morning they had carried out. Luzhin was returning from the station on foot – a stout, doleful gentleman, crushed by the heat and in shoes white with dust. He rested on all the benches and once or twice plucked a blackberry, grimacing from the sourness. While walking along the highway he noticed a fair-haired small boy following him with tiny steps, holding an empty beer bottle in his hands, and lagging behind on purpose and staring at him with unbearable childish concentration.

Luzhin halted. The boy also halted. Luzhin moved, the boy moved. Then Luzhin lost his temper and threatened him with his cane. The other froze, grinning with surprise and joy. 'I'll . . .' said Luzhin in a deep voice and went toward him, his cane raised. The small boy jumped and ran off. Grumbling to himself and breathing hard through the nose, Luzhin continued on his way. All at once an extremely well-aimed pebble hit him on the left shoulder blade. He let out a cry and turned around. Nobody – an empty road, woods, heather. 'I'll kill him,' he said loudly in German and walked on faster, trying to weave from side to side, the way, he had read somewhere, men do when they fear a shot in the back, and repeating his helpless threat. He was quite exhausted, panting and almost crying by the time he reached the hotel. 'Changed my mind,' he said, addressing the office grille as he went by. 'I'm staying, changed my mind. . . .'

'She's sure to be in her room,' he said as he went up the stairs. He burst in upon her as if he had butted the door with his head, and dimly catching sight of her reclining in a pink dress on the couch, he said hastily: 'H'llo – h'llo,' and strode all around the room, supposing that everything was working out very easily, wittily and entertainingly, and simultaneously suffocating with excitement. 'And therefore in continuance of the above I have to inform you that you will be my wife, I implore you to agree to this, it was absolutely impossible to go away, now everything will be different and wonderful,' and at this point he settled on a chair by the radiator and, covering his face with his hands, burst into tears; then trying to spread one hand so that it covered his face he began with the other to search for his handkerchief, and through the trembling wet chinks between his fingers he perceived in duplicate a blurry pink dress that noisily moved toward him. 'Now, now, that's enough, that's enough,' she repeated in a soothing voice. 'A grown man and crying like that.' He seized her by the elbow and kissed something hard and cold – her wristwatch. She removed his straw hat and stroked his forehead – and swiftly retreated, evading his clumsy, grabbing movements.

Luzhin trumpeted into his handkerchief, once, once more, loudly and juicily; then he wiped his eyes, cheeks and mouth and sighed with relief, leaning on the radiator, his moist bright eyes looking in front of him. It was then that she realized clearly that this man, whether you liked him or not, was not one you could thrust out of your life, that he had sat himself down firmly, solidly and apparently for a long time. But she also wondered how she could show this man to her father and mother, how could he be visualized in their drawing room – a man of a different dimension, with a particular form and coloring that was compatible with nothing and no one.

At first she tried fitting him this way and that in her family, among their milieu and even among the furnishings of their flat: she made an imaginary Luzhin enter the rooms, talk with her mother, eat home-cooked kulebiaka and be reflected in the sumptuous samovar purchased abroad – and these imaginary calls ended with a monstrous catastrophe, Luzhin with a clumsy motion of his shoulder would knock the house down like a shaky piece of scenery that emitted a sigh of dust. Their apartment was an expensive, well appointed one, on the first floor of an enormous Berlin apartment house. Her parents, rich once more, had first decided to start living in strict Russian style which they somehow associated with ornamental Slavic scriptory, postcards depicting sorrowing boyar maidens, varnished boxes bearing gaudy pyrogravures of troikas or firebirds, and the admirably produced, long since expired art magazines containing such wonderful photographs of old Russian manors and porcelain. Her father used to say to his friends that it was particularly pleasant after business meetings and conversations with people of dubious origin to immerse himself in genuine Russian comfort and eat genuine Russian food. At one time their servant had been a genuine Russian orderly taken from an émigré shelter near Berlin, but for no apparent reason he became extraordinarily rude and was replaced by a German-Polish girl. The mother, a stately lady with plump arms, used to call herself affectionately an 'enfant terrible' and a 'Cossack' (a result

82

of vague and distorted reminiscences from *War and Peace*);
she played the Russian housewife superbly, had a weakness for theosophy and denounced the radio as a Jewish
invention. She was very kind and very tactless, and sincerely
loved the daubed, artificial Russia she had rigged up around
her, but sometimes she became unbearably bored, not knowing exactly what was missing, for, as she put it, she for one
had brought her own Russia with her. The daughter was
completely indifferent to this gimcrack apartment, so unlike their quiet St. Petersburg house, where the furniture
and other things had their own soul, where the icon-
cabinet harbored an unforgettable garnet gleam and mysterious orange tree blossoms, where a fat, intelligent cat
was embroidered on the silk back of an armchair, and where
there were a thousand trifles, smells and shades that all together constituted something ravishing, and heartrending,
and completely irreplaceable.

The young Russians who visited them in Berlin considered her a nice but not very interesting girl, while her
mother said of her (in a low-pitched voice with a trace of
derision) that she represented in the family 'the intelli-
gentsia and avant-garde literature' -- whether because she
knew by heart a few poems of the 'Symbolist' Balmont that
she had found in the *Poetry Reader* or whether for some
other reason, remained unknown. Her father liked her in-
dependence, her quietness, and her particular way of lowering her eyes when she smiled. But nobody yet had been able
to dig down to what was most captivating about her: this
was the mysterious ability of her soul to apprehend in life
only that which had once attracted and tormented her in
childhood, the time when the soul's instinct is infallible;
to seek out the amusing and the touching; to feel constantly an intolerable, tender pity for the creature whose
life is helpless and unhappy; to feel across hundreds of miles
that somewhere in Sicily a thin-legged little donkey with a
shaggy belly is being brutally beaten. Whenever she did
come across a creature that was being hurt, she experienced a kind of legendary eclipse – when inexplicable night
comes down and ash flies and blood appears on the walls –

and it seemed that if at once, at once, she did not help, did not cut short another's torture (the existence of which it was absolutely impossible to explain in a world so conducive to happiness), her heart would not stand it, and she would die. Hence, she lived in perpetual, secret agitation, constantly anticipating a new delight or a new pity, and it was said of her that she adored dogs and was always ready to lend money – and listening to these trivial rumors she felt as she had in childhood during that game where you go out of the room and the others talk about you, and you have to guess who said what. And among the players, among those whom she joined after a stay in the next room (where you sat waiting to be called and conscientiously sang something so as not to overhear, or else opened a chance book – and like a Jack-in-the-box a passage from a novel would spring up, the end of an unintelligible conversation), among those people whose opinion she had to guess there was now a rather taciturn man, difficult to budge and thinking completely unknown things about her. She suspected that he had no opinion at all, that he had no conception whatsoever of her milieu or the circumstances of her life, and so might blurt out something dreadful.

Deciding that she had been absent long enough, she gently passed her hand over the back of her head, smoothing down her hair, and returned smiling to the lobby. Luzhin and her mother, whom she had only just introduced to one another, were sitting in wicker armchairs beneath a potted palmetto, and Luzhin, his brows knitted, was examining his disgraceful straw hat which he was holding in his lap, and at that moment she was equally terrified by the thought of what words Luzhin was using about her (if, indeed, he was using any) and the thought of what impression Luzhin himself was making on her mother. The day before, as soon as her mother had arrived and begun to complain that her window faced north and the bedside lamp was not working, the daughter had related, trying to keep all her words on the same level, how she had become great friends with the famous chess player Luzhin. 'No doubt a pseudonym,' said her mother, burrowing in her toilet case. 'His real name is Rubinstein or Abramson.' 'Very, very famous,' continued the daughter, 'and very nice.' 'Help me rather to find my soap,' said her mother. And now, having introduced them and left them alone on the pretext of ordering some lemonade, she experienced as she returned to the lobby such a feeling of horror, of the irreparability of already completed catastrophes that while still some distance away she began to speak loudly, then tripped on the edge of the carpet and laughed, waving her hands to keep her balance. His senseless fiddling with the boater, the silence, her mother's amazed, gleaming eyes, and the sudden recollection of how he had sobbed the other day, his arms round the radiator – all this was very hard to bear, but suddenly Luzhin raised his head, his mouth twisted into that familiar, morose smile – and at once her fear vanished and the potential disaster seemed something that was extraordinarily amusing, changing nothing. As if he had waited for her return in order to retire, Luzhin grunted, stood up and gave a remarkable nod ('boorish', she thought gaily, translating this nod into her mother's idiom) before proceeding toward the staircase. On the way he met the waiter bringing three glasses of lemonade on a tray. He stopped him, took one of the glasses, and holding it carefully in front of him, mimicking the swaying level of the liquid with his eyebrows, began slowly to mount the stairs. When he had disappeared round the bend she began with exaggerated care to peel the thin paper from her straw. 'What a boor!' said her mother loudly, and the daughter felt the kind of satisfaction you get when you find in the dictionary the meaning of a foreign term you have already guessed. 'That's not a real person,' continued her mother in angry perplexity. 'What is he? Certainly not a real person. He calls me madame, just madame, like a shop assistant. He's God knows what. And I'll guarantee he has a Soviet passport. A Bolshevik, just a Bolshevik. I sat there like an idiot. And his small talk ...! His cuffs are quite soiled, by the way. Did you notice? Soiled and frayed.'

'What kind of small talk?' she asked, smiling from beneath lowered brows.

' "Yes madame, no madame". "There's a nice atmosphere here". Atmosphere! Quite a word, eh? I asked him – to say something – if it was long since he had left Russia. He simply was silent. Then he remarked about you that you like cooling "beverages". Cooling "beverages"! And what a mug, what a mug! No, no, let us steer clear of such characters . . .'

Continuing the game of opinions she hastened to Luzhin. In the course of his botched departure his room had been given to someone else and he had been assigned to another one higher up. He was sitting with his elbows on the table, as if grief-stricken, and in the ashtray an insufficiently stubbed cigarette was struggling to send up smoke. On the table and floor were scattered sheets of paper covered with writing in pencil. For a second she thought they were bills and she wondered at their number. The wind blowing in through the open window gusted as she opened the door and Luzhin, coming out of his reverie, picked up the sheets of paper from the floor and neatly folded them, smiling at her and blinking. 'Well? How did it go?' she asked. 'It'll take shape during the game,' said Luzhin. 'I'm simply jotting down a few possibilities.' She had the feeling she had opened the wrong door, entered where she had not intended to enter, but it was nice in this unexpected world and she did not want to go to that other one where the game of opinions was played. But instead of continuing to talk about chess Luzhin moved up to her together with his chair, grasped her by the waist with hands shaking from tenderness and not knowing what to undertake, attempted to seat her on his knees. She pushed her hands against his shoulders and averted her face, pretending to look at the sheets of paper. 'What's that?' she asked. 'Nothing, nothing,' said Luzhin, 'notes on various games.' 'Let me go,' she demanded in a shrill voice. 'Notes on various games, notes . . .' repeated Luzhin, pressing her to him, his narrowed eyes looking up at her neck. A sudden spasm distorted his face and for an instant his eyes lost all expression; then his features relaxed oddly, his hands unclenched of themselves, and she moved away from him, angry without knowing exactly why she was angry, and surprised that he had let her go. Luzhin cleared his throat and greedily lit a cigarette, watching her with incomprehensible mischievousness. 'I'm sorry I came,' she said. 'First, I interrupted your work . . .' 'Not a bit of it,' replied Luzhin with unexpected merriment and slapped his knees.

'Second, I wanted to get your impressions.'

'A lady of high society,' answered Luzhin, 'you can see that right away.'

'Listen,' she exclaimed, continuing to be cross, 'were you ever educated ? Where did you go to school ? Have you ever met people at all, talked to people ?'

'I've voyaged a great deal,' said Luzhin. 'Here and there. Everywhere a little bit.'

'Where am I ? Who is he ? What next ?' she asked herself mentally and looked round at the room, the table covered with sheets of paper, the crumpled bed, the washbasin – on which a rusty safety blade had been left lying – and a half-open drawer from which, snakelike, a green, red-spotted tie came crawling. And in the middle of this bleak disorder sat the most unfathomable of men, a man who occupied himself with a spectral art, and she tried to stop, to grasp at all his failings and peculiarities, to tell herself once for all that this man was not the right one for her – and at the same time she was quite distinctly worried about how he would behave in church and how he would look in tails.

CHAPTER SEVEN

THEIR meetings, of course, continued. The poor lady began to notice with horror that her daughter and the shady Mr. Luzhin were inseparable – there were conversations between them, and glances, and emanations that she was unable to determine with exactness; this seemed to her so dangerous that she overcame her repugnance and resolved to keep Luzhin by her as much as possible, partly in order to get a thorough look at him but chiefly so that her daughter would not vanish too often. Luzhin's profession was trivial, absurd. . . . The existence of such professions was explicable only in terms of these accursed modern times, by the modern urge to make senseless records (these airplanes that want to fly to the sun, marathon races, the Olympic games . . .). It seemed to her that in former times, in the Russia of her youth, a man occupying himself exclusively with chess would have been an unthinkable phenomenon. However, even nowadays such a man was so strange that she conceived a vague suspicion that perhaps chess was a cover, a blind, that perhaps Luzhin's occupation was something quite different, and she felt faint at the thought of that dark, criminal – perhaps Masonic – activity which the cunning scoundrel concealed behind a predilection for an innocent pastime. Little by little, however, this suspicion dropped away. How could you expect any trickery from such an oaf? Besides, he was genuinely famous. She was staggered and somewhat irritated that a name should be familiar to many when it was completely unknown to her (unless as a chance sound in her past, connected with a distant relative who had been acquainted with a certain Luzhin, a St. Petersburg landowner). The Germans who lived in the hotel at the resort, heroically mastering the difficulty of an alien sibilant, pronounced his name with reverence. Her daughter showed her the latest number of a Berlin illustrated magazine, where in the section devoted to puzzles and crosswords they published a for some reason remarkable game that Luzhin had recently won. 'But can a man really devote himself to such trifles,' she exclaimed, looking at her daughter distractedly, 'throw one's whole life away on such trifles ? . . . Look, you had an uncle who was also good at all sorts of games – chess, cards, billiards – but at least he had a job and a career and everything.' 'He has a career too,' replied the daughter, 'and really he's very well known. Nobody's to blame that you never took an interest in chess.' 'Conjurors can also be well known,' said she peevishly, but nonetheless after some thought she concluded that Luzhin's reputation partially justified his existence. His existence, however, was oppressive. What particularly angered her was that he constantly contrived to sit with his back to her. 'He even talks with his back,' she complained to her daughter. 'With his back. He doesn't talk like a human being. I tell you there's something downright abnormal there.' Not once did Luzhin address a question to her, not once did he attempt to support a collapsing conversation. There were unforgettable walks along sun-dappled footpaths, where here and there in the pleasant shade a thoughtful genius had set out benches – unforgettable walks during which it seemed to her that Luzhin's every step was an insult. Despite his stoutness and short wind he would suddenly develop extraordinary speed, his companions would drop back and the mother, compressing her lips, would look at the daughter and swear in a hissing whisper that if this record-breaking run continued she would immediately – immediately, you understand – return home. 'Luzhin,' the girl would call, 'Luzhin ? Slow up or you'll get tired.' (And the fact that her daughter called him by his surname was also unpleasant – but when she remarked upon it the other replied with a laugh: 'Turgenev's heroines did it. Am I worse than they ?') Luzhin would suddenly turn around, give a wry smile and plop down on a bench. Beside it would stand a wire basket. He would invariably rummage in his pockets, find some piece of paper or other, tear it neatly into sections and throw it into the basket, after which he would laugh jerkily. A perfect specimen of his little jokes.

Nonetheless, despite those joint walks Luzhin and her daughter used to find time to seclude themselves and after each such seclusion the angry lady would ask: 'Well, have you two been kissing? Kissing? I'm convinced you kiss.' But the other only sighed and answered with assumed boredom: 'Oh Mamma, how can you say such things . . .' 'Good long kisses,' she decided, and wrote to her husband that she was unhappy and worried because their daughter was conducting an impossible flirtation – with a gloomy and dangerous character. Her husband advised her to return to Berlin or go to another resort. 'He doesn't understand a thing,' she reflected. 'Ah well, it doesn't matter. All this will soon come to an end. Our friend will leave.'

And suddenly, three days before Luzhin's departure for Berlin, one little thing happened that did not exactly change her attitude to Luzhin but vaguely moved her. The three of them had gone out for a stroll. It was a still August evening with a magnificent sunset, like a mangled blood-orange pressed out to the very last drop. 'I feel a bit chilly,' she said. 'Bring me something to put on.' And the daughter nodded her head, said 'uh-huh' through the stalk of grass she was sucking and left, walking fast and slightly swinging her arms as she returned to the hotel.

'I have a pretty daughter, don't I? Nice legs.'

Luzhin bowed.

'So you're leaving on Monday? And then, after the game, back to Paris?'

Luzhin bowed again.

'But you won't stay in Paris long, will you? Somebody will again invite you to play somewhere?'

This is when it happened. Luzhin looked around and held out his cane.

'This footpath,' he said. 'Consider this footpath. I was walking along. And just imagine whom I met. Whom did I meet? Out of the myths. Cupid. But not with an arrow – with a pebble. I was struck.'

'What do you mean?' she asked with alarm.

'No, please, please,' exclaimed Luzhin, raising a finger. 'I must have audience.'

He came close to her and strangely half-opened his mouth, which caused an unusual expression of martyred tenderness to appear on his face.

'You are a kind, sensitive woman,' said Luzhin slowly. 'I have the honor, the honor of begging you to give me her hand.'

He turned away as if having finished a speech on the stage and began to gouge a small pattern in the sand with his cane.

'Here's your shawl,' said her daughter's breathless voice from behind and a shawl settled over her shoulders.

'Oh no, I'm hot, I don't need it, what do I want with a shawl . . .'

Their walk that evening was particularly silent. Through her mind ran all the words she would have to say to Luzhin – hints about the financial side – he was probably not well off, he had the cheapest room in the hotel. And a very serious talk with her daughter. An unthinkable marriage, a most idiotic venture. But despite all this she was flattered that Luzhin had so earnestly and old-fashionedly addressed himself to her first.

'It's happened, congratulations,' she said that evening to her daughter. 'Don't look so innocent, you understand perfectly well. Our friend wishes to marry.'

'I'm sorry he told you,' replied her daughter. 'It concerns only him and me.'

'To accept the first rogue you come across . . .' began the offended lady.

'Don't you dare,' said her daughter calmly. 'It's none of your business.'

And what had seemed an unthinkable venture began to develop with amazing celerity. On the eve of his departure Luzhin stood on the tiny balcony of his room in his long nightshirt and looked at the moon, which was tremblingly disengaging itself from some black foliage, and while thinking of the unexpected turn taken by his defense against Turati, he listened through these chess reflections to the voice that still continued to ring in his ears, cutting across

91

his being in long lines and occupying all the chief points. This was an echo of the conversation he had just had with her; she had again sat on his lap and promised – promised – that in two or three days she would return to Berlin, and would go alone if her mother decided to stay. And to hold her on his lap was nothing compared to the certainty that she would follow him and not disappear, like certain dreams that suddenly burst and disperse because the gleaming dome of the alarm clock has floated up through them. With one shoulder pressed against his chest she tried with a cautious finger to raise his eyelids a little higher and the slight pressure on his eyeball caused a strange back light to leap there, to leap like his black Knight which simply took the Pawn if Turati moved it out on the seventh move, as he had done at their last meeting. The Knight, of course, perished, but this loss was recompensed with a subtle attack by black and here the chances were on his side. There was, true, a certain weakness on the Queen's flank, or rather not a weakness but a slight doubt lest it was all fantasy, fireworks, and would not hold out, nor the heart hold out, for perhaps after all the voice in his ears was deceiving him and was not going to stay with him. But the moon emerged from behind the angular black twigs, a round, full-bodied moon – a vivid confirmation of victory – and when finally Luzhin left the balcony and stepped back into his room, there on the floor lay an enormous square of moonlight, and in that light – his own shadow.

CHAPTER EIGHT

THAT to which his fiancée was so indifferent produced on Luzhin an impression nobody could have foreseen. He visited the famous apartment, in which the very air seemed colored with phony folklore, immediately after obtaining his first point by defeating an extremely tenacious Hungarian; the game, it is true, had been postponed after forty moves, but the continuation was perfectly clear to Luzhin. To a faceless taxi driver he read aloud the address on the postcard ('We've come. *Zhdyom vas vecherom* – Expecting you this evening') and having imperceptibly surmounted the dim accidental distance, he cautiously tried to pull the ring out of the lion's jaws. The bell leapt into action immediately: the door flew open. 'What, no overcoat? I won't let you in . . .' but he had already stepped over the threshold, and was waving his arm and shaking his head in an attempt to overcome his shortness of breath. '*Pfoof, pfoof,*' he gasped, preparing himself for a wonderful embrace, and then suddenly noticed that his left hand, already extended to one side, held an unnecessary cane and his right his billfold, which he had evidently been carrying since he paid his taxi fare. 'Wearing that black monster of a hat again . . . Well, why are you standing there? This way.' His cane dived safely into a vaselike receptacle; his billfold, at the second thrust, found the right pocket; and his hat was hung on a hook. 'Here I am,' said Luzhin, '*pfoof, pfoof.*' She was already far away at the far end of the entrance hall; she pushed a door sidewise, her bare arm extended along the jamb, bending her head and gaily looking up at Luzhin. And over the door, immediately over the lintel, there was a large, vivid oil painting that caught the eye. Luzhin, who normally did not notice such things, gave his attention to it because it was greasily glossed with electric light and the colors dazed him, like a sunstroke. A village

93

girl in a red kerchief coming down to her eyebrows was eating an apple, and her black shadow on a fence was eating a slightly larger apple. 'A Russian *baba*,' said Luzhin with relish and laughed. 'Well, come in, come in. Don't upset that table.' He entered the drawing room and went all limp with pleasure, and his stomach, beneath the velvet waistcoat that for some reason he always wore during tournaments, quivered touchingly with laughter. A chandelier with pale translucent pendants answered him with an oddly familiar vibration; and on the yellow parquetry that reflected the legs of Empire armchairs, a white bearskin with spread paws lay in front of the piano, as if flying in the shiny abyss of the floor. All sorts of festive-looking knickknacks were on numerous small tables, shelves and consoles, while something resembling big heavy rubles gleamed silver in a cabinet and a peacock feather stuck out from behind the frame of a mirror. And there were lots of pictures on the walls – more country girls in flowered kerchiefs, a golden bogatyr on a white draft horse, log cabins beneath blue featherbeds of snow. . . . All this for Luzhin merged into an affecting glitter of color, from which a separate object would momentarily leap out – a porcelain moose or a dark-eyed icon – and then again there would be that gay rippling in his eyes, and the polar skin, which he tripped over causing one edge to reverse, turned out to have a scalloped red lining. It was more than ten years since he had been in a Russian home and now, finding himself in a house where a gaudy Russia was boldly put on display, he experienced a childish elation, a desire to clap his hands – never in his life had he felt so cozy and so at ease. 'Left over from Easter,' he said with conviction, pointing with his auricular finger at a large gold-patterned wooden egg (a tombola prize from a charity ball). At that moment a white double-leafed door burst open and a very upright gentleman with his hair *en brosse* and a pince-nez came swiftly into the room, one hand already stretched out. 'Welcome,' he said. 'Pleased to meet you.' Here, like a conjuror, he opened a handmade cigarette case that had an Alexander-the-First eagle on the lid. 'With mouthpieces,' said Luzhin, squinting at the cigarettes. 'I don't smoke that kind. But look . . .' He began to burrow in his pockets, extracting some thick cigarettes that were spilling from a paper pack; he dropped several of them and the gentleman nimbly picked them up. 'My pet,' he said, 'get us an ashtray. Please take a seat. Excuse me . . . er . . . I don't know your name and patronymic.' A crystal ashtray came down between them and simultaneously dipping their cigarettes they knocked the ends together 'J'adoube,' said the chess player good-naturedly, straightening his bent cigarette. 'Never mind, never mind,' said the other quickly and expelled two thin streams of smoke through the nostrils of his suddenly narrowed nose. 'Well, here you are in good old Berlin. My daughter tells me you came for a contest.' He freed a starched cuff, placed one hand on his hip and continued: 'By the way, I have always wondered, is there a move in chess that always enables one to win? I don't know if you understand me, but what I mean is . . . sorry . . . your name and patronymic?' 'I understand,' said Luzhin, conscientiously considering for a moment. 'You see, we have quiet moves and strong moves. A strong move . . .' 'Ah yes, yes, so that's it,' nodded the gentleman. 'A strong move is one that,' continued Luzhin loudly and enthusiastically, 'that immediately gives us an undoubted advantage. A double check, for example, with the taking of a heavyweight piece, or say, when a Pawn is queened. Et cetera. Et cetera. And a quiet move . . .' 'I see, I see,' said the gentleman. 'About how many days will the contest last?' 'A quiet move implies trickery, subversion, complication,' said Luzhin, trying to please but also entering into the spirit of things. 'Let's take some position. White . . .' He pondered, staring at the ashtray. 'Unfortunately,' said his host nervously, 'I don't understand anything about chess. I only asked you . . . But that does not matter at all, at all. In a moment we'll proceed to the dining room. Tell me, my pet, is tea ready?' 'Yes!' exclaimed Luzhin. 'We'll simply take the endgame position at the point it was interrupted today. White: King c3, Rook a1, Knight d5, Pawns b3 and c4. Black . . .' 'A complicated thing, chess,' interjected the gentleman and jumped buoyantly to his feet, trying to cut off the flood of letters and numbers having some kind of relation to black. 'Let us suppose now,' said Luzhin weightily, 'that black makes the best possible move in this position – e6 to g5. To this I reply with the following quiet move . . .' Luzhin narrowed his eyes and almost in a whisper, pursing his lips as for a careful kiss, emitted not words, not the mere designation of a move, but something most tender and infinitely fragile. The same expression was on his face – the expression of a person blowing a tiny feather from the face of an infant – when the following day he embodied this move on the board. The Hungarian, sallow-cheeked after a sleepless night, during which he had managed to check all the variations (leading to a draw), but had failed to notice just this one hidden combination, sank into deep meditation over the board while Luzhin, with a finicky little cough, lovingly noted his own move on a sheet of paper. The Hungarian soon resigned and Luzhin sat down to play with a Russian. The game began interestingly and soon a solid ring of spectators had formed around their table. The curiosity, the pressure, the crackling of joints, the alien breathing and most of all the whispering – whispering interrupted by a still louder and more irritating 'shush!' – frequently tormented Luzhin: he used to be keenly affected by this crackling and rustling, and smelly human warmth if he did not retreat too deeply into the abysses of chess. Out of the corner of his eye he now saw the legs of the bystanders and found particularly irritating, among all those dark trousers, a pair of woman's feet in gleaming gray stockings and bluish shoes. These feet obviously understood nothing of the game, one wondered why they had come. . . . Those pointed shoes with transverse straps or something would be better clicking along the sidewalk . . . as far away as possible from here. While stopping his clock, jotting down a move or putting a captured piece aside he would glance askance at these motionless feminine feet, and only an hour and a half later, when he had won the game and stood up, tugging his waistcoat down, did Luzhin see that these feet belonged to his fiancée. He experienced a keen sense of happiness that she had been there to see him win and he waited avidly for the

chessboards and all these noisy people to disappear in order
the sooner to caress her. But the chessboards did not disappear immediately, and even when the bright dining
room appeared together with its huge brassy bright samovar, indistinct regular squares showed through the white
tablecloth and similar squares – chocolate and cream ones
– were indubitably there on the frosted cake. His fiancée's
mother met him with the same condescending, slightly
ironic indulgence with which she had greeted him the night
before, when her appearance had put an end to the conversation about chess – and the person with whom he had
talked, her husband evidently, now started to tell him what
a model country estate he had owned in Russia. 'Let's go to
your room,' whispered Luzhin hoarsely to his betrothed
and she bit her lip and looked surprised. 'Let's go,' he repeated. But she adroitly placed some heavenly raspberry
jam on his glass plate and this sticky, dazzlingly red sweetness, which ran over the tongue like granular fire and
gummed the teeth with fragrant sugar, took immediate
effect. '*Merci, merci*,' Luzhin bowed as he was served a
second helping, and amid deathly silence smacked his lips
again, licking his spoon that was still hot from the tea for
fear of losing even a single drop of the entrancing syrup.
And when finally he got his own way and found himself
alone with her, not, it is true, in her room, but in the gaudy
drawingroom, he drew her to him and sat down heavily,
holding her by the wrists, but she silently freed herself,
circled and sat down on a hassock. 'I have not at all made up
my mind yet whether to marry you,' she said. 'Remember
that.' 'Everything's decided,' said Luzhin. 'If they won't
let you, we'll use force to make them sign.' 'Sign what?' she
asked with surprise. 'I don't know . . . But it seems we need
some kind of signature or other.' 'Stupid, stupid,' she repeated several times. 'Impenetrable and incorrigible stupidity. What am I to do with you, what course of action shall
I take with you? . . . And how tired you look. I'm sure it's
bad for you to play so much.' '*Ach wo*,' said Luzhin, 'a
couple of little games.' 'And at night you keep thinking.
You mustn't do it. It's already late you know. Go home. You

G   97

need sleep, that's what.' He remained sitting on the striped sofa, however, and she thought in dismay about the kind of conversations they had – a poke here, a dab there, and disconnected words. And not once so far had he kissed her properly, all was bizarre and distorted, and when he touched her, not a single movement of his resembled a normal human embrace. But that forlorn devotion in his eyes, that mysterious light that had illumined him when he bent over the chessboard ... And the following day she again felt the urge to visit those silent premises on the second floor of a large café on a narrow, noisy street This time Luzhin noticed her at once: he was conversing in low tones with a broad-shouldered, clean-shaven man, whose short-cropped hair seemed to have been closely fitted to his head and came onto his forehead in a small peak; his thick lips were infolding and sucking an extinguished cigar. An artist who had been sent by his newspaper, lifting and lowering his face like a brass doll with a movable head, was swiftly sketching the profile with the cigar. Glancing at his pad as she passed, she saw next to this rudimentary Turati an already completed Luzhin – exaggeratedly doleful nose, darkstippled double chin, and on the temple that familiar lock, which she called a curl. Turati sat down to play with a German grandmaster and Luzhin came up to her and gloomily, with a guilty smile, said something long and clumsy. She realized with surprise that he was asking her to leave. 'I'm glad, I'm very glad *post factum*,' explained Luzhin pleadingly, 'but for the moment ... for the moment it somehow disturbs me.' He followed her with his eyes as she obediently withdrew between the rows of chess tables and after nodding briskly to himself, he made his way to the board where his new opponent was already seating himself, a grizzled Englishman who played with invariable sangfroid and invariably lost. Neither was he lucky this time and Luzhin again won a point, and the next day he achieved a draw and then again won – and by that time he no longer felt distinctly the boundary between chess and his fiancée's home, as if movement had been speeded up, and what at first had seemed an alternation of strips was now a flicker.

He moved in step with Turati. Turati scored a point and he scored a point; Turati scored a half and he scored a half. Thus they proceeded with their separate games, as if mounting the sides of an isosceles triangle and destined at the decisive moment to meet at the apex.

The nights were somehow bumpy. He just could not manage to force himself not to think of chess, and although he felt drowsy, sleep could find no way into his brain; it searched for a loophole, but every entrance was guarded by a chess sentry and he had the agonizing feeling that sleep was just there, close by, but on the outside of his brain: the Luzhin who was wearily scattered around the room slumbered, but the Luzhin who visualized a chessboard stayed awake and was unable to merge with his happy double. But still worse – after each session of the tournament it was with ever greater difficulty that he crawled out of the world of chess concepts, so that an unpleasant split began to appear even in daytime. After a three-hour game his head ached strangely, not all of it but in parts, in black squares of pain, and for a while he could not find the door, which was obscured by a black spot, nor could he remember the address of the cherished house: luckily his pocket still preserved that old postcard, folded in two and already tearing along the crease ('. . . *vas vecherom*—' 'expecting you this evening.'). He still continued to feel joy when he entered this house filled with Russian toys, but the joy, too, was spotty. Once, on a day with no play, he came earlier than usual when only the mother was at home. She decided to continue the conversation that had taken place at sunset in the beech coppice, and overestimating her own highly prized ability to speak her mind (for which the young men who visited their house considered her tremendously intelligent and were very much afraid of her), she swooped on Luzhin, lecturing him first of all on the cigarette butts found in all the vases and even in the jaws of the spreadeagled bear, and then suggested that there and then, this Saturday evening, he take a bath at their place after her husband had finished his own weekly ablutions. 'I dare say you don't wash often,' she said without circumlocution. 'Not too often ? Admit it, now.' Luzhin gloomily shrugged his shoulders looking at the floor, where a slight movement was taking place perceptible to him alone, an evil differentiation of shadows. 'And in general,' she continued, 'you must pull yourself together.' And having thus put her hearer in the right mood she went on to the main subject. 'Tell me,' she asked, 'I imagine you've managed to debauch my little girl thoroughly ? People like you are great lechers. But my daughter is chaste, not like today's girls. Tell me, you're a lecher, aren't you ?' 'No, madame,' replied Luzhin with a sigh, and then he frowned and quickly drew the sole of his shoe over the floor, obliterating a certain grouping that was already quite distinct. 'Why, I don't know you at all,' continued the swift, sonorous voice. 'I shall have to make inquiries about you – yes, yes, inquiries – to see if you haven't one of those special diseases.' 'Shortness of breath,' said Luzhin, 'and also a bit of rheumatism.' 'I'm not talking about that,' she interrupted crossly. 'It's a serious matter. You evidently consider yourself engaged, you come here and you spend time alone with her. But I don't think there can be any talk of marriage for a while.' 'And last year I had the piles,' said Luzhin dully. 'Listen, I'm talking to you about extremely important things. You would probably like to get married today, right away. I know you. Then she'll be going about with a big belly, you'll brutalize her immediately.' Having stamped out a shadow in one place, Luzhin saw with despair that far from where he was sitting a new combination was taking shape on the floor. 'If you are in the least interested in my opinion then I must tell you I consider this match ridiculous. You probably think my husband will support you. Admit it: you do think that ?' 'I am in straitened circumstances,' said Luzhin. 'I would need very little. And a magazine has offered me to edit its chess section . . .' Here the nuisances on the floor became so brazen that Luzhin involuntarily put out a hand to remove shadow's King from the threat of light's Pawn. From that day on he avoided sitting in that drawing room, where there were too many knickknacks of polished wood that assumed very definite features if you looked at them long enough.

His fiancée noticed that with each day of the tournament he looked worse and worse. His eyes were ringed with dull violet and his heavy lids were inflamed. He was so pale that he always seemed ill-shaven, although on his fiancée's insistence he shaved every morning. She awaited the end of the tournament with great impatience and it pained her to think what fabulous, harmful exertions he had to make to gain each point. Poor Luzhin, mysterious Luzhin. ... All through those autumn days, while playing tennis in the mornings with a German girl friend, or listening to lectures on art that had long since palled on her, or leafing through a tattered assortment of books in her room – Andreyev's *The Ocean*, a novel by Krasnov and a pamphlet entitled 'How to Become a Yogi' – she was conscious that right now Luzhin was immersed in chess calculations, struggling and suffering – and it vexed her that she was unable to share in the torments of his art. She believed in his genius unconditionally and was convinced moreover that this genius could not be exhausted by the mere playing of chess, however wonderful it might be, and that when the tournament fever had passed and Luzhin had calmed down, he would rest, and within him some kind of still unfathomed forces would come into play and he would blossom out and display his gift in other spheres of life as well. Her father called Luzhin a narrow fanatic, but added that he was undoubtedly a very naïve and very respectable person. Her mother, on the other hand, maintained that Luzhin was going out of his mind not by the day but by the hour and that lunatics were forbidden by law to marry and she concealed the inconceivable fiancé from all her friends, which was easy at first – they thought she was at the resort with her daughter – but then, very soon, there reappeared all those people who usually frequented their house – such as a charming old general who always maintained that it was not Russia we expatriates regretted but youth, youth; a couple of Russian Germans; Oleg Sergeyevich Smirnovski – theosophist and proprietor of a liqueur factory; several former officers of the White Army; several young ladies; the singer Mme. Vozdvishenski; the Alfyorov couple; and also the aged Princess

Umanov, whom they called the Queen of Spades (after the well-known opera). She it was who was the first to see Luzhin, concluding from a hasty and unintelligible explanation by the mistress of the house that he had some kind of connection with literature, with magazines – was, in a word, an author. 'And that thing, do you know it?' she asked, politely striking up a literary conversation. 'From Apukhtin – one of the new poets ... slightly decadent ... something about yellow and red cornflowers ...' Smirnovski lost no time in asking him for a game of chess, but unfortunately there proved to be no set in the house. The young people among themselves called him a ninny, and only the old general treated him with the most cordial simplicity, exhorting him at length to go see the little giraffe that had just been born at the zoo. Once the visitors began to come, appearing every evening now in various combinations, Luzhin was unable to be alone with his fiancée for a single moment and his struggle with them, his efforts to penetrate through the thick of them to her, immediately took on a tinge of chess. However, it proved impossible to overcome them, more and more of them would appear, and he fancied it was they, these numberless, faceless visitors, who densely and hotly surrounded him during the hours of the tournament.

An explanation of all that was happening came one morning when he was sitting on a chair in the middle of his hotel room and trying to concentrate his thoughts on one thing alone: yesterday he had won his tenth point and to-day he had to beat Moser. Suddenly his fiancée entered the room. 'Just like a little idol,' she laughed. 'Sitting in the middle while sacrificial gifts are brought to him.' She stretched out a box of chocolates to him and suddenly the laughter disappeared from her face. 'Luzhin,' she cried. Luzhin, wake up! What's the matter with you?' 'Are you real?' asked Luzhin softly and unbelievingly. 'Of course I'm real. What a thing to do, putting your chair in the middle of the room and sitting there. If you don't rouse yourself immediately I'm leaving.' Luzhin obediently roused himself, moving his shoulders and head about, then transferred his seat to the couch, and a happiness that was not quite sure of itself, not quite settled, shone and swam in his eyes. 'Tell me, when will this end?' she asked. 'How many games to go?' 'Three,' replied Luzhin. 'I read today in the newspaper that you are bound to win the tournament, that this time you are playing extraordinarily.' 'But there's Turati,' said Luzhin and raised his finger. 'I feel sick to my stomach,' he added mournfully. 'Then no candies for you,' she said quickly and tucked the square package under her arm again. 'Luzhin, I'm going to call a doctor. You'll simply die if it goes on like this.' 'No, no,' he said sleepily. 'It's already passed. There's no need for a doctor.' 'It worries me. That means till Friday, till Saturday . . . this hell. And at home things are pretty grim. Everyone's agreed with Mamma that I mustn't marry you. Why were you feeling sick, have you eaten something or other?' 'It's gone, completely,' muttered Luzhin and put his head down on her shoulder. 'You're simply very tired, poor boy. Are you really going to play today?' 'At three o'clock. Against Moser. In general I'm playing . . . how did they put it?' 'Extraordinarily.' She smiled. The head lying on her shoulder was large, heavy – a precious apparatus with a complex, mysterious mechanism. A minute later she noticed that he had fallen asleep and she began to think how to transfer his head now to some cushion or other. With extremely careful movements she managed to do it; he was now half lying on the couch, uncomfortably doubled up, and the head on the pillow was waxen. For a moment she was seized with horror lest he had died suddenly and she even felt his wrist, which was soft and warm. When she straightened up she felt a tinge of pain in her shoulder. 'A heavy head,' she whispered as she looked at the sleeper, and quietly left the room, taking her unsuccessful present with her. She asked the chambermaid she met in the corridor to wake Luzhin in an hour, and descending the stairs soundlessly she set off through sunlit streets to the tennis club – and caught herself still trying not to make a noise or any sharp movements. The chambermaid did not have to wake Luzhin – he awoke by himself and immediately made strenuous efforts to recall the delightful dream he had dreamed, knowing from experience that if you didn't begin immediately to recall it, later would be too late. He had dreamed he was sitting strangely – in the middle of the room – and suddenly, with the absurd and blissful suddenness usual in dreams, his fiancée entered holding out a package tied with red ribbon. She was dressed also in the style of dreams – in a white dress and soundless white shoes. He wanted to embrace her, but suddenly felt sick, his head whirled, and she in the meantime related that the newspapers were writing extraordinary things about him but that her mother still did not want them to marry. Probably there was much more of this and that, but his memory failed to overtake what was receding – and trying at least not to disperse what he had managed to wrest from his dream, Luzhin stirred cautiously, smoothed down his hair and rang for dinner to be brought. After dinner he had to play, and that day the universe of chess concepts revealed an awesome power. He played four hours without pause and won, but when he was already sitting in the taxi he forgot on the way where it was he was going, what postcard address he had given the driver to read and waited with interest to see where the car would stop.

The house, however, he recognized, and again there were guests, guests – but here Luzhin realized that he had simply returned to his recent dream, for his fiancée asked him in a whisper: 'Well, how are you, has the sickness gone?' – and how could she have known about this in real life? 'We're living in a fine dream,' he said to her softly. 'Now I understand everything.' He looked about him and saw the table and the faces of people sitting there, their reflection in the samovar – in a special samovarian perspective – and added with tremendous relief: 'So this too is a dream? These people are a dream? Well, well . . .' 'Quiet, quiet, what are you babbling about?' she whispered anxiously, and Luzhin thought she was right, one should not scare off a dream, let them sit there, these people, for the time being. But the most remarkable thing about this dream was that all around, evidently, was Russia, which the sleeper himself had left ages ago. The inhabitants of the dream, gay people drinking tea, were conversing in Russian and the sugar bowl was identical with the one from which he had spooned powdered sugar on the veranda on a scarlet summer evening many years ago. Luzhin noted this return to Russia with interest, with pleasure. It diverted him especially as the witty repetition of a particular combination, which occurs, for example, when a strictly problem idea, long since discovered in theory, is repeated in a striking guise on the board in live play.

The whole time, however, now feebly, now sharply, shadows of his real chess life would show through this dream and finally it broke through and it was simply night in the hotel, chess thoughts, chess insomnia and meditations on the drastic defense he had invented to counter Turati's opening. He was wide-awake and his mind worked clearly, purged of all dross and aware that everything apart from chess was only an enchanting dream, in which, like the golden haze of the moon, the image of a sweet, clear-eyed maiden with bare arms dissolved and melted. The rays of his consciousness, which were wont to disperse when they came into contact with the incompletely intelligible world surrounding him, thereby losing one half of their force, had grown stronger and more concentrated now that this world had dissolved into a mirage and there was no longer any need to worry about it. Real life, chess life, was orderly, clear-cut, and rich in adventure, and Luzhin noted with pride how easy it was for him to reign in this life, and the way everything obeyed his will and bowed to his schemes. Some of his games at the Berlin tournament had been even then termed immortal by connoisseurs. He had won one after sacrificing in succession his Queen, a Rook and a Knight; in another he had placed a Pawn in such a dynamic position that it had acquired an absolutely monstrous force and had continued to grow and swell, balefully for his opponent, like a furuncle in the tenderest part of the board; and finally in a third game, by means of an apparently absurd move that provoked a murmuring among the spectators, Luzhin constructed an elaborate trap for his opponent that the latter divined too late. In these games and in all the others that he played at this unforgettable tournament, he manifested a stunning clarity of thought, a merciless logic. But Turati also played brilliantly, Turati also scored point after point, somewhat hypnotizing his opponents with the boldness of his imagination and trusting too much, perhaps, to the chess luck that till now had never deserted him His meeting with Luzhin was to decide who would get first prize and there were those who said that the limpidity and lightness of Luzhin's thought would prevail over the Italian's tumultuous fantasy, and there were those who forecast that the fiery, swift-swooping Turati would defeat the far-sighted Russian player. And the day of their meeting arrived.

Luzhin awoke fully dressed, even wearing his overcoat; he looked at his watch, rose hastily and put on his hat, which had been lying in the middle of the room. At this point he recollected himself and looked round the room, trying to understand what exactly he had slept on. His bed was unrumpled and the velvet of the couch was completely smooth. The only thing he knew for sure was that from time immemorial he had been playing chess – and in the darkness of his memory, as in two mirrors reflecting a candle, there was only a vista of converging lights with Luzhin sitting at a chessboard, and again Luzhin at a chessboard, only smaller, and then smaller still, and so on an infinity of times. But he was late, he was late, and he had to hurry. He swiftly opened the door and stopped in bewilderment. According to his concept of things, the chess hall, and his table, and the waiting Turati should have been right here. Instead of this he saw an empty corridor and a staircase beyond it. Suddenly from that direction, from the stairs, appeared a swiftly running little man who caught sight of Luzhin and spread out his hands, 'Maestro,' he exclaimed, 'what is this? They are waiting for you, they are waiting for you, Maestro. . . . I telephoned you three times and they said you didn't answer their knocks. Signor Turati has been at his post a long time.' 'They removed it,' said Luzhin sourly, pointing to the empty corridor with his cane. 'How was I to know that everything would be removed?' 'If you don't feel well ...' began the little man, looking sadly at Luzhin's pale, glistening face. 'Well, take me there!' cried Luzhin in a shrill voice and banged his cane on the floor. 'With pleasure, with pleasure,' muttered the other distractedly. His gaze concentrated on the little overcoat with its raised collar running in front of him, Luzhin began to conquer the incomprehensible space. 'We'll go on foot,' said his guide, 'it's exactly a minute's walk.' With a feeling of relief Luzhin recognized the revolving doors of the café and then the staircase, and finally he saw what he had been looking for in the hotel corridor. Upon entering he immediately felt fullness of life, calm, clarity, and confidence. 'There's a big victory coming,' he said loudly, and a crowd of dim people parted in order to let him through. '*Tard, tard, très tard*,' jabbered Turati, materializing suddenly and shaking his head. '*Avanti*,' said Luzhin and laughed. A table appeared between them and upon it was a board with pieces set out ready for battle. Luzhin took a cigarette from his waistcoat pocket and unconsciously lit up.

At this point a strange thing happened. Turati, although having white, did not launch his famous opening and the defense Luzhin had worked out proved an utter waste. Whether because Turati had anticipated possible complications or else had simply decided to play warily, knowing the calm strength which Luzhin had revealed at this tournament, he began in the most banal way. Luzhin momentarily regretted the work done in vain, but nevertheless he was glad: this gave him more freedom. Moreover, Turati was evidently afraid of him. On the other hand there was undoubtedly some trick concealed in the innocent, jejune opening proposed by Turati, and Luzhin settled down to play with particular care. At first it went softly, softly, like muted violins. The players occupied their positions cautiously, moving this and that up but doing it politely, without the slightest sign of a threat – and if there was any threat it was entirely conventional – more like a hint to one's opponent that over there he would do well to build a cover, and the opponent would smile, as if all this were an insignificant joke, and strengthen the proper place and himself move forward a fraction. Then, without the least warning, a chord sang out tenderly. This was one of Turati's forces occupying a diagonal line. But forthwith a trace of melody very softly manifested itself on Luzhin's side also. For a moment mysterious possibilities were quivering, and then all was quiet again: Turati retreated, drew in. And once more for a while both opponents, as if having no intention of advancing, occupied themselves with sprucing up their own squares – nursing, shifting, smoothing things down at home – and then there was another sudden flare up, a swift combination of sounds: two small forces collided and both were immediately swept away: a momentary, masterly motion of the fingers and Luzhin removed and placed on the table beside him what was no longer an incorporeal force but a heavy, yellow Pawn; Turati's fingers flashed in the air and an inert, black Pawn with a gleam of light on its head was in turn lowered onto the table. And having got rid of these two chess quantities that had so suddenly turned into wood the players seemed to calm down and forget the momentary flare-up the vibration in this part of the board, however, had not yet quite died down, something was still endeavoring to take shape. . . . But these sounds did not succeed in establishing the desired relationship – some other deep dark note chimed elsewhere and both players abandoned the still quivering square and became interested in another part of the board. But here too everything ended abortively. The weightiest elements on the board called to one another several times with trumpet voices and again there was an exchange, and again two chess forces were transformed into carved, brightly lacquered dummies. And then there was a long, long interval of thought, during which Luzhin bred from one spot on the board and lost a dozen illusionary games in succession, and then his fingers groped for and found a bewitching, brittle, crystalline combination – which with a gentle tinkle disintegrated at Turati's first reply. But neither was Turati able to do anything after that and playing for time (time is merciless in the universe of chess), both opponents repeated the same two moves, threat and defense, threat and defense – but meanwhile both kept thinking of a most tricky conceit that had nothing in common with these mechancial moves. And Turati finally decided on this combination – and immediately a kind of musical tempest overwhelmed the board and Luzhin searched stubbornly in it for the tiny, clear note that he needed in order in his turn to swell it out into a thunderous harmony. Now everything on the board breathed with life, everything was concentrated on a single idea, was rolled up tighter and tighter; for a moment the disappearance of two pieces eased the situation and then again – *agitato*. Luzhin's thought roamed through entrancing and terrible labyrinths, meeting there now and then the anxious thought of Turati, who sought the same thing as he. Both realized simultaneously that white was not destined to develop his scheme any further, that he was on the brink of losing rhythm. Turati hastened to propose an exchange and the number of forces on the board was again reduced. New possibilities appeared, but still no one could say which side had the advantage. Luzhin, preparing an attack for which it was first necessary to explore a maze of variations, where his every step aroused a perilous echo, began a long meditation: he needed, it seemed, to make one last prodigious effort and he would find the secret move leading to victory. Suddenly, something occurred outside his being, a scorching pain – and he let out a loud cry, shaking his hand stung by the flame of a match, which he had lit and forgotten to apply to his cigarette. The pain immediately passed, but in the fiery gap he had seen something unbearably awesome, the full horror of the abysmal depths of chess. He glanced at the chessboard and his brain wilted from hitherto unprecedented weariness. But the chessmen were pitiless, they held and absorbed him. There was horror in this, but in this also was the sole harmony, for what else exists in the world besides chess? Fog, the unknown, non-being ... He noticed that Turati was no longer sitting; he stood stretching himself. 'Adjournment, Maestro,' said a voice from behind. 'Note down your next move.' 'No, no, not yet,' said Luzhin pleadingly, his eyes searching for the person who spoke. 'That's all for today,' the same voice went on, again from behind, a gyratory kind of voice. Luzhin wanted to stand up but was unable to. He saw that he had moved backwards somewhere together with his chair and that people had hurled themselves rapaciously upon the position on the chessboard, where the whole of his life had just been, and were wrangling and shouting as they nimbly moved the pieces this way and that. He again tried to stand up and again was unable to. 'Why, why?' he said plaintively, trying to distinguish the board between the narrow, black backs bent over it. They dwindled completely away and disappeared. On the board the pieces were mixed up now and stood about in disorderly groups. A phantom went by, stopped and began swiftly to stow the pieces away in a tiny coffin. 'It's all over,' said Luzhin and groaning from the effort, wrenched himself out of the chair. A few phantoms still stood about discussing something. It was cold and fairly dark. Phantoms were carrying off the boards and chairs. Tortuous and transparent chess images roamed about in the air, wherever you looked – and Luzhin, realizing that he had got stuck, that he had lost his way in one of the combinations he had so recently pondered, made a desperate attempt to free himself, to break out somewhere – even if into nonexistence. 'Let's go, let's go,' cried someone and disappeared with a bang. He remained alone. His vision became darker and darker and in relation to every vague object in the hall he stood in check. He had to escape; he moved, the whole of his fat body shaking, and was completely unable to imagine what people did in order to get out of a room – and yet there should be a simple method – abruptly a black shade with a white breast began to hover about him, offering him his coat and hat. 'Why is this necessary?' he muttered, getting into the sleeves and revolving together with the obliging ghost. 'This way,' said the host briskly and Luzhin stepped forward and out of the terrible hall. Catching sight of the stairs he began to creep upward, but then changed his mind and went down, since it was easier to descend than to climb up. He found himself in a smoky establishment where noisy phantoms were sit-

ting. An attack was developing in every corner – and pushing aside tables, a bucket with a gold-necked glass Pawn
sticking out of it and a drum that was being beaten by an
arched, thick-maned chess Knight, he made his way to a
gently revolving glass radiance and stopped, not knowing
where to go next. People surrounded him and wanted to
do something with him. 'Go away, go away,' a gruff voice
kept repeating. 'But where?' said Luzhin, weeping. 'Go
home,' whispered another voice insinuatingly and something pushed against Luzhin's shoulder. 'What did you
say?' he asked again, suddenly ceasing to sob. 'Home, home,'
repeated the voice, and the glass radiance, taking hold of
Luzhin, threw him out into the cool dusk. Luzhin smiled.
'Home,' he said softly. 'So that's the key to the combination.'

And it was necessary to hurry. At any minute these chess
growths might ring him in again. For the time being he
was surrounded by twilight murk, thick, cotton-wool air.
He asked a ghost slipping by how to get to the manor. The
ghost did not understand and passed on. 'One moment,'
said Luzhin, but it was already too late. Then, swinging his
short arms, he quickened his step. A pale light sailed past
and disintegrated with a mournful rustle. It was difficult,
difficult to find one's way home in this yielding fog. Luzhin
felt he should keep left, and then there would be a big wood,
and once in the wood he would easily find the path. Another
shadow slipped by. 'Where's the wood, the wood?' Luzhin
asked insistently and since this word evoked no reply he
cast around for a synonym: 'Forest? Wald?' he muttered.
'Park?' he added indulgently. Then the shadow pointed to
the left and disappeared from view. Upbraiding himself
for his slowness, anticipating pursuit at any minute, Luzhin
strode off in the direction indicated. And indeed – he was
suddenly surrounded by trees, ferns crepitated underfoot,
it was quiet and damp. He sank down heavily on the ground
and squatted there for he was quite out of breath, and tears
poured down his face. Presently he got up, removed a wet
leaf from his knee and after wandering among tree trunks
for a short time he found the familiar footpath. *'Marsch,*

marsch,' Luzhin kept repeating, urging himself on as he walked over the sticky ground. He had already come half-way. Soon there would be the river, and the sawmill, and then the manor house would peep through the bare bushes. He would hide there and would live on the contents of large and small glass jars. The mysterious pursuit had been left far behind. You wouldn't catch him now. Oh no. If only it were easier to breathe, and one could get rid of this pain in the temples, this numbing pain. .. The path twisted through the wood and came out onto a transverse road, while farther on a river glinted in the darkness. He also saw a bridge and a dim pile of structures on the other side of it, and at first, for one moment, it seemed to him that over there against the dark sky was the familiar triangular roof of the manor with its black lightning conductor. But immediately he realized that this was some subtle ruse on the part of the chess gods, for the parapet of the bridge produced the rain-glistening, trembling shapes of great female figures and a queer reflection danced on the river. He walked along the bank, trying to find another bridge, the bridge where you sink up to your ankles in sawdust. He looked for a long time and finally, quite out of the way, he found a narrow, quiet little bridge and thought that here at least he could cross peacefully. But on the other bank everything was unfamiliar, lights flashed past and shadows slid by. He knew the manor was somewhere here, close by, but he was approaching it from an unfamiliar angle and how difficult everything was. . . . His legs from hips to heels were tightly filled with lead, the way the base of a chessman is weighted. Gradually the lights disappeared, the phantoms grew sparser, and a wave of oppressive blackness washed over him. By the light of a last reflection he made out a front garden and a couple of round bushes, and it seemed to him he recognized the miller's house. He stretched out a hand to the fence but at this point triumphant pain began to overwhelm him, pressing down from above on his skull, and it was as if he were becoming flatter and flatter, and then he soundlessly dissipated.

CHAPTER NINE

THE sidewalk skidded, reared up at a right angle and swayed back again. Günther straightened himself up, breathing heavily, while his comrade, supporting him and also swaying, kept repeating 'Günther, Günther, try to walk.' Günther stood up quite straight and after this brief stop, which was not the first, both of them continued farther along the deserted night street, which alternately rose up smoothly to the stars and then sloped down again. Günther, a big sturdy fellow, had drunk more than his comrade: the latter, Kurt by name, supported Günther as best he could, although the beer was throbbing thunderously in his head. 'Where are . . . where are . . .' Günther strove to ask, 'Where are the others ?' A moment before they had all been sitting around an oaken table, thirty fellows or so, happy, level-headed, hard-working men celebrating the fifth anniversary of their leaving school with a good sing and the sonorous ringing of clinked glasses – whereas now, as soon as they had started to disperse to their homes, they found them-selves beset by nausea, darkness, and the hopeless unsteadi-ness of this sidewalk. 'The others are there,' said Kurt with a broad gesture, which unpleasantly called into life the near-est wall: it leaned forward and slowly straightened up again. 'They've gone, gone,' elucidated Kurt sadly. 'But Karl is in front of us,' said Günther slowly and distinctly, and a resili-ent, beery wind caused them both to sway to one side: they halted, took a step backwards and again went on their way. 'I'm telling you Karl is there,' repeated Günther sulkily. And truly a man was sitting on the edge of the sidewalk with his head lowered. They miscalculated their impetus and were carried past. When they succeeded in approaching him the man smacked his lips and slowly turned toward them. Yes, it was Karl, but what a Karl – his face blank, his eyes glazed! 'I'm just taking a rest,' he said in a dull voice.

'I'll continue in a minute.' Suddenly a taxi with its flag up came rolling slowly over the deserted asphalt. 'Stop him,' said Karl. 'I want him to take me.' The car drew up. Günther kept tumbling over Karl, trying to help him get up and Kurt tugged at somebody's gray-spatted foot. From his seat the driver encouraged all this good-naturedly and then climbed out and also began to help. The limply floundering body was squeezed through the aperture of the door and the car immediately pulled away. 'And we're nearly there,' said Kurt. The figure standing next to him sighed and Kurt, looking at him, saw that it was Karl – which meant that the taxi had carried off Günther instead. 'I'll give you a hand,' he said guiltily. 'Let's go.' Looking in front of him with empty, childlike eyes, Karl leaned toward him and they both moved off and started to cross to the other side of the heaving asphalt. 'Here's another,' said Kurt. A fat man without a hat lay all hunched up on the sidewalk, beside a garden fence. 'That's probably Pulvermacher,' muttered Kurt. 'You know he's changed an awful lot in recent years.' 'That's not Pulvermacher,' replied Karl, sitting down on the sidewalk beside him. 'Pulvermacher's bald.' 'It doesn't matter,' said Kurt. 'He also has to be taken home.' They tried to raise the man by his shoulders and lost their equilibrium. 'Don't break the fence,' cautioned Karl. 'He has to be taken,' repeated Kurt. 'Perhaps it's Pulvermacher's brother. He was there, too.'

The man was evidently sound asleep. He was wearing a black overcoat with strips of velvet on the lapels. His fat face with its heavy chin and convex eyelids was glossy in the light of the streetlamp. 'Let's wait for a taxi,' said Kurt and followed the example of Karl, who had squatted on the curbing.' This night will come to an end,' he said confidently and added, looking at the sky: 'How they revolve.' 'Stars,' explained Karl and both sat still, staring upward at the wonderful, pale nebulous abyss, where the stars flowed in an arc. 'Pulvermacher's also looking,' said Kurt after a silence. 'No, he's sleeping,' objected Karl, glancing at the fat, motionless face. 'Sleeping,' agreed Kurt.

A light glided over the asphalt and the same good-natured

taxi that had taken Günther away somewhere, softly pulled in alongside the sidewalk. 'Another one?' laughed the driver. 'They could have gone together.' 'But where?' Karl asked Kurt sleepily. 'There must be an address of some kind – let's look in his pockets ...' the latter answered vaguely. Swaying and involuntarily nodding, they bent over the motionless man and the fact that his overcoat was unbuttoned facilitated their further explorations. 'Velvet waistcoat,' said Kurt. 'Poor fellow, poor fellow ...' In the very first pocket they found a postcard folded in two, which parted in their hands, and one half with the receiver's address on it slipped down and vanished without trace. On the remaining half, however, they found another address that had been written across the card and thickly underlined. On the other side there was just a single level line, cut short at the left; but even if it had been possible to place it side by side with the fallen-off and lost half the meaning of this line would hardly have become any clearer. 'Bac berepom,' read Kurt mistaking the Russian letters for Latin ones, which was excusable. The address found on the postcard was told to the driver and then they had to thrust the heavy, lifeless body in the car, and again the driver came to their aid. On the door large chess squares – the blazon of Berlin taxis – showed in the light of the street-lamp. Finally the jam-packed motorcar moved off.

Karl fell asleep on the way. His body and the unknown's body and the body of Kurt, who was sitting on the floor, came into soft, involuntary contact at every turn and subsequently Kurt finished up on the seat and Karl and most of the unknown fellow on the floor. When the car stopped and the driver opened the door he was unable at first to make out how many people were inside. Karl woke up immediately, but the hatless man was as motionless as before. 'I'm curious to know what you'll do with your friend now,' said the driver. 'They're probably waiting for him,' said Kurt. The driver, considering he had done his job and carried enough heavyweights for the night, raised his flag and announced the fare. 'I'll pay,' said Karl. 'No, I will,' said Kurt. 'I found him first,' This argument convinced Karl. The car was emptied with difficulty, and departed. Three people remained on the sidewalk: one of them lying with his head resting against a stone step.

Swaying and sighing, Kurt and Karl moved to the middle of the street and then, addressing themselves to the sole lighted window in the house, shouted hoarsely, and immediately, with unexpected responsiveness, the light-slashed blind trembled and was pulled up. A young woman looked out of the window. Not knowing how to begin, Kurt smirked, then, pulling himself together, said boldly and loudly: 'Miss, we've brought Pulvermacher.' The woman gave no answer and the blind descended with a rattle. One could see, however, that she stayed by the window. 'We found him in the street,' said Karl uncertainly, addressing the window. The blind went up again. 'A velvet waistcoat,' Kurt considered it necessary to explain. The window emptied, but a moment later the darkness behind the front door disintegrated and through the glass appeared an illuminated staircase, marble as far as the first landing, and this newborn staircase had not had time to congeal completely before swift feminine legs appeared on the stairs. A key grated in the lock and the door opened. On the sidewalk with his back to the steps lay a stout man in black.

Meanwhile the staircase continued to spawn people. . . . A gentleman appeared wearing bedroom slippers, black trousers and a collarless starched shirt, and behind him came a pale, stocky maid with scuffers on her bare feet. Everybody bent over Luzhin, and the guiltily grinning, completely drunk strangers kept explaining something, while one of them insistently proffered half a postcard, like a visiting card. The five of them carried Luzhin up the stairs and his fiancée, supporting the heavy, precious head, let out a cry when the light over the staircase suddenly went out. In the darkness everything swung, there was a knocking and a shuffling and a puffing, someone took a step backwards and invoked God's name in German, and when the light came on again one of the strangers was sitting on a stair and the other was being crushed by Luzhin's body, while higher up, on the landing, stood Mother in a gaudily embroidered robe, surveying with bright prominent eyes the lifeless body that her husband, groaning and muttering, was supporting, and the large awful head that lay on her daughter's shoulder. They carried Luzhin into the drawing room. The young strangers clicked their heels, trying to introduce themselves to someone, and shied away from the little tables laden with porcelain. They were seen at once in all the rooms. No doubt they wanted to leave but were unable to make it to the front hall. They were found on all the divans, in the bathroom and on the trunk in the hallway, and there was no way of getting rid of them. Their number was unclear – a fluctuating, blurred number. But after a while they disappeared, and the maid said that she had let two of them out and that the rest must still be sprawling around somewhere, and that drunkenness ruins a man, and that her sister's fiancé also drank.

'Congratulations, he's pickled,' said the mistress of the house, looking at Luzhin, who was lying like a corpse, half-undressed and covered with a laprobe, on a couch in the drawing room. 'Congratulations.' And strange thing: the fact that Luzhin was drunk pleased her, evoked a warm sentiment with regard to Luzhin. In such revelry she detected something human and natural, and even a certain daring, a breadth of spirit. This was a situation in which people she knew found themselves, good people, merry people. (And why not, she reasoned, these troubled times knock one off balance so no wonder our Russian lads turn to drink, the green dragon and comforter, from time to time. . . .) But when it turned out there was no smell of vodka or wine coming from Luzhin, and he was sleeping queerly, not at all like a drunken man, she was disappointed and chided herself for being able to presuppose a single natural inclination in Luzhin. While the doctor, who came at dawn, was examining him, a change occurred in Luzhin's face, his eyelids lifted and dim eyes looked out from beneath them. And only then did his fiancée come out of that numbness of the soul that had possessed her ever since she saw the body lying by the front steps. It is true she had been expecting something terrible, but this precise horror had been beyond her imagination. Last night when Luzhin had not visited them as usual she had called the chess café and had been told that play had finished long ago. Then she called the hotel and they replied that Luzhin had still not returned. She went out onto the street, thinking that perhaps Luzhin was waiting by the locked door, and then called the hotel again, and then consulted her father about notifying the police. 'Nonsense,' her father said decisively. 'There must be plenty of friends of his around. The man's gone to a party.' But she knew perfectly well that Luzhin had no friends and that there was something senseless about his absence.

And now, looking at Luzhin's large, pale face, she so brimmed with aching, tender pity that it seemed as if without this pity inside her there would be no life either. It was impossible to think of this inoffensive man sprawling in the street and his soft body being handled by drunks; she could not bear to think that everybody had taken his mysterious swoon for the flabby, vulgar sleep of a reveler and had expected a devil-may-care snore from his helpless quietude. Such pity, such pain. And this outmoded, eccentric waistcoat that one could not bear to look at without tears, and that poor curl, and the bare, white neck all creased like a child's. . . . And all this had happened because of her . . . she had not kept an eye on him, had not kept an eye on him. She should have stayed by him the whole time, not allowed him to play too much . . . and how was it he had not been run-over yet by a car, and why had she not guessed that at any minute he might topple over, paralyzed by this chess fatigue ? . . . 'Luzhin,' she said smiling, as if he could see her smile. 'Luzhin, everything's all right. Luzhin, do you hear me ?'

As soon as he was taken to the hospital she went to the hotel for his things, and at first they would not let her into his room, and this led to long explanations and a telephone call to the hospital by a rather cheeky hotel employee, after which she had to pay Luzhin's bill for the last week, and she did not have enough money and more explanations were necessary, and it seemed to her that the mockery of Luzhin was continuing, and it was difficult to hold back her tears. And when, refusing the coarse help of the hotel chambermaid, she began to gather up Luzhin's things, the feeling of pity rose to an extreme pitch. Among his things were some that he must have been carrying around with him for ages, not noticing them and never throwing them out – unnecessary, unexpected things: a canvas belt with a metallic buckle in the shape of a letter S and with a leather pocket on the side, a miniature penknife for a watch chain, inlaid with mother of pearl, a collection of Italian postcards – all blue sky and madonnas and a lilac haze over Vesuvius; and unmistakably St. Petersburg things: a tiny abacus with red and white counters, a desk calendar with turn-back pages for a completely non-calendar year – 1918. All this was kicking about in a drawer, among some clean but crumpled shirts, whose colored stripes and starched cuffs evoked a picture of long-gone years. There also she found a collapsible opera hat bought in London, and in it the visit-ing card of somebody named Valentinov. . . . The toilet articles were in such a state that she resolved to leave them behind – and to buy him a rubber sponge in place of that unbelievable loofah. A chess set, a cardboard box full of notes and diagrams, and a pile of chess magazines she wrap-ped up in a separate package: he did not need this now. When the valise and small trunk were full and locked, she looked once more into all the corners and retrieved from under the bed a pair of astonishingly old, torn laceless brown shoes that served Luzhin in place of bedroom slip-pers. Carefully she pushed them back under the bed.

From the hotel she went to the chess café, remembering that Luzhin had been without his cane and hat and think-ing that perhaps he had left them there. There were lots of people in the tournament hall, and Turati, standing by the coat rack, was jauntily taking off his overcoat. She realized that she had come just as play was about to be resumed, and that nobody knew of Luzhin's illness. Never mind, she thought with a certain malicious satisfaction. Let them wait. She found the cane but there was no hat. And after glancing with hatred at the small table, where the pieces had already been set out, and at the broad-shouldered

Turati, who was rubbing his hands and deeply clearing his throat like a bass singer, she swiftly left the café, reentered the taxi on top of which Luzhin's checked little trunk showed touchingly green, and returned to the sanatorium.

She was not at home when yesterday's young men reappeared. They came to apologize for their tempestuous nocturnal intrusion. They were well dressed, they scraped and bowed and asked after the gentleman they had brought home the night before. They were thanked for delivering him and were told for the sake of decorum that he had slept it off wonderfully after some friendly revels, at which his colleagues had honored him on the occasion of his betrothal. After sitting for ten minutes the young men rose and went away quite satisfied. At about the same time a distracted little man having some connection with the organization of the tournament arrived at the sanatorium. He was not admitted to see Luzhin; the composed young lady who spoke to him informed him coldly that Luzhin had overtired himself and it was uncertain when he would resume his chess activities. 'That's awful, that's incredible,' plaintively repeated the little man several times. 'An unfinished game! And such a good game! Give the Maestro . . . give the Maestro my anxious wishes, my best wishes . . .' He waved a hand hopelessly and plodded to the exit, shaking his head.

And the newspapers printed an announcement that Luzhin had had a nervous breakdown before finishing the deciding game and that, according to Turati, black was bound to lose because of the weakness of the Pawn on f4. And in all the chess clubs the experts made long studies of the positions of the pieces, pursued possible continuations and noted white's weakness at d3, but nobody could find the key to indisputable victory.

CHAPTER TEN

ONE night soon after this, there took place a long
brewing, long rumbling and at last breaking, futile, disgrace-
fully loud, but unavoidable scene. She had just returned
from the sanatorium and was hungrily eating hot buck-
wheat cereal and relating that Luzhin was better. Her
parents exchanged looks and then it began.

'I hope,' said her mother resonantly, 'that you have re-
nounced your crazy intention.' 'More please,' she asked,
holding out her plate. 'Out of a certain feeling of delicacy,'
continued her mother, and here her father quickly took up
the torch. 'Yes,' he said, 'out of delicacy your mother has
said nothing to you these past days – until your friend's
situation cleared up. But now you must listen to us. You
yourself know that our main desire, and care, and aim, and
in general . . . desire is for you to be all right, for you to be
happy, et cetera. But for this . . .' 'In my time parents would
simply have forbidden it,' put in her mother, 'that's all.'
'No, no, what's forbidding got to do with this? You listen
to me, my pet. You're not eighteen years old, but twenty-
five, and I can see nothing whatsoever enticing or poetic
in all that has happened.' 'She just likes to annoy us,' interrupted her mother again. 'It's just one continuous nightmare. . . .' 'What exactly are you talking about?' asked the
daughter finally and smiled from beneath lowered brows,
resting her elbows softly on the table and looking from
her father to her mother. 'About the fact that it's time you
ceased to be silly,' cried her mother. 'About the fact that
marriage to a penniless crackpot is nonsense.' 'Ach,' uttered
the daughter, and stretching her arm out on the table she
put her head upon it. 'Here's what,' her father began again.
'We suggest you go to the Italian lakes. Go with Mamma to
the Italian lakes. You can't imagine what heavenly spots
there are there. I remember the first time I saw Isola

Bella ...' Her shoulders began to twitch from half-suppressed laughter; then she lifted her head and continued to laugh softly, keeping her eyes closed. 'What is it you want?' asked her mother and banged on the table. 'First,' she replied, 'that you stop shouting. Second, that Luzhin gets completely well.' 'Isola Bella means Beautiful Island,' continued her father hastily, trying with a meaningful grimace to intimate to his wife that he alone would manage it. 'You can't imagine ... An azure sky, and the heat, and magnolias, and the superb hotels at Stresa – and of course tennis, dancing ... And I particularly remember – what do you call them – those insects that light up ...' 'Well and what then?' asked the mother with rapacious curiosity. 'What then, when your friend – if he doesn't die ...' 'That depends on him,' said the daughter, trying to speak calmly. 'I can't abandon him. And I won't. Period.' 'You'll be in the mad house with him – that's where you'll be, my girl!' 'Mad or not ...' began the daughter with a trembling smile. 'Doesn't Italy tempt you?' cried her father. 'The girl is crazy. You won't marry this chess moron!' 'Moron yourself. If I want to I'll marry him. You're a narrow-minded, and wicked woman ...' 'Now, now, now, that's enough, that's enough,' mumbled her father. 'I won't let him set foot in here again,' panted her mother; 'that's final.' The daughter began to cry soundlessly and left the dining room, banging into a corner of the sideboard as she passed and letting out a plaintive 'damn it!' The offended sideboard went on vibrating for a long time.

'That was a little too harsh,' said the father in a whisper. 'I'm not defending her, of course. But you know, all kinds of things happen. The man overtired himself, and had a breakdown. Perhaps after this shock he'll really change for the better. Look, I think I'll go to see what she's doing.'

And the following day he had a long conversation with the famous psychiatrist in whose sanatorium Luzhin was staying. The psychiatrist had a black Assyrian beard and moist, tender eyes that shimmered marvelously as he listened to his interlocutor. He said that Luzhin was not an epileptic and was not suffering from progressive paralysis, that his condition was the consequence of prolonged strain, and that as soon as it was possible to have a sensible conversation with Luzhin, one would have to impress upon him that a blind passion for chess was fatal for him and that for a long time he would have to renounce his profession and lead an absolutely normal mode of life. 'And can such a man marry?' 'Why not – if he's not impotent.' The professor smiled tenderly. 'Moreover, there's an advantage for him in being married. Our patient needs care, attention and diversion. This is a temporary clouding of the senses, which is now gradually passing. As far as we can judge, a complete recovery is under way.'

The psychiatrist's words produced a small sensation at home. 'That means chess is kaput?' noted the mother with satisfaction. 'What will be left of him then – pure madness?' 'No, no,' said the father. 'There's no question of madness. The man will be healthy. The devil's not as black as his painters. I said "painters" – did you hear, my pet?' But the daughter did not smile and only sighed. To tell the truth she felt very tired. She spent the larger part of the day at the sanatorium and there was something unbelievably exhausting in the exaggerated whiteness of everything surrounding her and in the noiseless white movements of the nurses. Still extremely pale, with a growth of bristle and wearing a clean shirt, Luzhin lay immobile. There were moments, it is true, when he raised one knee under the sheet or gently moved an arm, and changing shadows would flit over his face, and sometimes an almost rational light would appear in his eyes – but nonetheless all that could be said of him was that he was immobile – a distressing immobility, exhausting for the gaze that sought a hint of conscious life in it. And it was impossible to tear one's gaze away – one so wanted to penetrate behind this pale yellowish forehead wrinkling from time to time with a mysterious inner movement, to pierce the mysterious fog that stirred with difficulty, endeavoring, perhaps, to disentangle itself, to condense into separate human thoughts. Yes, there was movement, there was. The formless fog thirsted for contours, for embodiments, and once something, a mirror-like glint, appeared in the darkness, and in this dim ray Luzhin perceived a face with a black, curly beard, a familiar image, an inhabitant of childish nightmares. The face in the dim little mirror came closer, and immediately the clear space clouded over and there was foggy darkness and slowly dispersing horror. And upon the expiry of many dark centuries – a single earthly night – the light again came into being, and suddenly something burst radiantly, the darkness parted and remained only in the form of a fading shadowy frame, in the midst of which was a shining, blue window. Tiny yellow leaves gleamed in this blueness, throwing a speckled shadow on a white tree trunk, that was concealed lower down by the dark green paw of a fir tree; and immediately this vision filled with life, the leaves began to quiver, spots crept over the trunk and the green paw oscillated, and Luzhin, unable to support it, closed his eyes, but the bright oscillation remained beneath his lids. I once buried something under those trees, he thought blissfully. And he seemed on the point of recalling exactly what it was when he heard a rustle above him and two calm voices. He began to listen, trying to understand where he was and why something soft and cold was lying on his forehead. After a while he opened his eyes again. A fat woman in white was holding her palm on his forehead – and there in the window was the same happy radiance. He wondered what to say, and catching sight of a little watch pinned on her breast, he licked his lips and asked what time it was. Movement immediately began around him, women whispered, and Luzhin remarked with astonishment that he understood their language, could even speak it himself. 'Wie spät ist es – what time is it?' he repeated. 'Nine in the morning,' said one of the women. 'How do you feel?' In the window, if you lifted yourself a little, you could see a fence that was also spotted with shadow. 'Evidently I got home,' said Luzhin pensively and again lowered his light, empty head onto the pillow. For a while he heard whispers, the light tinkle of glass. . . . There was something pleasing in the absurdity of everything that was happening, and it was amazingly good to lie there without moving. Thus he imperceptibly fell asleep and when he awoke saw again the blue gleam of a Russian autumn. But something had changed, someone unfamiliar had appeared next to his bed. Luzhin turned his head: on a chair to the right sat a man in white, with a black beard, looking at him attentively with smiling eyes. Luzhin thought vaguely that he resembled the peasant from the mill, but the resemblance immediately vanished when the man spoke: '*Karasho?*' he inquired amiably. 'Who are you?' asked Luzhin in German. 'A friend,' replied the gentleman, 'a faithful friend. You have been sick but now you are well. Do you hear? You are quite well.' Luzhin began to meditate on these words, but the man did not allow him to finish and said sympathetically: 'You must lie quiet. Rest. Get lots of sleep.'

Thus Luzhin came back from a long journey, having lost en route the greater part of his luggage, and it was too much bother to restore what was lost. These first days of recovery were quiet and smooth: women in white gave him tasty food to eat; the bewitching bearded man came and said nice things to him and looked at him with his agate gaze which bathed one's body in warmth. Shortly Luzhin began to notice that there was someone else in the room – a palpitating, elusive presence. Once when he woke up someone noiselessly and hastily went away, and once when he half dozed, someone's extremely light and apparently familiar whisper started beside him and immediately stopped. And hints began to flicker in the bearded man's conversation about something mysterious and happy; it was in the air around him and in the autumn beauty of the window, and it trembled somewhere behind the tree – an enigmatic, evasive happiness. And Luzhin gradually began to realize that the heavenly void in which his transparent thoughts floated was being filled in from all sides.

Warned of the imminence of a wonderful event, he looked through the railed head of his bed at the white door and waited for it to open and the prediction to come true. But the door did not open. Suddenly, to one side, beyond his field of vision, something stirred. Under the cover of a large

125

screen someone was standing and laughing. 'I'm coming, I'm coming, just a moment,' muttered Luzhin, freeing his legs from the sheet and looking with bulging eyes under the chair beside the bed for something to put on his feet. 'You're not going anywhere,' said a voice and a pink dress instantaneously filled the void.

The fact that his life was illumined first of all from this side eased his return. For a short while longer those harsh eminences, the gods of his being, remained in shadow. A tender optical illusion took place: he returned to life from a direction other than the one he had left it in, and the work of redistributing his recollections was assumed by the wondrous happiness that welcomed him first. And when, finally, this area of his life had been fully restored and suddenly, with the roar of a crumbling wall, Turati appeared, together with the tournament and all the preceding tournaments – this happiness was able to remove Turati's protesting image and replace the twitching chessmen in their box. As soon as they came to life, the lid was reslammed upon them – and the struggle did not continue for long. The doctor assisted, the precious stones of his eyes coruscating and melting; he spoke of the fact that all around them was a bright, free world, that chess was a cold amusement that dries up and corrupts the brain, and that the passionate chess player is just as ridiculous as the madman inventing a *perpetuum mobile* or counting pebbles on a deserted ocean shore. 'I shall stop loving you,' said his fiancée, 'if you start thinking about chess – and I can see every thought, so behave yourself.' 'Horror, suffering, despair,' said the doctor quietly, 'those are what this exhausting game gives rise to.' And he proved to Luzhin that Luzhin himself was well aware of this, that Luzhin was unable to think of chess without a feeling of revulsion, and in some mysterious fashion Luzhin, melting and coruscating, and blissfully relaxing, agreed with his reasoning. And in the vast, fragrant garden of the sanatorium Luzhin went strolling in new bedroom slippers made of soft leather and registered his approval of the dahlias, while beside him walked his fiancée and thought for some reason of a book she had read in

126

childhood in which all the difficulties in the life of a school-boy, who had run away from home together with a dog he had saved, were resolved by a convenient (for the author) fever – not typhus, not scarlet fever, but just 'a fever' – and the young stepmother whom he had not loved hitherto so cared for him that he suddenly began to appreciate her and would call her Mamma, and a warm tearlet would roll down her face and everything was fine. 'Luzhin is well,' she said with a smile, looking at his ponderous profile (the profile of a flabbier Napoleon) as it bent apprehensively over a flower, which maybe might bite. 'Luzhin is well. Luzhin is out for a walk. Luzhin is very sweet.' 'It doesn't smell,' said Luzhin in a thick, small voice. 'Nor should it smell,' she replied taking him by the arm. 'Dahlias aren't supposed to. But see that white flower over there – that's Mister Tabacum – and *he* has a strong smell at night. When I was little I always used to suck the sap out of the corolla. Now I don't like it any more.' 'In our garden in Russia . . .' began Luzhin and became thoughtful, squinting at the flower beds. 'We had these flowers over here,' he said. 'Our garden was quite a presentable one.' 'Asters,' she explained. 'I don't like them. They're coarse. Now in our garden . . .'

In general there was a lot of talk about childhood. The professor talked about it too and questioned Luzhin. 'Your father owned land, didn't he?' Luzhin nodded. 'Land, the country – that's excellent,' continued the professor. 'You probably had horses and cows?' A nod. 'Let me imagine your house – ancient trees all around . . . the house large and bright. Your father returns from the hunt . . .' Luzhin recalled that his father had once found a fat, nasty little fledgling in a ditch. 'Yes,' replied Luzhin uncertainly. 'Some details,' asked the professor softly. 'Please, I beg you. I'm interested in the way you occupied yourself in childhood, what you played with. You had some tin soldiers, I'm sure. . . .'

But Luzhin rarely grew enlivened during these conversations. On the other hand, constantly nudged by such interrogations, his thoughts would return again and again to the sphere of his childhood. It was impossible to express his recollections in words – there simply were no grown-up words for his childish impressions – and if he ever related anything then he did so jerkily and unwillingly – rapidly sketching the outlines and marking a complex move, rich in possibilities, with just a letter and a number. His pre-school, pre-chess childhood, which he had never thought about before, dismissing it with a slight shudder so as not to find dormant horrors and humiliating insults there, proved now to be an amazingly safe spot, where he could take pleasant excursions that sometimes brought a piercing pleasure. Luzhin himself was unable to understand whence the excitement – why the image of the fat French governess with the three bone buttons on one side of her skirt, that drew together whenever she lowered her enormous croup into an armchair – why the image that had then so irritated him, now evoked in his breast a feeling of tender constriction. He recalled that in their St. Petersburg house her asthmatic obesity had preferred to the staircase the old-fashioned, water-powered elevator which the janitor used to set in motion by means of a lever in the vestibule. 'Here we go,' the janitor said invariably as he closed the door leaves behind her, and the heavy, puffing, shuddering elevator would creep slowly upwards on its thick velvet cable, and past it, down the peeling wall that was visible through the glass, would come dark geographic patches, those patches of dampness and age among which, as among the clouds in the sky, the reigning fashion is for silhouettes of Australia and the Black Sea. Sometimes little Luzhin would go up with her, but more often he stayed below and listened to the elevator, high up and behind the wall, struggling upwards – and he always hoped, did little Luzhin, that it would get stuck halfway. Often enough this happened. The noise would cease and from unknown, intermural space would come a wail for help: the janitor below would move the lever, with a grunt of effort, then open the door into blackness and ask briskly, looking upwards: 'Moving?' Finally something would shudder and stir and after a little while the elevator would descend – now empty. Empty.

Goodness knows what had happened to her – perhaps she had traveled up to heaven and remained there with her asthma, her liquorice candies and her pince-nez on a black cord. The recollection also came back empty, and for the first time in all his life, perhaps, Luzhin asked himself the question – where exactly had it all gone, what had become of his childhood, whither had the veranda floated, whither, rustling through the bushes, had the familiar paths crept away?

With an involuntary movement of the soul he looked for these paths in the sanatorium garden, but the flower beds had a different outline, the birches were placed differently, and the gaps in their russet foliage, filled with autumn blue, in no way correspond to the remembered gaps into which he tried to fit these cut-out pieces of azure. It seemed as though that distant world was unrepeatable; through it roamed the by now completely bearable images of his parents, softened by the haze of time, and the clockwork train with its tin car painted to look like paneling went buzzing under the flounces of the armchair, and goodness knows how this affected the dummy engine driver, too big for the locomotive and hence placed in the tender.

That was the childhood Luzhin now visited willingly in his thoughts. It was followed by another period, a long, chess period that both the doctor and his fiancée called lost years, a dark period of spiritual blindness, a dangerous delusion – lost, lost years. They did not bear recollection. Lurking there like an evil spirit was the somehow terrible image of Valentinov. All right, we agree, that will do – lost years – away with them – they are forgotten – crossed out of life. And once they were thus excluded, the light of childhood merged directly with the present light and its flow formed the image of his fiancée. Her being expressed all the gentleness and charm that could be extracted from his recollections of childhood – as if the dapples of light scattered over the footpaths of the manor garden had now grown together into a single warm radiance.

'Feeling happy?' asked her mother dejectedly, looking at her animated face. 'Shall we soon be celebratng a wedding?' 'Soon,' she replied and threw her small round gray hat on the couch. 'In any case he's leaving the sanatorium in a day or two.' 'It's costing your father a pretty penny – about a thousand marks.' 'I've just scoured through all the book stores,' sighed the daughter, 'he absolutely had to have Jules Verne and Sherlock Holmes. And it turns out he's never read Tolstoy.' 'Naturally, he's a peasant,' muttered her mother. 'I always said so.' 'Listen, Mamma,' she said, lightly slapping her glove against the package of books, 'let's make an agreement. From today on let's have no more of these cracks. It is stupid, degrading for you, and, above all, completely pointless.' 'Then don't marry him,' said the mother, her face working. 'Don't marry him. I beseech you. Why, if you like – I'll throw myself on my knees before you—' And leaning one elbow on the armchair she started with difficulty to bend her leg, slowly lowering her large, slightly creaking body. 'You'll cave the floor in,' said her daughter, and picking up the books went out of the room.

Luzhin read Fogg's journey and Holmes' memoirs in two days, and when he had read them he said they were not what he wanted – this was an incomplete edition. Of the other books, he liked *Anna Karenin* – particularly the pages on the zemstvo elections and the dinner ordered by Oblonski. *Dead Souls* also made a certain impression on him, moreover in one place he unexpectedly recognized a whole section that he had once taken down in childhood as a long and painful dictation. Besides the so-called classics his fiancée brought him all sorts of frivolous French novels. Everything that could divert Luzhin was good – even these doubtful stories, which he read, though embarrassed, with interest. Poetry, on the other hand (for instance a small volume of Rilke's that she had bought on the recommendation of a salesman) threw him into a state of severe perplexity and sorrow. Correspondingly, the professor forbade Luzhin to be given anything by Dostoevski, who, in the professor's words, had an oppressive effect on the psyche of contemporary man, for as in a terrible mirror –

'Oh, Mr. Luzhin doesn't brood over books,' she said cheerfully. 'And he understands poetry badly because of the rhymes, the rhymes put him off.'

And strangely enough: in spite of the fact that Luzhin had read still fewer books in his life than she in hers, had never finished high school and had been interested in nothing but chess – she felt in him the ghost of a culture that she herself lacked. There were titles of books and names of characters which for some reason were household words to Luzhin, although the books themselves he had never read. His speech was clumsy and full of shapeless, ridiculous words – but in it there sometimes quivered a mysterious intonation hinting at some other kind of words, which were living and charged with subtle meaning, but which he could not utter. Despite his ignorance, despite the meagerness of his vocabulary, Luzhin harbored within him a barely perceptible vibration, the shadow of sounds that he had once heard.

No more did her mother speak of his uncouthness or of his other defects after that day when, remaining in a genuflectory position, she had sobbed out everything to her heart's content, her cheek pressed against the arm of the chair. 'I would have understood everything,' she said later to her husband, 'understood and forgiven everything if only she really loved him. But that's the dreadful part—' 'No, I don't quite agree with you,' interrupted her husband. 'I also thought at first that it was all mental. But her attitude to his illness convinces me to the contrary. Of course such a union is dangerous, and she could also have made a better choice ... Although he's from an old, noble family, his narrow profession has left a certain mark on him. Remember Irina who became an actress? Remember how she had changed when she came to us afterwards? All the same, disregarding all these defects, I consider him a good man. You'll see, he'll take up some useful occupation now. I don't know about you, but I simply can't bring myself to dissuade her any longer. In my opinion we should brace ourselves and accept the inevitable.'

He spoke briskly and at length, holding himself very straight and playing with the lid of his cigarette case.

'I feel just one thing,' repeated his wife. 'She doesn't love him.'

IN a rudimentary jacket minus one sleeve Luzhin, who was being renovated, stood in profile before a cheval glass, while a bald-headed tailor either chalked his shoulder and back or else jabbed pins into him, which he took with astonishing deftness from his mouth, where they seemed to grow naturally. From all the samples of cloth arranged neatly according to color in an album, Luzhin had chosen a dark gray square, and his fiancée spent a long time feeling the corresponding bolt of cloth, which the tailor threw with a hollow thud onto the counter, unwrapped with lightning speed, and pressed against his protruding stomach, as if covering up his nakedness. She found that the material tended to crease easily, whereupon an avalanche of tight rolls of cloth began to cover the counter and the tailor, wetting his finger on his lower lip, unrolled and unrolled. Finally a cloth was chosen that was also dark gray, but soft and flexible, and even just a bit shaggy; and now Luzhin, distributed about the cheval glass in pieces, in sections, as if for visual instruction (. . . here we have a plump, clean-shaven face, here is the same face in profile, and here we have something rarely seen by the subject himself, the back of his head, fairly closely cropped, with folds in the neck and slightly protruding ears, pink where the light shines through . . .) looked at himself and at the material, failing to recognize its former smooth, generous, virgin integrity. 'I think it needs to be a bit narrower in front,' said his fiancée, and the tailor, taking a step backward, slit his eyes at Luzhin's figure, purred with the polite trace of a smile that the gentleman was somewhat on the stout side, and then busied himself with some newborn lapels, pulling this and pinning that, while Luzhin in the meantime, with a gesture peculiar to all people in his position, held his arm slightly away from his body or else bent it at the elbow and looked at his wrist, trying to get accustomed to the sleeve. In passing, the tailor slashed him over the heart with chalk to indicate a small pocket, then pitilessly ripped off the sleeve that had seemed finished and began quickly to remove the pins from Luzhin's stomach.

Besides a good business suit they made Luzhin a dress suit; and the old-fashioned tuxedo found at the bottom of his trunk was altered by the same tailor. His fiancée did not dare to ask why Luzhin had formerly needed a tuxedo and an opera hat, fearing to arouse chess memories, and therefore she never learned about a certain big dinner given in Birmingham, where incidentally Valentinov . . . Oh well, good luck to him.

The renovation of Luzhin's envelope did not stop here. Shirts, ties and socks appeared – and Luzhin accepted all this with carefree interest. From the sanatorium he moved into a small, gaily papered room that had been rented on the second floor of his fiancée's building, and when he moved in he had exactly the same feeling as in childhood when he had moved from country to town. It was always strange, this settling into town. You went to bed and everything was so new: on the silence of the night the wooden pavement would come to life for several seconds of slow clip-clop, the windows were curtained more heavily and more sumptuously than at the manor; in darkness slightly relieved by the bright line of the incompletely closed door, the objects stopped expectantly, still not fully warmed up, still not having completely renewed their acquaintanceship after the long summer interval. And when you woke up, there was sober, gray light outside the windows and the sun slipped through a milky haze in the sky, looking like the moon, and suddenly in the distance – a burst of military music: it approached in orange waves, was interrupted by the hurried beat of a drum, and soon everything died down, and in place of the puffed-out sounds of trumpets there came again the imperturbable clopping of hoofs and the subdued rattling of a St. Petersburg morning.

'You forget to put out the light in the corridor,' said, smiling, his landlady, an elderly German woman. 'You for-

134

get to close your door at night.' And she also complained to his fiancée – saying he was absentminded like an old professor.

'Are you comfortable, Luzhin?' his fiancée kept inquiring. 'Are you sleeping well, Luzhin? No, I know it's not comfortable, but it will all change soon.' 'There's no need to put it off any longer,' muttered Luzhin, putting his arms around her and interlacing his fingers on her hip. 'Sit down, sit down, there's no need to put it off. Let's do it tomorrow. Tomorrow. Most lawful matrimony.' 'Yes, soon, soon,' she replied. 'But it can't be done in a single day. There's still one more establishment. There you and I will hang on the wall for two weeks, and in the meantime your wife will come from Palermo, take a look at the names and say: 'Impossible – Luzhin's mine.'

'It's mislaid,' replied her mother when she inquired about her birth certificate. 'I put it away and mislaid it. I don't know. I don't know anything.' The document, however, was found pretty quickly. And in any case it was too late now to warn, to forbid, to think up difficulties. The wedding rolled up with fatal smoothness, and could not be stopped as if one were standing on ice – slippery, nothing to catch hold of. She was forced to submit and think up ways of embellishing and displaying her daughter's fiancé so as not to be ashamed before other people, and she had to pluck up the courage to smile at the wedding, to play the role of the satisfied mother and to praise Luzhin's honesty and goodness of heart. She also thought of how much money had gone on Luzhin and how much more was still to go, and she tried to expel a terrifying picture from her imagination: Luzhin disrobed, aflame with simian passion, and her stubbornly submissive, cold, cold daughter. Meanwhile the frame for this picture was also ready. A not very expensive but decently furnished apartment was rented in the vicinity – on the fifth floor, it is true, but that did not matter – there was an elevator for Luzhin's shortness of breath, and in any case the stairs were not steep and there was a chair on every landing beneath a stained-glass window. From the spacious entrance hall, conventionally enlivened by silhouette drawings in black frames, a door to the left opened into the bedroom and a door to the right into the study. Farther down the right-hand side of the entrance hall was the door to the drawing room; the adjoining dining room had been made a little longer at the expense of the entrance hall, which at this point neatly turned into a corridor – a transformation chastely concealed by a plush portière on rings. To the left of the corridor was the bathroom, then the servant's room and at the end, the kitchen.

The future mistress of the apartment liked the disposition of the rooms; their furniture was less to her taste. In the study stood some brown velvet armchairs, a bookcase crowned with a broad-shouldered, sharp-faced Dante in a bathing cap, and a large, emptyish desk with an unknown past and an unknown future. A rickety lamp on a black spiraled standard topped with an orange shade rose beside a small couch, on which someone had forgotten a light-haired teddy bear and a fat-faced toy dog with broad pink soles and a black spot over one eye. Above the couch hung an imitation Gobelin tapestry depicting some dancing rustics.

From the study – if the sliding doors were given a slight push – a through view opened up: the parquet floor of the drawing room and beyond it the dining room with its sideboard reduced by perspective. In the drawing room a palm gave off a glazed green light and little rugs were strewn about the floor. Finally came the dining room with the sideboard now grown to its natural size and with plates around the walls. Above the table a lone, fluffy, little toy devil was hanging from the low lamp. There was a bay window and from there one could see a small public garden with a fountain at the end of the street. Returning to the dining table she looked through the drawing room into the distant study, at the Gobelin now in turn reduced, and then went from the dining room into the corridor and passed through the entrance hall into the bedroom. There, pressing close up to one another, stood two flocculent beds. The lamp turned out to be in the Mauritanian style, the curtains over the windows were yellow, promising a deceptive sunlight in the mornings –and a woodcut in the wall space between the windows showed a child prodigy in a nightgown that reached to his heels playing on an enormous piano, while his father, wearing a gray dressing gown and carrying a candle, stood stock-still, with the door ajar.

Something had to be added and something taken away. A portrait of the landlady's grandfather was removed from the drawing room and the study was hastily cleared of an Oriental-looking small table inlaid with a mother-of-pearl chessboard. The bathroom window, whose lower part was of sparkly blue-frosted glass, turned out to be cracked in its upper, transparent part and a new pane had to be put in. In the kitchen and servant's room the ceilings were white-washed anew. A phonograph grew up in the shade of the drawing room palm tree. But generally speaking, as she inspected and arranged this apartment 'rented with a long view but at short notice' – as her father joked – she could not throw off the thought that all this was only temporary, that no doubt it would be necessary to take Luzhin away from Berlin, to amuse him with other countries. Any future is unknown – but sometimes it acquires a particular fogginess, as if some other force had come to the aid of destiny's natural reticence and distributed this resilient fog, from which thought rebounds.

But how gentle and sweet Luzhin was these days; how cozily he sat at the tea table in his new suit, adorned by a smoke-colored tie, and politely, if not always in the right places, agreed with his interlocutor. His future mother-in-law told her acquaintances that Luzhin had decided to abandon chess because it took up too much of his time, but that he did not like to talk about it – and now Oleg Sergeyevich Smirnovski no longer asked for a game, but disclosed to him with a gleam in his eye the secret machinations of the Masons and even promised to give him a remarkable pamphlet to read.

In the establishments that they visited to inform officials of their intention to enter into matrimony, Luzhin conducted himself like a grown-up, carried all the documents himself, reverently and considerately, and lovingly filled in the forms, distinctly tracing out each letter. His handwriting was small, round and extraordinarily neat, and not a little time was expended in unscrewing his new fountain pen, which he somewhat affectedly shook to one side before beginning to write, and then, when he had thoroughly enjoyed the glide of the gold nib, thrust back into his breast pocket with its gleaming clip outside. And it was with pleasure that he accompanied his fiancée around the stores and waited for the interesting surprise of the apartment, which she had decided not to show him until after the wedding.

During the two weeks that their names were hung up on view, various wide-awake firms began to send them offers, sometimes to the future groom and sometimes to the future bride: vehicles for weddings and funerals (with a picture of a carriage harnessed to a pair of galloping horses), dress suits for hire, top hats, furniture, wine, halls to rent and pharmaceutical appurtenances. Luzhin conscientiously examined the illustrated catalogues and stored them in his room, at a loss to know why his fiancée was so scornful of all these interesting offers. There were also offers of another kind. There was what Luzhin called 'a small *à parte*' with his future father-in-law, a pleasant conversation in the course of which the latter offered to get him a job in a commercial enterprise – later on, of course, not immediately, let them live in peace for a few months. 'Life, my friend, is so arranged,' it was said in this conversation, 'that every second costs a man, at the very minimum estimate, 1/432 of a pfennig, and that would be a beggar's life; but you have to support a wife who is used to a certain amount of luxury.' 'Yes, yes,' said Luzhin with a beaming smile, trying to disentangle in his mind the complex computation that his interlocutor had just made with such delicate deftness. 'For this you need a little more money,' the latter continued, and Luzhin held his breath in expectation of a new trick. 'A second will cost you . . . dearer. I repeat: I am prepared at first – the first year, let's say – to give you generous assistance, but with time . . . Look, come see me sometime at the office, I'll show you some interesting things.'

Thus in the most pleasant manner possible people and things around him tried to adorn the emptiness of Luzhin's life. He allowed himself to be lulled, spoiled and titillated, and with his soul rolled up in a ball he accepted the caressive live that enveloped him from all sides. The future appeared to him vaguely as a long, silent embrace in a blissful penumbra, through which the diverse playthings of this world of ours would pass by, entering a ray of light and then disappearing again, laughing and swaying as they went. But at unavoidable moments of solitude during his engagement, late at night or early in the morning, there would be a sensation of strange emptiness, as if the colorful jigsaw puzzle done on the tablecloth had proved to contain curiously shaped blank spots. And once he dreamt he saw Turati sitting with his back to him. Turati was deep in thought, leaning on one arm, but from behind his broad back it was impossible to see what it was he was bending over and pondering. Luzhin did not want to see what it was, afraid to see, but nonetheless he cautiously began to look over the black shoulder. And then he saw that a bowl of soup stood before Turati and that he was not leaning on his arm but was merely tucking a napkin into his collar. And on the November day which this dream preceded Luzhin was married

Oleg Sergeyevich Smirnovski and a certain Baltic baron were witnesses when Luzhin and his bride were led into a large room and seated at a long, cloth-covered table. An official changed his jacket for a worn frock coat and read the marriage sentence. At this everyone stood up. After which with a professional smile and a humid handshake the official paid his respects to the newlyweds and everything was over. A fat janitor by the door bowed to them in expectation of a tip, and Luzhin good naturedly proffered his hand, which the other received upon his palm, not realizing at first that this was a human hand and not a handout.

That same day there was also a church wedding. The

last time Luzhin had been in church was many years ago, at his mother's funeral. Peering further into the depths of the past he remembered nocturnal returns on Catkin Night, holding a candle whose flame darted about in his hands, maddened at being carried out of the warm church into the unknown darkness, and finally died of a heart attack at the corner of the street where a gust of wind bore down from the Neva. There had been confession at the chapel on Pochtamtskaya Street, and footfalls had a special way of resounding in its twilight emptiness and the chairs moved with the sound of throats being cleared, and the waiting people sat one behind the other, and from time to time a whisper would burst out from the mysteriously curtained corner. And he remembered the nights at Easter: the deacon would read in a sobbing bass voice, and still sobbing would close the enormous gospel with a sweeping gesture. . . . And he remembered how airy and penetrating, so that it evoked a sucking sensation in the epigaster, the Greek word 'pascha' (paschal cake) sounded on an empty stomach when it was pronounced by the emaciated priest; and he remembered how difficult it always was to catch the moment when the smoothly swaying censer was aimed at you, precisely at you and not at your neighbor, and to bow so that the bow came exactly on the thurible's swing. There was a smell of incense and the hot fall of a drop of wax on the knuckles of one's hand, and the dark, honey-hued luster of the icon awaiting one's kiss. Languorous recollections, duskiness, fitful gleams, saporous church air and pins and needles in the legs. And to all this now was added a veiled bride, and a crown that trembled in the air over his very head and looked as if it might fall at any minute. He squinted up at it cautiously and it seemed to him once or twice that the invisible hand of someone holding the crown passed it to another, also invisible, hand. 'Yes-yes,' he replied hastily to the priest's question and wanted to add how nice everything was, and strange, and heart-melting, but he only cleared his throat agitatedly and rays of light wheeled blurrily in his yes.

Afterwards, when everyone was sitting at the big table,

he had the same feeling you get when you come home after matins to the festive table with its gilt-horned ram made of butter, a ham, and a virgin-smooth pyramid of paschal cottage cheese that you want to start on right away, by-passing the ham and eggs. It was hot and noisy, and lots of people were sitting at table who must have been in church as well – never mind, never mind, let them stay a while for the time being. ... Mrs. Luzhin looked at her husband, at his curl, at his beautifully tailored dress suit and at the crooked half-smile with which he greeted the courses. Her mother, liberally powdered and wearing a very low dress that showed, as in the old days, the tight groove between her raised, eighteenth-century breasts, was bearing up heroically and even used the familiar second person singular ('*ty*') to her son-in-law, so that at first Luzhin did not realize to whom she was speaking. He drank two glasses of champagne in all and a pleasant drowsiness began to come over him in waves. They went out onto the street. The black, windy night struck him softly on the breast, which was un-protected by his underdeveloped dress waistcoat, and his wife requested him to button up his overcoat. Her father, who had been smiling the whole evening and silently rais-ing his glass in some special way – until it was level with his eyes – a mannerism he had adopted from a certain diplomat who used to say '*sköl*' very elegantly – now raised a bunch of door keys, glinting in the lamplight, as a mark of farewell, still smiling with his eyes alone. Her mother, with an ermine wrap on her shoulders, tried not to look at Luzhin's back as he climbed into the taxicab. The guests, all a little drunk, took leave of their hosts and one another and laughing discreetly surrounded the car, which finally moved off, and then someone yelled 'hurrah' and a late passerby, turning to his woman companion, remarked approvingly: '*zemly-achki shumyat* – fellow countrymen celebrating.'

Luzhin immediately fell asleep in the cab; reflected gleams of whitish light unfolded fanwise, bringing his face to life, and the soft shadow made by his nose circled slowly over his cheek and then his lip, and again it was dark until another light went by, stroking Luzhin's hand in passing, which appeared to slide into a dark pocket as soon as darkness returned. And then came a series of bright lights and each one flushed out a shadowy butterfly from behind his white tie, and then his wife carefully adjusted his muffler, since the cold of the November night penetrated even into the closed automobile. He woke up and screwed up his eyes, not realizing immediately where he was, but at that moment the taxi came to a halt and his wife said softly 'Luzhin, we're home.'

In the elevator he stood smiling and blinking, somewhat dazed but not in the least drunk, and looked at the row of buttons, one of which his wife pressed. 'Quite a way up,' he said and looked at the elevator ceiling, as if expecting to see the summit of their journey. The elevator stopped. 'Hic,' said Luzhin and dissolved into quiet laughter.

They were met in the entrance hall by the new servant – a plumpish wench who immediately held out her red, disproportionately large hand to them. 'Oh, why did you wait for us?' said his wife. Speaking rapidly the maid congratulated them, and reverently took Luzhin's opera hat. Luzhin, with a subtle smile, showed her how it banged flat. 'Amazing,' exclaimed the maid. 'You can go, go to bed,' repeated his wife anxiously. 'We'll lock up.'

The lights went on in turn in the study, drawing room and dining room. 'Extends like a telescope,' mumbled Luzhin sleepily. He did not look at anything properly – he could not keep his eyes open enough. He was already on his way into the dining room when he noticed he was carrying in his arms a large, plush dog with pink soles. He put it on the table and a fluffy imp hanging from the lamp immediately came down like a spider. The rooms went dark like the sections of a telescope being folded together and Luzhin found himself in the bright corridor. 'Go to bed,' again shouted his wife to someone who at the far end rustled and bid them good night. 'That's the servant's room,' said his wife. 'And the bathroom's here, to the left.' 'Where's the little place?' whispered Luzhin. 'In the bathroom, everything's in the bathroom,' she replied and Luzhin cautiously opened the door, and when he had convinced himself of something he speedily locked himself in. His wife passed through the hallway into the bedroom and sat down in an armchair, looking at the entrancingly flocculent beds. 'Oh, I'm tired.' She smiled and for a long time watched a big, sluggish fly that circled around the Mauretanian lamp, buzzing hopelessly, and then disappeared. 'This way, this way,' she cried, hearing Luzhin's uncertain, shuffling step in the hallway. 'Bedroom,' he said approvingly, and placing his hands behind his back he looked about him for a while. She opened the wardrobe where she had put away their things the day before, hesitated, and turned to her husband. 'I'll take a bath,' she said. 'All your things are in here.'

'Wait a minute,' said Luzhin and suddenly yawned with his mouth wide open. 'Wait a minute,' he repeated in a palatal voice, gulping down between syllables the elastic pieces of yawn. But picking up her pajamas and bedroom slippers she quickly left the room.

The water poured from the tap in a thick blue stream and began to fill the white bathtub, steaming tenderly and changing the tone of its murmur as the level rose. Looking at its gushing gleam she reflected with some anxiety that the limits of her feminine competency were now in sight and that there was one sphere in which it was not her place to lead. As she immersed herself in the bath she watched the tiny water bubbles gathering on her skin and on the sinking, porous sponge. Settling down up to the neck, she saw herself through the already slightly soapy water, her body thin and almost transparent, and when a knee came just barely out of the water, this round, glistening, pink island was somehow unexpected in its unmistakable corporeality. 'After all it's none of my affair,' she said, freeing one sparkling arm from the water and pushing the hair back from her forehead. She turned on the hot water again, reveling in the resilient waves of warmth as they passed over her stomach, and finally, causing a small storm in the bathtub, she stepped out and unhurriedly began to dry herself. 'Turkish beauty,' she said, standing only in her silk pajama pants before the slightly sweating mirror.

143

'Pretty well built on the whole,' she said after a while. Continuing to look at herself in the mirror, she began slowly to draw on her pajama top. 'A bit full in the hips,' she said. The water in the bath that had been flowing out with a gurgle suddenly squeaked and all was quiet: the bathtub was now empty, and only the plug-hole retained a tiny, soapy whirlpool. Suddenly she realized she was dawdling on purpose, standing in her pajamas before the mirror – and a shiver went through her breast, as when you are leafing through last year's magazine, knowing that in a second, in just a second, the door will open and the dentist will appear on the threshold.

Whistling loudly she walked to the bedroom, and the whistle was immediately cut short: Luzhin, covered to the waist by an eiderdown, his starched shirtfront undone and bulging was lying on the bed with his hands tucked under his head and emitting a purring snore. His collar hung on the foot of the bed, his trousers sprawled on the floor, their suspenders spread out, and his dress coat, set crookedly on the shoulders of a hanger, was lying on the couch with one tail tucked underneath it. All this she quietly picked up and put away. Before going to bed she moved back the window curtain to see if the blind had been lowered. It had not been. In the dark depths of the courtyard the night wind rocked a shrub and in the faint light shed from somewhere unknown something glistened, perhaps a puddle on the stone path that skirted the lawn, and in another place the shadow of some railings fitfully appeared and disappeared. And suddenly everything went dark and there was only a black chasm.

She thought she would fall asleep as soon as she jumped into bed but it turned out otherwise. The cooing snore beside her, a strange melancholy, and this dark, unfamiliar room kept her suspended and would not allow her to slip off into sleep. And for some reason the word 'match' kept floating through her brain – 'a good match,' 'find yourself a good match,' 'match,' 'match,' 'an unfinished, interrupted match,' 'such a good game.' 'Give the Maestro my anxiety, anxiety . . .' 'She could have made a brilliant match,' said

144

her mother clearly, floating past in the darkness. 'Let's drink a toast,' whispered a tender voice, and her father's eyes appeared round the edge of a glass, and the foam rose higher, higher, and her new shoes pinched a bit and it was so hot in the church.

CHAPTER TWELVE

THE long trip abroad was postponed until spring – the sole concession Mrs. Luzhin made to her parents, who wanted at least for the first few months to be near at hand. Mrs. Luzhin herself somewhat feared Berlin life for her husband, entwined as it was with chess memories; it turned out, however, not to be difficult to amuse Luzhin even in Berlin.

A long trip abroad, conversations about it, travel projects. In the study, which Luzhin had become very fond of, they found a splendid atlas in one of the bookcases. The world was shown at first as a solid sphere, tightly bound in a net of longitudes and latitudes, then it was rolled out flat, cut into two halves and served up in sections. When it was rolled out, some place like Greenland, which at first had been a small process, a mere appendix, suddenly swelled out almost to the dimensions of the nearest continent. There were white bald patches on the poles. The oceans stretched out smoothly azure. Even on this map there would be enough water to, say wash your hands – what then was it, actually – so much water, depth, breadth. Luzhin showed his wife all the shapes he had loved as a child – the Baltic Sea, like a kneeling woman, the jackboot of Italy, the drop of Ceylon falling from India's nose. He thought the equator was unlucky – its path lay mostly across oceans; it cut across two continents, true, but it had no luck with Asia, which had pulled up out of the way. Moreover it pressed down and squashed what it did manage to cross – the tips of one or two things and some untidy islands. Luzhin knew the highest mountain and the smallest state, and looking at the relative positions of the two Americas he found something acrobatic in their association. 'But in general, all this could have been arranged more piquantly,' he said, pointing to the map of the world. 'There's no idea behind it, no

146

point.' And he even grew a little angry that he was unable to find the meaning of all these complicated outlines, and he spent hours looking, as he had looked in childhood, for a way of going from the North Sea to the Mediterranean along a labyrinth of rivers, or of tracing some kind of rational pattern in the disposition of the mountain ranges.

'Now where shall we go?' said his wife and clucked slightly, the way adults do to indicate pleasant anticipation when they begin to play with children. And then she loudly named the romantic spots. 'First down here, to the Riviera,' she suggested. 'Monte Carlo, Nice. Or, say, the Alps.' 'And then this way a bit,' said Luzhin. 'They have very cheap grapes in the Crimea.' 'What are you saying, Luzhin, the Lord have mercy on you, it's impossible for us to go to Russia.' 'Why?' asked Luzhin. 'They invited me to go.' 'Nonsense, stop it please,' she said, angered not so much by Luzhin's talking of the impossible as by his referring obliquely to something connected with chess. 'Look down here,' she said, and Luzhin obediently transferred his gaze to another place on the map. 'Here, for instance, is Egypt, the pyramids. And here is Spain where they do horrible things to bulls. . . .'

Knowing that Luzhin had probably already been more than once in many of the towns they might have visited, she did not name the large cities in order to avoid any harmful reminiscences. A superfluous caution. The world in which Luzhin had traveled in his time was not depicted on the map, and if she had named him Rome or London, then from the sound of these names on her lips and from the big whole note on the map he would have imagined something completely new, never seen before, and not in any circumstance that vague chess café, which was always the same whether situated in Rome or London or even in that innocent Nice, so trustfully named by her. And when she brought innumerable folders back from the railroad office, the world of his chess-playing trips separated, as it were, still more sharply from this new world, where the tourist strolled in his white suit with a pair of binoculars on a strap. There were black palms silhouetted against a rosy sunset and the reversed silhouettes of the same palms in the rosy Nile. There was an almost indecently blue gulf, and a sugary white hotel with a multicolored flag waving in the opposite direction to the smoke of a steamer on the horizon. There were snowy mountaintops and suspension bridges, and lagoons with gondolas, and an infinite number of ancient churches, and a narrow cobbled lane, and a small donkey with two thick bales on its sides. . . . Everything was attractive, everything was entertaining, everything sent the unknown author of the brochures into transports of praise. . . . The musical names, the millions of saints, the waters that cured all sickness, the age of a town rampart, hotels of the first, second, third class – all this rippled before the eyes and everything was fine, Luzhin was awaited everywhere, they called him in voices of thunder, they were driven wild by their own hospitality, and without asking the owner they distributed the sun.

It was during these first first days of married life that Luzhin visited his father-in-law's office. His father-in-law was dictating something, but the typewriter stuck to its own version – repeating the word 'tot' in a rapid chatter with something like the following intonation: tot Hottentot tot tot tot do not totter – and then something would move across with a bang. His father-in-law showed him sheafs of forms, account books with Z-shaped lines on the pages, books with little windows on their spines, the monstrously thick tomes of Commercial Germany, and a calculating machine, very clever and quite tame. However, Luzhin liked Tot-tot best of all, the words spilling swiftly out onto the paper, the wonderful evenness of the lilac lines – and several copies at the same time. 'I wonder if I took . . . One needs to know,' he said, and his father-in-law nodded approvingly and the typewriter appeared in Luzhin's study. It was proposed to him that one of the office employees come and explain how to use it, but he refused, replying that he would learn on his own. And so it was: he fairly quickly made out its construction, learned to put in the ribbon and roll in the sheet of paper, and made friends with all the little levers. It proved to be more difficult to remember the distribution of the letters, the typing went very slowly; there was none of Tot-tot's rapid chatter and for some reason – from the very first day – the exclamation mark dogged him – it leapt out in the most unexpected places. At first he copied out half a column from a German newspaper, and then composed a thing or two himself. A brief little note took shape with the following contents: 'You are wanted on a charge of murder. Today is November 27th. Murder and arson. Good day, dear Madam. Now when you are needed, dear, exclamation mark, where are you? The body has been found. Dear Madam! Today the police will come!!' Luzhin read this over several times, re-inserted the sheet and, groping for the right letters, typed out, somewhat jumpily, the signature: 'Abbé Busoni.' At this point he grew bored, the thing was going too slowly. And somehow he had to find a use for the letter he had written. Burrowing in the telephone directory he found a Frau Louisa Altman, write out the address by hand and sent her his composition.

The phonograph also provided him with a certain amount of entertainment. Its chocolate-colored cabinet under the palm tree used to sing with a velvety voice and Luzhin, one arm around his wife, would sit on the sofa and listen, and think it would soon be night. She would get up and change the record, holding the disc up to the light, and one sector of it would be a silky shimmer, like moonlight on the sea. And again the cabinet would exude music, and again his wife would sit next to him, and lower her chin onto interlaced fingers and listen, blinking. Luzhin remembered the airs and even attempted to sing them. There were moaning, clattering and ululating dances and a most tender American who sang in a whisper, and there was a whole opera on fifteen records – *Boris Godunov* – with church bells ringing in one place and with sinister pauses.

His wife's parents used to drop in frequently and it was established that the Luzhins would dine with them three times a week. The mother tried several times to learn from her daughter a detail or two about their marriage and would ask inquisitively: 'Are you pregnant? I'm sure you're going to have a baby soon.' 'Nonsense,' replied the daughter, 'I've just had twins.' She was still her usual calm self, still smiled the same way with her brows lowered and still addressed Luzhin by his surname and by the second person plural. 'My poor Luzhin,' she would say, tenderly pursing her lips, 'my poor, poor man.' And Luzhin would rub his cheek on her shoulder, and she would think vaguely that there were probably greater joys than the joys of compassion, but that these were no concern of hers. Her only care in life was a minute-by-minute effort to arouse Luzhin's curiosity about things in order to keep his head above the dark water, so that he could breathe easily. She asked Luzhin in the mornings what he had dreamed, enlivened his matutinal appetite with a cutlet or English marmalade, took him for walks, lingered with him before shopwindows, read *War and Peace* aloud to him after dinner, played jolly geography with him and dictated sentences for him to type. Several times she took him to the museum and showed him her favorite pictures and explained that in Flanders, where they had rain and fog, painters used bright colors, while it was in Spain, a country of sunshine, that the gloomiest master of all had been born. She said also that the one over there had a feeling for glass objects, while this one liked lilies and tender faces slightly inflamed by colds caught in heaven, and she directed his attention to two dogs domestically looking for crumbs beneath the narrow, poorly spread table of 'The Last Supper.' Luzhin nodded and slit his eyes conscientiously, and was a very long time examining an enormous canvas on which the artist had depicted all the torments of sinners in hell – in great detail, very curiously. They also visited the theater and the zoo, and the movies, at which point it turned out that Luzhin had never been to the movies before. The picture ran on in a white glow and finally, after many adventures, the girl returned – now a famous actress to her parents' house, and paused in the doorway, while in the room, not seeing her yet, her grizzled father was playing chess with the doctor, a faithful friend of the family who had remained completely unchanged over the years. In the darkness came the sound of Luzhin laughing abruptly. 'An absolutely impossible position for the pieces,' he said, but at this point, to his wife's relief, everything changed and the father, growing in size, walked toward the spectators and acted his part for all he was worth; his eyes widened, then came a slight trembling, his lashes flapped, there was another bit of trembling, and slowly his wrinkles softened, grew kinder, and a slow smile of infinite tenderness appeared on his face, which continued to tremble – and yet, gentlemen, the old man had cursed his daughter in his time. . . . But the doctor – the doctor stood to one side, he remembered – the poor, humble doctor – how as a young girl at the very beginning of the picture she had thrown flowers over the fence at him, while he, lying on the grass, had been reading a book: he had then raised his head and had seen only a fence; but suddenly a girl's head with parted hair rose on the other side and then came a pair of eyes growing ever bigger – ah, what mischievousness, what playfulness! Go on, Doctor, jump over the fence – there she runs, the sweet nymph, she's hiding behind those trees – catch her, catch her, Doctor! But now all this is gone. Head bowed, hands limply hanging, one of them holding a hat, stands the famous actress (a fallen woman, alas!). And the father, continuing the trembling, slowly opens his -arms, and suddenly she kneels before him. Luzhin began to blow his nose. When they left the movie house he had red eyes and he cleared his throat and denied that he had been crying. And the following day over morning coffee he leaned an elbow on the table and said thoughtfully: 'Very, very good – that picture.' He thought a bit more and added: 'But they don't know how to play.' 'What do you mean, they don't know?' said his wife with surprise. 'They were first-class actors.' Luzhin looked at her sideways and immediately averted his eyes, and there was something about this she did not like. Suddenly she realized what was up and began to debate with herself, how to make Luzhin forget this unfortunate game of chess, which that fool of a director had seen fit to introduce for the sake of 'atmosphere.' But Luzhin, evidently, immediately forgot it himself – he was engrossed in some genuine Russian bread that his mother-in-law had sent, and his eyes were again quite clear.

In this way a month passed, a second. The winter that year was a white, St. Petersburg one. Luzhin was made a wadded overcoat. Indigent refugee Russians were given certain of Luzhin's old things – including a green woolen scarf of Swiss origin. Mothballs exuded a rough-edged melancholy smell. In the entrance hall hung a condemned jacket. 'It was so comfortable,' implored Luzhin, 'so very comfortable.' 'Leave it alone,' said his wife from the bedroom 'I haven't looked at it yet. It's probably teeming with moths.' Luzhin took off the dinner jacket he had been trying on to see whether he had filled out much during the past month (he had filled out, he had – and tomorrow there was a big Russian ball, a charitable affair) and slipped lovingly into the sleeves of the condemned one. A darling jacket, not the slightest trace of moth in it. Here was a tiny hole in the pocket, but not right through like they sometimes were. 'Wonderful,' he cried in a high voice. His wife, sock in hand, looked out into the entrace hall. 'Take it off, Luzhin. It's torn and dusty, goodness knows how long it's lain about.' 'No, no,' said Luzhin. She inspected it from all sides; Luzhin stood and slapped himself on to the hips, and it felt, incidentally, as if there were something in his pocket; the thrust his hand in – no, nothing, only a hole. 'It's very decrepit,' said his wife, frowning, 'but perhaps as a work coat . . .' 'I beg you,' said Luzhin. 'Well, as you wish – only give it to the maid afterwards so she can give it a good beating.' 'No, it's clean,' said Luzhin to himself and resolved to hang it somewhere in his study, in some little nook, to take it off and hang it up the way civil servants do. In taking it off he again felt as if the jacket were a trifle heavier on the left side, but he remembered that the pockets were empty and did not investigate the cause of the heaviness. As to the dinner jacket here, it had become tightish – yes, definitely tightish. 'A ball,' said Luzhin, and imagined to himself lots and lots of circling couples.

The ball turned out to be taking place in one of the best hotels in Berlin. There was a crush near the cloakrooms, and the attendants were accepting things and carrying them away like sleeping children. Luzhin was given a neat metal number. He missed his wife, but found her immediately: she was standing in front of a mirror. He placed the metal disk against the tender hollow of her smooth, powdered back. 'Brr, that's cold,' she exclaimed, moving her shoulder blade. 'Arm in arm, arm in arm,' said Luzhin. 'We have to enter arm in arm.' And that is how they entered. The first thing Luzhin saw was his mother-in-law, looking much younger, rosy red, and wearing a magnificent, sparkling headdress – a Russian woman's *kokoshnik*. She was selling punch, and an elderly Englishman (who had simply come down from his room) was quickly becoming drunk, one elbow propped on her table. At another table, near a fir tree adorned with colored lights, there was a pile of lottery prizes: a dignified samovar with red and blue reflected lights on the tree side, dollas dressed in *sarafans*, a phonograph, and liqueurs (donated by Smirnovski). A third table had sandwiches, Italian salad, caviar – and a beautiful blond lady was calling to someone: 'Marya Vasilyevna, Marya Vasilyevna, why did they take it away again . . . I had asked . . .' 'A very good evening to you,' said somebody close by, and Mrs. Luzhin raised an arched, swanlike hand. Farther on, in the next room, there was music, and dancers circled and marked time in the space between the tables; someone's back banged into Luzhin at full speed, and he grunted and stepped back. His wife had disappeared, and searching for her with his eyes he set off back to the first room. Here the tombola again attracted his attention. Paying out a mark every time, he would plunge his hand into the box and fish out a tiny cylinder of rolled-up paper. Snuffling through his nose and protruding his lips, he would take a long time to unroll the paper, and finding no number inside would look to see if there was one on the other, outer side – a useless but very normal procedure. In the end he won a children's book, *Purry-Cat* or something, and not knowing what to do with it, left it on a table, where two full glasses were awaiting the return of a dancing couple. The crush and the movement and the bursts of music now got on his nerves and there was nowhere to hide, and everyone, probably, was looking at him and wondering why he did not dance. In the intervals between dances his wife looked for him in the other room, but at every step she was stopped by acquaintances. A great many people attended this ball – there was a foreign consul, obtained with great difficulty, and a famous Russian singer, and two movie actresses. Somebody pointed out their table to her: the ladies wore artificial smiles, and their escorts – three well-fed men of the producer-businessman type – kept clucking their tongues and snapping their fingers and abusing the pale, sweating waiter for his slowness and inefficiency. One of these men seemed particularly obnoxious to her: he had very white teeth and shining brown eyes; having dealt with the waiter he began to relate something in a loud voice, sprinkling his Russian with the most hackneyed German expressions. All at once, she felt depressed that everyone was looking at these movie people, at the singer and at the consul, and nobody seemed to know that a chess genius was present at the ball, a man whose name had been in millions of newspapers and whose games had already been called immortal. 'You are amazingly easy to dance with. They have a good floor here. Excuse me. It's terribly crowded. The receipts will be excellent. This man over here is from the French Embassy. It is amazingly easy dancing with you.' With this the conversation usually ended, they liked to dance with her but they did not know exactly what to talk about. A rather pretty but boring young lady. And that strange marriage to an unsuccessful musician, or something of that sort. 'What did you say – a former socialist? A what? A player? A card player? Do you ever visit them, Oleg Sergeyevich?'

In the meantime Luzhin had found a deep armchair not far from the staircase and was looking at the crowd from behind a column and smoking his thirteenth cigarette. Into another armchair next to him, after making a preliminary inquiry as to whether it was taken or not, settled a swarthy gentleman with a tiny mustache. People still continued to go by and Luzhin gradually became frightened. There was

154

nowhere he could look without meeting inquisitive eyes and from the accursed necessity of looking somewhere he fixed on the mustache of his neighbor, who evidently was also staggered and perplexed by all this noisy and unnecessary commotion. This person, feeling Luzhin's gaze on him, turned his face to him. 'It's a long time since I was at a ball,' he said amiably and grinned, shaking his head. 'The main thing is not to look,' uttered Luzhin hollowly, using his hands as a form of blinkers. 'I've come a long way,' explained the man. 'A friend dragged me here. To tell the truth, I'm tired.' 'Tiredness and heaviness,' nodded Luzhin. 'Who knows what it all means? It surpasses my conception. 'Particularly when you work, as I do, on a Brazilian plantation,' said the gentleman. 'Plantation,' repeated Luzhin after him like an echo. 'You have an odd way of living here,' continued the stranger. 'The world is open on all four sides and here they are pounding out Charlestons on an extremely restricted fragment of floor.' 'I'm also going away,' said Luzhin. 'I've got the travel folders.' 'There is nothing like freedom,' exclaimed the stranger. 'Free wanderings and a favorable wind. And what wonderful countries. . . . I met a German botanist in the forest beyond Rio Negro and lived with the wife of a French engineer on Madagascar.' 'I must get their folders, too,' said Luzhin. 'Very attractive things – folders. Everything in great detail.'

'Luzhin, so that's where you are!' suddenly cried his wife's voice; she was passing quickly by on her father's arm. 'I'll be back immediately, I'll just get a table for us,' she cried, looking over her shoulder, and disappeared. 'Is your name Luzhin?' asked the gentleman curiously. 'Yes, yes,' said Luzhin 'but it's of no importance.' 'I knew one Luzhin,' said the gentleman, screwing up his eyes (for memory is shortsighted). 'I knew one. You didn't happen to go to the Balashevski school, did you?' 'Suppose I did,' replied Luzhin, and seized by an unpleasant suspicion he began to examine his companion's face. 'In that case we were classmates!' exclaimed the other. 'My name is Petrishchev. Do you remember me? Oh, of course you remember! What a coincidence. I would never have recognized you by your face.

Tell me, Luzhin ... Your first name and patronymic ?...
Ah, I seem to remember – Tony ... Anton. ... What next?'
'You're mistaken, mistaken,' said Luzhin with a shudder.
'Yes, my memory is bad,' continued Petrishchev. 'I've forgotten lots of names. For instance, do you remember that
quiet boy we had? Later he lost an arm fighting under
Wrangel, just before the evacuation. I saw him in church
in Paris. Hm, what's his name now?' 'Why is all this necessary?' said Luzhin. 'Why talk about it so much?' 'No, I
don't remember,' sighed Petrishchev, tearing his palm from
his forehead. 'But then, for instance, there was Gromov:
he's also in Paris now; fixed himself up nicely, it seems. But
where are the others? Where are they all? Dispersed, gone
up in smoke. It's odd to think about it. Well, and how are
you getting on, Luzhin, how are you getting on, old boy?'
'All right,' said Luzhin and averted his eyes from the ex-
pansive Petrishchev, seeing his face suddenly as it had been
then: small, pink, and unbearably mocking. 'Wonderful
times, they were,' cried Petrishchev. 'Do you remember
our geographer, Luzhin? How he used to fly like a hurricane into the classroom, holding a map of the world? And
that little old man – oh, again I've forgotten the name – do
you remember how he used to shake all over and say: "Get
on with you, pshaw, you noodle"? Wonderful times. And
how we used to whip down those stairs, into the yard, you
remember? And how it turned out at the school party that
Arbuzov could play the piano? Do you remember how his
experiments never used to come off? And how we thought
up a rhyme for him – "booze off"?' '... just don't react,'
Luzhin said quickly to himself. 'And all that's vanished,'
continued Petrishchev. 'Here we are at a ball. ... Oh, by the
way, I seem to remember ... you took up something some
occupation, when you left school. What was it? Yes, of
course – chess!' 'No, no,' said Luzhin. 'Why on earth must
you ...' 'Oh excuse me,' said Petrishchev affably. 'Then
I'm getting mixed up. Yes, yes, that's how it is. ... The ball's
in full swing, and we're sitting here talking about the past.
You know I've traveled the whole world. ... What women
in Cuba! Or that time in the jungle, for instance ...'

156

'It's all lies,' sounded a lazy voice from behind. 'He was never in any jungle whatsoever. . . .'

'Now why do you spoil everything?' drawled Petrishchev, turning around. 'Don't listen to him,' continued a bald, lanky person, the owner of the lazy voice. 'He has been living in France since the Revolution and left Paris for the first time the day before yesterday.' 'Luzhin, allow me to introduce you,' began Petrishchev with a laugh; but Luzhin hastily made off, tucking his head into his shoulders and weaving strangely and quivering from the speed of his walk.

'Gone,' said Petrishchev in astonishment, and added thoughtfully, 'After all, it may be I took him for somebody else.'

Stumbling into people and exclaiming in a tearful voice '*pardon, pardon!*' and still stumbling into people and trying not to see their faces, Luzhin looked for his wife, and when he finally caught sight of her he seized her by the elbow from behind, so that she started and turned around; but at first he was unable to say anything, he was puffing too much. 'What's the matter?' she asked anxiously. 'Let's go, let's go,' he muttered, still holding her by the elbow. 'Calm down, please, Luzhin, that's not necessary,' she said, nudging him slightly to one side so that the bystanders could not hear. 'Why do you want to go?' 'There's a man there,' said Luzhin, breathing jerkily. 'And such an unpleasant conversation.' '. . . whom you knew before?' she asked quietly. 'Yes, yes,' nodded Luzhin. 'Let's go. I beg you.'

Half closing his eyes so that Petrishchev would not notice him, he pushed his way through to the vestibule, began to rummage in his pockets, looking for his tag, found it at last after several enormous seconds of confusion and despair and shuffled this way and that impatiently while the cloakroom attendant, like a somnambulist, looked for his things. . . . He was the first to get dressed and the first to go out and his wife swiftly followed him, pulling her moleskin coat together as she went. Only in the car did Luzhin begin to breathe freely, and his expression of distracted sullenness gave way to a guilty half-smile. 'Dear Luzhin met a nasty person,' said his wife, stroking his hand. 'A schoolfellow – a suspicious character,' explained Luzhin. 'But now dear Luzhin's all right,' whispered his wife and kissed his soft hand. 'Now everything's gone,' said Luzhin.

But this was not quite so. Something remained – a riddle, a splinter. At nights he began to meditate over why this meeting had made him so uneasy. Of course there were all sorts of individual unpleasantnesses – the fact that Petrishchev had once tormented him in school and had now referred obliquely to a certain torn book about little Tony, and the fact that a whole world, full of exotic temptations, had turned out to be a braggart's rigmarole, and it would no longer be possible in future to trust travel folders. But it was not the meeting itself that was frightening but something else – this meeting's secret meaning that he had to divine. He began to think intensely at nights, the way Sherlock had been wont to do over cigar ash – and gradually it began to seem that the combination was even more complex than he had at first thought, that the meeting with Petrishchev was only the continuation of something, and that it was necessary to look deeper, to return and replay all the moves of his life from his illness until the ball.

CHAPTER THIRTEEN

ON a grayish-blue rink (where there were tennis courts in summer), lightly powdered with snow, the townsfolk were disporting themselves cautiously, and at the very moment the Luzhins passed by on their morning stroll, the sprightliest of the skaters, a besweatered young fellow, gracefully launched into a Dutch step and sat down hard on the ice. Farther, in a small public garden, a three-year-old boy all in red, walking unsteadily on woolen legs, made his way to a stirrup-stone, scraped off with one fingerless little hand some snow that was lying there in an appetizing hillock and raised it to his mouth, for which he was immediately seized from behind and spanked. 'Oh, you poor little thing,' said Mrs. Luzhin, looking back. A bus went along the whitened asphalt, leaving two thick, black stripes behind it. From a shop of talking and playing machines came the sound of fragile music and someone closed the door so the music would not catch cold. A dachshund with a patched, blue little overcoat and low-swinging ears stopped and sniffed the snow and Mrs. Luzhin just had time to stroke it. Something light, sharp and whitish kept striking them in the face, and when they peered at the empty sky, bright specks danced before their eyes. Mrs. Luzhin skidded and looked reproachfully at her gray snowboots. By the Russian food store they met the Alfyorov couple. 'Quite a cold snap,' exclaimed Alfyorov with a shake of his yellow beard. 'Don't kiss it, the glove's dirty,' said Mrs. Luzhin, and looking with a smile at Mrs. Alfyorov's enchanting, always animated face she asked why she never came to visit them. 'And you're putting on weight, sir,' growled Alfyorov, squinting playfully at Luzhin's stomach, exaggerated by his wadded overcoat. Luzhin looked imploringly at his wife. 'Remember, you're always welcome,' she said, nodding. 'Wait, Mashenka, do you know their telephone number?' asked

Alfyorov. 'You know ? Fine. Well, so long – as they say in Soviet Russia. My deepest respect to your mother.'

'There's something a little mean and a little pathetic about him,' said Mrs. Luzhin, taking her husband's arm and changing step in order to match his. 'But Mashenka ... what a darling, what eyes. ... Don't walk so fast, dear Luzhin – it's slippery'

The light snow ceased to fall, a spot of sky gleamed through palely, and the flat, bloodless disk of the sun floated out. 'You know what, let's go to the right today,' suggested Mrs. Luzhin. 'We've never been that way, I believe.' 'Look, oranges,' said Luzhin with relish and recalled how his father had asserted that when you pronounce '*leemon*' (lemon) in Russian, you involuntarily pull a long face, but when you say '*apelsin*' (orange) – you give a broad smile. The sales-girl deftly spread the mouth of the paper bag and rammed the cold, pocked-red globes into it. Luzhin began to peel an orange as he walked, frowning in anticipation that the juice would squirt in his eye. He put the peel in his pocket, because it would have stood out too vividly on the snow, and because, perhaps, you could make jam with it. 'Is it good ?' asked his wife. Luzhin smacked his lips on the last segment and with a contended smile was about to take his wife's arm again, but suddenly he stopped and looked around. Having thought for a moment, he walked back to the corner and looked at the name of the street. Then he quickly caught up with his wife again and thrust out his cane in the direction of the nearest house, an ordinary gray stone house separated from the street by a small garden behind iron railings. 'My dad used to reside here,' said Luzhin. 'Thirty-five A.' 'Thirty-five A,' his wife repeated after him, not knowing what to say and looking up at the windows. Luzhin walked on, cutting snow away from the railings with his cane. Presently he stopped stock-still in front of a stationery store where the wax dummy of a man with two faces, one sad and the other joyful, was throwing open his jacket alternately to left and right: the fountain pen clipped into the left pocket of his white waistcoat had sprinkled the whiteness with ink, while on the right was the pen that never ran. Luzhin took a great fancy to the bifacial man and even thought of buying him. 'Listen, Luzhin,' said his wife when he had had his fill of the window. 'I've wanted to ask you for a long time – haven't some things remained after your father's death? Where are they all?' Luzhin shrugged his shoulders. 'There was a man called Khrushchenko,' he muttered after a while. 'I don't unders and,' said his wife questioningly. 'He wrote to me in Paris,' explained Luzhin reluctantly, 'about the death and funeral and all that, and that he preserved the things left after the late father.' 'Oh, Luzhin,' she sighed, 'what you do to the language.' She reflected a moment and added: 'It doesn't matter to me, but I just thought it might be pleasant for you to have those things – as having belonged to your father.' Luzhin remained silent. She imagined those unwanted things – perhaps the pen that old man Luzhin wrote his books with, some documents or other, photographs – and she grew sad and mentally reproached her husband for hardheartedness. 'But one thing has to be done without fail,' she said decisively. 'We must go to the cemetery to see his grave, to see that it's not neglected.' 'Cold and far,' said Luzhin. 'We'll do it in a day or two,' she decided. 'The weather is bound to change. Careful, please – there's a car coming.'

The weather got worse and Luzhin, remembering that depressing waste patch and the cemetery wind, begged for their trip to be postponed to the following week. The frost, incidentally, was extraordinary. They closed the ice-rink, which was always unlucky: last winter it had been thaw after thaw and a pool in place of ice, and now such a cold spell that not even schoolboys were up to skating. In the parks little, high-breasted birds lay on the snow with feet in the air. The helpless mercury under the influence of its surroundings, fell ever lower and lower. And even the polar bears in the zoo found that the management had overdone it.

The Luzhin apartment turned out to be one of those fortunate flats with heroic central heating, where one did not have to sit around in fur coats and blankets. His wife's parents, driven insane by the cold, were remarkably willing guests of the central heating, Luzhin, wearing the old jacket that had been saved from destruction, sat at his desk, assiduously drawing a white cube standing before him. His father-in-law walked about the study telling long, perfectly proper anecdotes or else sat on the sofa with a newspaper, from time to time breathing deep and then clearing his throat. His mother-in-law and wife stayed by the tea table and from the study, across the dark drawing room, one could see the bright yellow lampshade in the dining room, his wife's illuminated profile on the brown background of the sideboard and her bare arms, which, with her elbows a long way in front of her on the table, she bent back to one shoulder, her fingers interlaced, or suddenly she would smoothly stretch an arm out and touch some gleaming object on the tablecloth. Luzhin put the cube aside, took a clean sheet of paper, prepared a tin box with buttons of watercolor in it and hastened to draw this vista, but while he was painstakingly tracing out the lines of perspective with the aid of a ruler, something changed at the far end, his wife disappeared from the vivid rectangle of the dining room and the light went out and came on again closer, in the drawing room, and no perspective existed any longer. In general he rarely got to the colors, and, indeed, preferred pencil. The dampness of watercolors made the paper buckle unpleasantly and the wet colors would run together; on occasion it would be impossible to get rid of some extraordinarily tenacious Prussian blue – no sooner would you get a small bit of it on the very tip of your brush than it would already be running all over the enamel inside of the box, devouring the shade you had prepared and turning the water in the glass a poisonous blue. There were thick tubes with India ink and ceruse, but the caps invariably got lost, the necks would dry up, and when he pressed too hard the tube would burst at the bottom and thence would come crawling and writhing a fat worm of goo. His daubings were fruitless and even the simplest things – a vase with flowers or a sunset copied from a travel folder of the Riviera – came out spotty, sickly, horrible. But drawing was nice. He drew his mother-in-law, and she was offended; he drew his wife in

162

profile, and she said that if she looked like that there was no reason to marry her; on the other hand his father-in-law's high, starched collar came out very well. Luzhin took great pleasure in sharpening pencils and in measuring things before him, screwing up one eye and raising his pencil with his thumb pressed against it, and he would move his eraser over the paper with care, pressing with his palm on the sheet, for he knew from experience that otherwise there would come a loud crack and the sheet would crease. And he would blow off the particles of rubber very delicately, fearing to smudge the drawing by touching it with his hand. Most of all he liked what his wife had advised him to begin with and what he constantly returned to – white cubes, pyramids, cylinders, and a fragment of plaster ornament that reminded him of drawing lessons at school – the sole, acceptable subject. He was soothed by the thin lines that he drew and redrew a hundred times, achieving a maximum of sharpness, accuracy and purity. And it was remarkably nice to shade, tenderly and evenly, not pressing too hard, in regularly applied strokes.

'Finished,' he said, holding the paper away from him and looking at the completed cube through his eyelashes. His father-in-law put on his pince-nez and looked at it for a long time, nodding his head. His mother-in-law and wife came from the drawing room and also looked. 'It even casts a tiny shadow,' said his wife. 'A very, very handsome cube.' 'Well done, you're a real cubist,' said his mother-in-law. Luzhin, smiling on one side of his mouth, took the drawing and looked round the walls of his study. By the door one of his productions was already hanging: a train on a bridge spanning an abyss. There was also something in the drawing room: a skull on a telephone directory. In the dining room there were some extremely round oranges which everyone for some reason took for tomatoes. And the bedroom was adorned by a bas-relief done in charcoal and a confidential conversation between a cone and a pyramid. He went out of the study, his eyes roving over the walls, and his wife said with a sigh: 'I wonder where dear Luzhin will hang this one.'

'You haven't yet deigned to inform me,' began her mother, pointing with her chin to a heap of gaudy travel folders lying on the desk. 'But I don't know myself,' said Mrs. Luzhin. 'It's very difficult to decide, everywhere's beautiful. I think we'll go to Nice first.' 'I would advise the Italian lakes,' said her father, and, folding up the newspaper and removing his pince-nez, he began to relate how beautiful the lakes were. 'I'm afraid he has grown rather tired of the talk about our journey,' said Mrs. Luzhin. 'One fine day we'll simply get in the train and go.' 'Not before April,' said her mother imploringly. 'You promised me, you know. . . .'

Luzhin returned to the study. 'I had a box of thumb-tacks somewhere,' he said, looking at the desk and slapping his pockets (whereupon he again, for the third or fourth time, had a feeling there was something in his left pocket – but not the box – and there was not time to investigate). The tacks were found on the desk. Luzhin took them and hastily went out.

'Oh, I quite forgot to tell you. Just imagine, yesterday morning . . .' and she began to tell her daughter that she had been called by a woman who had unexpectedly arrived from Russia. This woman had often visited them as a young girl in St. Petersburg. It turned out that several years ago she had married a Soviet businessman or official – it had been impossible to understand exactly – and on her way to a spa, where her husband was going to gather new strength, she had stopped off for a week or two in Berlin. 'I feel a bit awkward, you know, about a Soviet citizen coming to our place, but she's so persistent. I'm amazed she's not afraid to telephone. Why, if they learn in Sovietia that she rang me up . . .' 'Oh, Mamma, she's probably a very unhappy woman – she's broken out temporarily to freedom and she feels like seeing somebody.' 'Well then, I'll pass her on to you,' said her mother with relief, 'especially as it's warmer at your place.'

And several days afterward, at midday, the lady appeared. Luzhin was still slumbering, since he had slept badly the night before. Twice he woke up with choking cries, suffocated by a nightmare, and now Mrs. Luzhin somehow did not feel up to guests. The visitor turned out to be a slim, animated, nicely made-up, nicely bobbed lady who was dressed, like Mrs. Luzhin, with expensive simplicity. Loudly, interrupting one another, and assuring one another that neither had changed a bit, except perhaps to grow prettier, they went through to the study, which was cozier than the drawing room. The newcomer remarked to herself that Mrs. Luzhin ten to twelve years ago had been a rather graceful, lively little girl and now had grown plumper, paler and quieter, while Mrs Luzhin found that the modest, silent young lady who used to visit them and was in love with a student, later shot by the Reds, had turned into a very interesting, confident lady. 'So this is your Berlin ... thank you kindly. I almost died with cold. At home in Leningrad it's warmer, really warmer.' 'How is it, St. Petersburg? It must have changed a lot?' asked Mrs. Luzhin. 'Oh of course it's changed,' replied the newcomer jauntily. 'And a terribly difficult life,' said Mrs. Luzhin, nodding thoughtfully. 'Oh, what nonsense! Nothing of the sort. They're working at home, building. Even my boy – what, you didn't know I had a little boy? – well, I have, I have, a cute little squirt – well, even he says that at home in Leningrad "they wuk, while in Bellin the boulzois don't do anything." And in general he finds Berlin far worse than home and doesn't even want to look at anything. He's so observant, you know, and sensitive. . . . No, speaking seriously, the child's right. I myself feel how we've outstripped Europe. Take our theater. Why, you in Europe don't have a theater, it just doesn't exist. I'm not in the least, you understand, not in the least praising the communists. But you have to admit one thing: they look ahead, they build. Intensive construction.' 'I don't understand politics,' said Mrs. Luzhin slowly and plaintively. 'But it just seems to me ...' 'I'm only saying that one has to be broad-minded,' continued the visitor hastily. 'Take this, for instance. As soon as I arived I bought an émigré paper. Of course my husband said, joking, you know – "Why do you waste money, my girl, on such filth?" He expressed himself worse than that, but let's call it that for the sake of decency – but me: "No,"

I said, "you have to look at everything, find out everything absolutely impartially." And imagine – I opened the paper and began to read, and there was such slander printed there, such lies, and everything so crude.' 'I rarely see the Russian newspapers,' said Mrs. Luzhin. 'Mamma, for instance, gets a Russian newspaper from Serbia, I believe—' 'It is a conspiracy,' continued the lady. 'Nothing but abuse, and nobody dares to utter a peep in our favor.' 'Really, let's talk about something else,' said Mrs. Luzhin distractedly. 'I can't express it, I'm very poor at speaking about these matters, but I feel you're mistaken. Now if you want to talk about it with my parents some day . . .' (And saying this, Mrs. Luzhin imagined to herself, not without a certain pleasure, her mother's bulging eyes and strident cries.) 'Well, you're still little.' The lady indulgently smiled. 'Tell me what you are doing, what does your husband do, what is he?' 'He used to play chess,' replied Mrs. Luzhin. 'He was a remarkable player. But then he overstrained himself and now he is resting; and please, you mustn't talk to him about chess.' 'Yes, yes, I know he's a chess player,' said the newcomer. 'But what is he? A reactionary? A White Guardist?' 'Really I don't know,' laughed Mrs. Luzhin. 'I've heard a thing or two about him,' continued the newcomer. 'When your *maman* told me you had married a Luzhin I thought immediately that it was he. I had a good acquaintance in Leningrad and she told me – with such naïve pride, you know – how she had taught her little nephew to play chess and how he later became a remarkable . . .'

At this point in the conversation a strange noise occurred in the next room, as if someone had knocked against something there and let out a cry. 'One moment,' said Mrs. Luzhin, jumping up from the sofa, and was about to slide open the door to the drawing room, but changing her mind she went via the hall. In the drawing room she saw a completely unexpected Luzhin. He was in his dressing gown and bedroom slippers and holding a piece of white bread in one hand – but it was not this of course, that was surprising – the surprising thing was the trembling excitement distorting his face, the wide-open, gleaming eyes, and the forehead looking as if it had grown lumpier, the vein as if it had swollen, and catching sight of his wife he appeared to pay no attention to her at first, but continued to stand looking with open mouth in the direction of the study. An instant later it turned out his excitement was joyful. He clicked his teeth joyfully at his wife, then turned heavily in a circle, almost knocking the palm over, lost a slipper which slithered, like a live thing, into the dining room, where some cocoa was steaming, and speedily went after it.

'Nothing, nothing,' said Luzhin slyly, and like a man reveling in a secret find he slapped himself on the knees, and closing his eyes began to shake his head. 'That lady is from Russia,' said his wife probingly. 'She knows your aunt who – well, just an aunt of yours.' 'Excellent, excellent,' said Luzhin and suddenly choked with laughter. What am I frightened of? she thought. He's simply feeling jolly, he woke up in a good mood and wanted, perhaps . . . 'Is it some private joke, Luzhin?' 'Yes, yes,' said Luzhin and added, finding a way out: 'I wanted to introduce myself in my dressing gown.' 'So then we're feeling jolly, that's good,' she said with a smile. 'Have something to eat and then get dressed. It seems to be a little warmer this morning.' And leaving her husband in the dining room, Mrs. Luzhin quickly returned to the study. Her visitor was sitting on the couch and looking at some views of Switzerland on the pages of a travel leaflet. 'Listen,' she said, catching sight of Mrs. Luzhin, 'I'm going to take advantage of you. I need to buy a few things and I have absolutely no idea where the best stores are here. Yesterday I stood a solid hour in front of a store window, standing and thinking that perhaps there are stores that are even better. And then my German isn't up to much. . . .'

Luzhin remained sitting in the dining room and continued from time to time to slap himself on the knees. And there was really something to celebrate. The combination he had been struggling to discern since the ball, had suddenly revealed itself to him, thanks to a chance phrase that had come flying out of the next room. During these first minutes he had still only had time to feel the keen delight of

being a chess player, and pride, and relief, and that physio-
logical sensation of harmony which is so well known to
artists. He still made many more small motions before he
realized the true nature of his unusual discovery – finished
his cocoa, shaved, transferred his studs to a clean shirt. And
suddenly the delight vanished and he was overcome by
other sensations. Just as some combination, known from
chess problems, can be indistinctly repeated on the board in
actual play – so now the consecutive repetition of a familiar
pattern was becoming noticeable in his present life. And as
soon as his initial delight in having established the actual
fact of the repetition had passed, as soon as he began to go
carefully over his discovery, Luzhin shuddered. With
vague admiration and vague horror he observed how awe-
somely, how elegantly and how flexibly, move by move,
the images of his childhood had been repeated (country
house . . . town . . . school . . . aunt), but he still did not quite
understand why this combinational repetition inspired his
soul with such dread. He felt one thing keenly, a certain
vexation that he had gone so long without noticing the
cunning sequence of moves; and now, recalling some trifle
– and there had been so many of them, and at times so skillfully presented, that the repetition was almost concealed –
Luzhin was indignant with himself for not having reflected,
for not taking the initiative, but with trustful blindness
letting the combination unfold. But now he resolved to be
more circumspect, to keep an eye on the further development of these moves, if there was to be one – and of course,
to maintain his discovery in impenetrable secret, to be
merry, extraordinarily merry. But from that day on there
was no rest for him – he had, if possible, to contrive a defense against this perfidious combination, to free himself of
it, and for this he had to foresee its ultimate aim, its dire
direction, but this did not yet appear feasible. And the
thought that the repetition would probably continue was
so frightening that he was tempted to stop the clock of life,
to suspend the game for good, to freeze, and at the same
time he noticed that he continued to exist, that some kind of
preparation was going on, a creeping development, and that

168

he had no power to halt this movement.

Perhaps his wife would have noticed the change in Luzhin sooner, his wooden jollity between intervals of sullenness, had she been with him more these days. But it so happened that it was precisely during these days that she was taken advantage of, as had been promised, by the importunate lady from Russia – who forced her to spend hours taking her from store to store, and unhurriedly tried on hats, dresses and shoes, and then paid the Luzhin's prolonged visits. She continued to maintain as before that there was no theater in Europe and to pronounce 'Leningrad' (instead of 'Petersburg') with cold glibness, and for some reason Mrs. Luzhin took pity on her, accompanied her to cafés and bought her son, a fat, gloomy little boy deprived of the gift of speech in the presence of strangers, toys which he accepted fearfully and unwillingly, whereupon his mother affirmed that there was nothing here that he liked and that he yearned to return to his little co-Pioneers. She also met Mrs. Kuzhin's parents, but unfortunately the conversation about politics did not take place; they reminisced about former acquaintances, while Luzhin silently and concentratedly fed chocolates to little Ivan, and Ivan silently and concentratedly ate them, and then turned deep red and was hastily led out of the room. Meanwhile the weather got warmer, and once or twice Mrs. Luzhin said to her husband that once this unfortunate woman with her unfortunate child and unpresentable husband had finally left, they should go the very first day, without putting it off, and visit the cemetery, and Luzhin nodded with an assiduous smile. The typewriter, geography and drawing were abandoned, for he knew now that all this was part of the combination, was an intricate repetition of all the moves that had been taken down in his childhood. Ridiculous days: Mrs. Luzhin felt she was not paying enough attention to her husband's moods, something was slipping out of control, and yet she continued to listen politely to the newcomer's chatter and to translate her demands to shop assistants, and it was particularly unpleasant when a pair of shoes that had already been worn once turned out to be unsuitable, and she had to accompany her to the store while the purple-faced lady bawled out the firm in Russian and demanded the shoes be changed, and then she had to be soothed and her caustic expressions considerably toned down in the German version. On the evening before her departure she came, together with little Ivan, to say good-bye. She left Ivan in the study while she went to the bed-room with Mrs. Luzhin who for the hundredth time showed her wardrobe. Ivan sat on the couch and scratched his knee, trying not to look at Luzhin, who also did not know where to look and was thinking how to occupy the flabby child. 'Telephone!' exclaimed Luzhin finally in a high voice, and pointing to it with his finger he began to laugh with delib-erate astonishment. But Ivan, after looking sullenly in the direction of Luzhin's finger, averted his eyes, his lower lip hanging. 'Train and precipice!' tried Luzhin again and stretched out his other hand, pointing to his own picture on the wall. Ivan's left nostril filled with a glistening droplet and he sniffed, looking apathetically before him. 'The author of a certain divine comedy!' bellowed Luzhin, raising a hand to the bust of Dante. Silence, a slight sniffing. Luzhin was tired by his gymnastic movements and also grew still. He began to wonder whether there was any candy in the dining room or whether to play the phonograph in the drawing room, but the little boy on the couch hypno-tized him with his mere presence and it was impossible to leave the room. 'A toy would do it,' he said to himself, then looked at his desk ,measured the paper knife against the little boy's curiosity, found that his curiosity would not be roused by it, and began in despair to burrow in his pockets. And here again, as many times before, he felt that his left pocket, although empty, mysteriously retained some intan-gible contents. Luzhin thought that such a phenomenon was capable of interesting little Ivan. He sat down on the edge of the couch beside him and winked slyly. 'Conjuring trick,' he said and started by showing that the pocket was empty. 'This hole has no connection with the trick,' he ex-plained. Listlessly and malevolently Ivan watched his move-ments. 'But nevertheless there *is* something here,' said

170

Luzhin rapturously and winked. 'In the lining,' snorted Ivan, and with a shrug of his shoulders turned away. 'Right!' cried Luzhin, miming delight, and thrust one hand through the hole, holding on to the bottom of the jacket with his other one. At first some kind of a red corner came into view, and then the whole object – something in the shape of a flat leather notebook. Luzhin looked at it with raised brows, turned it around in his hands, pulled a little flap out of its slit and cautiously opened the thing. It was not a notebook, but a small, folding chessboard of morrocco leather. Luzhin immediately recalled that it had been given to him at a club in Paris – all the participants in that tournament were given this knickknack – some firm's advertisement, not simply a souvenir from the club. Lateral compartments on both leaves of this pocket board contained little celluloid pieces resembling fingernails and each one bore the picture of a chess figure. These were placed in position on the board by inserting the pointed end into a tiny crack at the lower edge of each square so that the rounded top of the piece with the drawn figure on it lay flat on the square. The effect was very elegant and neat – one could not help admiring the little red and white board, the smooth celluloid fingernails, and also the stamped gold letters along the horizontal edge of the board and the golden numbers along the vertical one. Opening his mouth wide with pleasure, Luzhin began to slip in the pieces – at first just a row of Pawns along the second rank – but then he changed his mind, and with the tips of his fingers taking the tiny, insertable figures out of their compartments, he set out the position of his game with Turati at the point where it had been interrupted. This setting out was accomplished almost instantaneously and immediately the whole material side of the matter dropped away: the tiny board lying open in the palm of his hand became intangible and weightless, the morocco dissolved in a pink and cream haze and everything disappeared save the chess position itself, complex, pungent, charged with extraordinary possibilities. Luzhin, one finger pressed to his temple, was so immersed in thought that he did not notice that Ivan, for lack of something to do, had clambered down from the couch and had started to rock the black upright of the standard lamp. It heeled over and the light went out. Luzhin came to his senses in complete darkness and for the first moment did not realize where he was or what was going on around him. An invisible creature was fidgeting and grunting close by, and suddenly the orange shade lit up again with transparent light, and a pale little boy with a shaven head was kneeling and straightening out the cord. Luzhin started and banged the board shut. His terrible little double, little Luzhin, for whom the chess pieces had been set out, crawled over the carpet on his knees. . . . All this had happened once before. . . . And again he had been caught, had not understood how exactly the repetition of a familiar theme would come out in practice. The following instant everything regained its balance: Ivan, snuffling, clambered back onto the couch; in the slight gloom beyond the orange light floated Luzhin's study, swaying gently; the red morocco notebook lay innocently on the carpet – but Luzhin knew that this was all a trick, the combination had still not completely developed, and soon a new, dire repetition would manifest itself. Bending down quickly he picked up and thrust into his pocket the material symbol of what had so voluptuously and so horribly possessed his imagination again, and he wondered where would be a surer place to hide it; but just then voices were heard, his wife came in with their visitor and both swam toward him as if through cigarette smoke. 'Ivan, get up, it's time to go. Yes, yes, my dear, I still have so much to pack,' said the lady and then came up to Luzhin and began to take leave of him.'Very pleased to have made your acquaintance,' she said, and between the words managed to think what she had more than once thought before: What a dunderhead, what a queer fish! 'Very pleased. Now I can tell your aunt I've seen her little chess player, big now, and famous –' 'You must not fail to come and see us on your way back,' interruped Mrs. Luzhin hastily and loudly, for the first time looking with hatred at the woman's smiling, wax-red lips and mercilessly stupid eyes. 'But of course, it goes without saying. Ivan, get up and

172

say goodbye!' Ivan carried this out with some reluctance and they all went into the entrance hall. 'There's always a lot of fuss with letting people out here in Berlin,' she said ironically, watching Mrs. Luzhin take the keys from the pier table. 'No, we have an elevator,' replied Mrs. Luzhin irrelevantly, yearning with fierce impatience for the lady's departure, and she signed to Luzhin with her eyebrow to offer the sealskin coat. Luzhin instead took down the child's overcoat from the hallstand ... but fortunately the maid turned up at this moment. 'Good-bye, good-bye,' said Mrs. Luzhin, standing in the doorway while the departing visitors, accompanied by the maid, arranged themselves in the elevator. From behind his wife's shoulder Luzhin saw Ivan clamber onto the little bench but then the doors closed and the elevator sank down in its iron cage Mrs. Luzhin ran into the study and fell face down on the couch. He sat beside her and began deep down inside him, with difficulty, to produce, glue together and sew up a smile, preparing it for the moment when his wife turned to him His wife turned. The smile came out completely successfully. 'Ouf,' sighed Mrs. Luzhin, 'we're finally rid of them,' and quickly embracing her husband, she began to kiss him – on the right eye, then the chin, then the left ear – observing a strict sequence that had once been approved by him. 'Well, cheer up, cheer up,' she repeated. 'That madam's gone away now, disappeared.' 'Disappeared,' said Luzhin obediently and with a sigh kissed the hand that was patting his neck. 'What tenderness,' whispered his wife, 'ah, what sweet tenderness . . .'

It was time to go to bed, she went to undress, and Luzhin walked through all three rooms, looking for a place to hide the pocket chess set. Everywhere was insecure. The most unexpected places were invaded in the mornings by the snout of that rapacious vacuum cleaner. It is difficult, difficult to hide a thing the other things are jealous and inhospitable, holding on firmly to their places and not allowing a homeless object, escaping pursuit, into a single cranny. Thus he did not manage to hid the morocco notebook that night, and subsequently he decided not to hide it at all but simply to get rid of it, but this also proved to be far from

173

easy; so it remained in his lining, and only after several months, when all danger was long, long past, only then was the pocket chess set found again, and by then its origin was obscure.

CHAPTER FOURTEEN

To herself Mrs. Luzhin admitted that the three-week visit of the lady from Russia had not passed without leaving a trace. The visitor's opinions were false and stupid – but how prove it ? She was horrified that in recent years she had taken so little interest in the science of exile, passively accepting the glossy, varnished and gold-lettered views of her parents and paying no attention to the speeches she heard at émigré political meetings, which it had once been the thing to attend. It occurred to her that Luzhin too, perhaps, would have a taste for political matters – would perhaps revel in them, the way millions of other intelligent people do. And a new occupation for Luzhin was essential. He had become strange, the familiar sullenness had re-appeared, and there often was in his eyes a kind of slippery expression, as if he were hiding something from her. She was worried that he had still not found a completely engrossing hobby and she reproached herself for the narrowness of her mental vision and her inability to find the sphere, the idea, the object which would provide work and food for Luzhin's inactive talents. She knew she had to hurry, and that every unoccupied minute in Luzhin's life was a loophole for phantoms. Before departing for picturesque lands it was necessary to find Luzhin an interesting game, and only afterwards to resort to the balsam of travel, that decisive factor used by romantic millionaires to cure their spleen.

She began with newspapers. She took out subscriptions to *Znamya* (*The Banner*), *Rossianin* (*The Russian*), *Zarubezhny Golos* (*The Voice of Exile*), *Ob'yedinyenie* (*Union*) and *Klich* (*The Clarion*), bought the latest numbers of émigré magazines and – for comparison – several Soviet magazines and newspapers. It was decided that every day after dinner they would read to one another aloud. Noticing that some newspapers printed a chess section, she wondered at first whether to cut out and destroy these bits, but she feared by this to insult Luzhin. Once or twice, as examples of interesting play, old games of Luzhin's would turn up. This was disagreeable and dangerous. She was unable to hide the issues with chess sections in them because Luzhin collected the newspapers with the aim of later binding them in the form of large books. Whenever he opened a newspaper which proved to contain a smudgy chess diagram she watched the expression on his face, but he felt her glance and merely skipped over it. And she did not know with what sinful impatience he awaited those Thursdays or Mondays when the chess section appeared, and did not know with what curiosity he looked through the printed games in her absence. In the case of chess problems he would glance sideways at the diagram and, with this glance grasping the disposition of the pieces, would memorize the problem instantly and then solve it it in his mind while his wife read the editorial aloud to him. '. . . The whole activity comes down to a fundamental transformation and augmentation, which are designed to insure . . .' read his wife in an even voice. (An interesting construction, thought Luzhin. Black's Queen is completely free.) '. . . draws a clear distinction between their vital interests, moreover it would not be superfluous to note that the Achilles heel of this punitive hand . . .' (Black has an obvious defense against the threat on h7, thought Luzhin, and smiled mechanically when his wife, interrupting her reading for a moment, said suddenly in a low voice: 'I don't understand what he means.') 'If in this respect,' she continued, 'nothing is respected . . .' (Oh, splendid! exclaimed Luzhin mentally, finding the key to the problem – a bewitchingly elegant sacrifice. '. . . and disaster is not far away,' his wife concluded the article, and finished, sighed. The thing was that the more closely she read the newspapers the more bored she grew, and a fog of words and metaphors, suppositions and arguments was used to obscure the clear truth, which she always felt but was never able to express. But when she turned to the newspapers of the other world, Soviet newspapers, her boredom then knew no bounds. From them came the chill of a sepul-

176

chral countinghouse, the boredom of flyblown offices, and they reminded her somehow of the lifeless features of a certain little official in one of the establishments she had had to visit in the days when she and Luzhin were being sent from department to department for the sake of some paltry document. The little official was seedy and touchy, and was eating a diabetic roll. He probably received a miserable salary, was married and had a child whose whole body was covered with a rash. The document they did not have and had to get he endowed with cosmic significance, the whole world hung on that piece of paper and would crumble hopelessly to dust if a person were deprived of it. And that was not all: it turned out the Luzhins could not obtain it until monstrous time spans, millennia of despair and emptiness, had elapsed, and the only means allowed one of easing this Weltschmerz was the writing of petitions. The official snapped at poor Luzhin for smoking in his office and Luzhin started and stuffed the butt into his pocket. Through the window could be seen a house under construction, all in scaffolding, and a slanting rain; in the corner of the room hung a black little jacket which the official changed during working hours for a lustrine one, and his desk gave a general impression of violet ink and that same transcendental hopelessness. They went away with empty hands, and she felt as if she had had to do battle with a gray and blind eternity, which had in fact conquered her, disdainfully brushing aside her timid earthly bribe – three cigars. In another establishment they received the piece of paper instantly. Later Mrs. Luzhin thought with horror that the little official who had sent them away was probably imagining them wandering like inconsolable specters through a vacuum, and perhaps was waiting for their submissive, sobbing return. It was unclear to her why precisely this image floated before her as soon as she picked up a Moscow newspaper. The same sense of boredom and pity, perhaps, but this was not enough for her, her mind was not satisfied – and suddenly she realized that she was also looking for a formula, the official embodiment of feeling, and this was not the point at all. Her mind was unable to grasp the complicated struggle among the hazy opinions expressed by various émigré news-papers; this diversity of opinion particularly stunned her, used as she was to suppose apathetically that everyone who did not think like her parents thought like that amusing lame fellow who had spoken of sociology to a crowd of giggly girls. There turned out to be the most subtle shades of opinion and the most viperous hostility – and if all this was too complex for the mind, then the heart began to grasp one thing quite distinctly: both here and in Russia people tortured, or desired to torture, other people, but there the torture and desire to torture were a hundred times greater than here and therefore here was better.

When Luzhin's turn came to read aloud she would choose for him a humorous article, or else a brief, heartfelt story. He read with a funny stammer, pronouncing some of the words oddly and at times going past a period, or else not reaching it, and raising or lowering the tone of his voice for no logical reason. It was not difficult for her to realize that the news-papers did not interest him; whenever she engaged him in a conversation concerning an article they had just read, he hastily agreed with all her conclusions, and when, in order to check on him, she said deliberately that all the émigré papers were lying, he also agreed.

Newspapers were one thing, people another; it would be nice to listen to these people. She imagined how people of various tendencies – 'a bunch of intellectuals' as her mother put it – would gather in their apartment, and how Luzhin, listening to these live disputes and conversations on new themes, would if not blossom out then at least find a tem-porary diversion. Of all her mother's acquaintances the most enlightened and even 'Leftist,' as her mother affirmed with a certain coquetry, was considered to be Oleg Ser-geyevich Smirnovski – but when Mrs. Luzhin asked him to bring to her place some interesting, freethinking people, who read not only *Znamya* but also *Ob'yedinyenie* and *Zarubezhny Golos*, Smirnovski replied that he, she should understand, did not revolve in such circles and then began to censure such revolving and quickly explained that he revolved in other circles in which revolving was essential, and Mrs. Luzhin's head began to spin as it used to in the amusement park on the revolving disk. After this failure she began to extract from various tiny chambers of her memory people whom she had chanced to meet and who might be of aid to her now. She recalled a Russian girl who used to sit next to her at the Berlin school of applied arts, the daughter of a political worker of the democratic group; she recalled Alferov who had been everywhere and liked to relate how an old poet had once died in his arms; she recalled an unappreciated relative working in the office of a liberal Russian newspaper, the name of which was gutturally rouladed every evening by the fat paperwoman on the corner. She chose one or two other people. It also occurred to her that many intellectuals probably remembered Luzhin the writer or knew of Luzhin the chess player and would visit her home with pleasure.

And what did Luzhin care about all this? The only thing that really interested him was the complex, cunning game in which he somehow had become enmeshed. Helplessly and sullenly he sought for signs of the chess repetition, still wondering toward what it was tending. But to be always on his guard, to strain his attention constantly, was also impossible: something would temporarily weaken inside him, he would take carefree pleasure in a game printed in the newspaper – and presently would note with despair that he had been unwary again and that a delicate move had just been made in his life, mercilessly continuing the fatal combination. Then he would decide to redouble his watchfulness and keep track of every second of his life, for traps could be everywhere. And he was oppressed most of all by the impossibility of inventing a rational defense, for his opponent's aim was still hidden.

Too stout and flabby for his years, he walked this way and that among people thought up by his wife, tried to find a quiet spot and the whole time looked and listened for a hint as to the next move, for a continuation of the game that had not been started by him but was being directed with awful force against him. It happened that such a hint would occur, something would move forward, but it did not make the general meaning of the combination any clearer. And a quiet spot was difficult to find – people addressed questions to him that he had to repeat several times to himself before understanding their simple meaning and finding a simple answer. In all three untelescoped rooms it was very bright – not one was spared by the lamps – and people were sitting in the dining room, and on uncomfortable chairs in the drawing room, and on the divan in the study, and one man wearing pale flannel pants strove repeatedly to settle himself on the desk, moving aside in the interests of comfort the box of paints and a pile of unsealed newspapers. An elderly actor with a face manipulated by many roles, a mellow, mellow-voiced person (who surely gave his best performances in carpet slippers, in parts demanding grunts, groans, grimaceful hangovers and quirky, fruity expressions), was sitting on the divan next to the corpulent, black-eyed wife of the journalist Bars, an ex-actress, and reminiscing with her about the time they had once played together in a Volga town in the melodrama *A Dream of Love*. 'Do you remember that mix-up with the top hat and the neat way I got out of it ?' said the actor mellowly. 'Endless ovations,' said the black-eyed lady, 'they gave me such ovations as I shall never forget. . . .' In this way they interrupted one another, each with his or her own recollections, and the man in the pale pants for the third time asked a musing Luzhin for 'one small cigarette.' He was a beginning poet and read his poems with fervor, with a singsong lilt, slightly jerking his head and looking into space. Normally he held his head high, as a result of which his large, mobile Adam's apple was very noticeable. He never got that cigarette, since Luzhin moved absentmindedly into the drawing room, and the poet, looking with reverence at his fat nape, thought what a wonderful chess player he was and looked forward to the time when he would be able to talk with a rested, recovered Luzhin about chess, of which he was a great enthusiast, and then, catching sight of Luzhin's wife through the gap of the door, he debated with himself for a while whether it was worth while trying to dangle after her. Mrs. Luzhin was listening smilingly to what was being said

180

by the tall, pockmarked journalist Bars, and thinking how difficult it would be to seat these guests around one tea table and would it not be better in future simply to serve them wherever they sat? Bars spoke very fast and always as if he were obliged to express a tortuous idea with all its riders and slippery appendages in the shortest possible period of time, to prop up and readjust all this, and if his listener happened to be attentive, then little by little he began to realize that this maze of rapid words was gradually revealing an astonishing harmony, and that the speech itself with its occasional incorrect stresses and journalese was suddenly transformed, as if acquiring its grace and nobility from the idea expressed. Mrs. Luzhin, catching sight of her husband, thrust a plate into his hand with a beautifully peeled orange on it and went past him into the study. 'And note,' said a plain-looking man who had listened to the whole of the journalist's idea and appreciated it, 'note that Tyutchev's night is cool and the stars in it are round and moist and glossy, and not simply bright dots.' He did not say any more, since in general he spoke little, not so much out of modesty, it seemed, as out of a fear of spilling something precious that was not his but had been entrusted to him. Mrs. Luzhin, incidentally, liked him very much, and precisely because of his plainness, the neutrality of his features, as if he were himself only the outside of a vessel filled with something so sacred and rare that it would be a sacrilege to paint the clay. His name was Petrov, not a single thing about him was remarkable, he had written nothing, and he lived like a beggar, but never talked about it to anyone. His sole function in life was to carry, reverently and with concentration, that which had been entrusted to him, something which it was necessary at all costs to preserve in all its detail and in all its purity, and for that reason he even walked with small careful steps trying not to bump into anyone, and only very seldom, only when he discerned a kindred solicitude in the person he was talking to did he reveal for a moment – from the whole of that enormous something that he carried mysteriously within him – some tender, priceless little trifle, a line from Pushkin or the pea-

181

sant name of a wild flower. 'I remember our host's father,' said the journalist when Luzhin's back retreated into the dining room. 'He doesn't look like him but there's something analogous in the set of the shoulders. He was a good soul, a nice fellow, but as a writer . . . What ? Do you really find that those oleographic tales for youngsters . . .' 'Please, please, to the dining room,' said Mrs. Luzhin, returning from the study with three guests she had found there. 'Tea is served. Come, I beg you.' Those already at table were sitting at one end, while at the other a solitary Luzhin, his head bent gloomily, sat chewing a segment of orange and stirring the tea in his glass. Alferov was there with his wife, then there was a swarthy, brightly made-up girl who drew marvelous firebirds, and a bald young man who jokingly called himself a worker for the press but secretly yearned to be a political ringleader, and two women, the wives of lawyers. And also sitting at table was delightful Vasiliy Vasilievich, shy, stately, pure-hearted, with a fair beard and wearing an old-man's prunella shoes. Under the Tsar he had been exiled to Siberia and then abroad, whence he had returned in 1917 and succeeded in catching a brief glimpse of the revolution before being exiled again, this time by the Bolshevists. He talked earnestly about his work in the underground, about Kautsky and Geneva, and was unable to look at Mrs. Luzhin without emotion, for in her he found a resemblance to the clear-eyed, ideal maidens who had worked with him for the good of the people.

As usually happened, at these gatherings, when all the guests had been rounded up and placed at table together silence ensued. The silence was such that the maid's breathing was clearly audible as she served the tea. Mrs. Luzhin several times caught herself with the impossible thought that it would be a good idea to ask the maid why she breathed so loudly, and could she not do it more quietly. She was not very efficient in general, this pudgy wench – telephone calls were particularly disastrous. As she listened to the breathing, Mrs. Luzhin recalled briefly how the maid had laughingly informed her a few days beforehand: 'A Mr. Fa . . . Felt . . . Felty. Here, I wrote down the number.'

Mrs Luzhin called the number, but a sharp voice replied that this was a movie company's office and that no Mr. Felty was there. Some kind of hopeless muddle. She was about to start criticizing German maids in order to break her neighbor's silence when she noticed that a conversation had already flared up, that they were talking about a new novel. Bars was asserting that it was elaborately and subtly written and that every word betrayed a sleepless night; a woman's voice said, 'Oh no, it reads so easily'; Petrov leaned over to Mrs. Luzhin and whispered a quotation from Zhukovsky: 'That which took pains to write is read with ease'; and the poet, interrupting someone in mid-word and rolling his "r"s vehemently, shouted that Zhukovsky was a brainless parrot; at which Vasiliy Vasilievich, who had not read the novel, shook his head reproachfully. Only when they were already in the front hall and everyone was taking leave of the others in a kind of dress rehearsal, for they all took leave of one another again in the street, though they all had to go in the same direction – only then did the actor with the well-manipulated face suddenly clap his hand to his forehead: 'I almost forgot, darling,' he said to Mrs. Luzhin, squeezing her hand at each word. 'The other day a man from the movie kingdom asked me for your telephone number—' Whereupon he made a surprised face and released Mrs. Luzhin's hand. 'What, you don't know I'm in the movies now? Oh yes, yes. Big parts with close-ups.' At this point he was shouldered aside by the poet and thus Mrs. Luzhin did not find out what person the actor had meant.

The guests departed. Luzhin was sitting sideways at the table on which, frozen in various poses like the characters in the concluding scene of Gogol's *The Inspector General*, were the remains of the refreshments, empty and unfinished glasses. One of his hands lay spread heavily on the tablecloth. From beneath half-lowered, once more puffy lids he looked at the black match tip, writhing in pain after having just gone out in his fingers. His large face with loose folds around the nose and mouth was slightly shiny, and on his cheeks the constantly shaved, constantly sprouting bristle showed golden in the lamplight. His dark gray suit, shaggy to the touch, enfolded him tighter than before, although it had been planned with plenty of room. Thus Luzhin sat, not stirring, and the glass dishes with bonbons in them gleamed; and a teaspoon lay still on the tablecloth, far from any glass or plate, and for some reason a small cream puff that did not look especially enticing but was really very, very good had remained untouched. What's the matter? thought Mrs. Luzhin, looking at her husband. Goodness, what's the matter? And she had an aching feeling of impotence and hopelessness, as if she had taken on a job that was too difficult for her. Everything was useless – there was no point in trying, in thinking up amusements, in inviting interesting guests. She tried to imagine how she would take this Luzhin, blind and sullen once more, around the Riviera, and all she could imagine was Luzhin sitting in his room and staring at the floor. With a nasty sense of looking through the keyhole of destiny she bent forward to see her future – ten, twenty, thirty years – and it was all the same, with no change, the same, sullen, bowed Luzhin, and silence, and hopelessness. Wicked, unworthy thoughts! Her soul immediately straightened up again and around her were familiar images and cares: it was time to go to bed, better not buy that shortcake next time, how nice Petrov was, tomorrow morning they would have to see about their passports, the trip to the cemetery was being postponed again. Nothing could have been simpler, it seemed, than to take a taxi and drive out into the suburbs to the tiny Russian cemetery in its patch of wasteland. But it always happened that they were unable to go, either Luzhin's teeth ached or there was this passport business, or else something else – petty, imperceptible obstacles. And how many different worries there would be now . . . Luzhin definitely had to be taken to the dentist. 'Is it aching again?' she asked, putting her hand on Luzhin's. 'Yes, yes,' he said, and distorting his face, sucked one cheek in with a popping sound. He had invented the toothache the other day in order to explain his low spirits and silence. 'Tomorrow I'll ring up the dentist,' she said decisively. 'It's not necessary,' muttered Luzhin. 'Please, it's not necessary.' His lips trembled. He felt as if he were about to burst into tears, everything had become so terrifying now. 'What's not necessary?' she asked tenderly, and expressed the question mark with a little 'hm' sound pronounced with closed lips. He shook his head and, just in case, sucked his tooth again. 'Not necessary to go to the dentist? No, Luzhin is certainly going to be taken to the dentist. One should not neglect this.' Luzhin rose from his chair and holding his cheek went into the bedroom. 'I'll give him a pill,' she said, 'that's what I'll do.'

The pill did not work. Luzhin stayed awake for long after his wife fell asleep. To tell the truth, the hours of night, the hours of insomnia in the secure closed bedroom, were the only ones when he could think peacefully without the fear of missing a new move in the monstrous combination. At night, particularly if he lay without moving and with his eyes closed, nothing could happen. Carefully and as coolly as he could, Luzhin would go over all the moves already made against him, but as soon as he began to guess at what forms the coming repetition of the scheme of his past would take, he grew confused and frightened by the inevitable and unthinkable catastrophe bearing down on him with merciless precision. On this night more than ever he felt his helplessness in the face of this slow, elegant attack and he tried not to sleep at all, to prolong as much as possible this night, this quiet darkness, to arrest time at midnight. His wife slept absolutely soundlessly; most likely – she was not there at all. Only the ticking of the little clock on the bedside table proved that time continued to exist. Luzhin listened to these tiny heartbeats and became lost in thought again, and then he started, noticing that the ticking of the clock had stopped. It seemed to him that the night had stopped forever, there was not a single sound now that would indicate its passing, time was dead, everything was all right, a velvet hush. Sleep imperceptibly took advantage of this happiness and relief but now, in sleep, there was no rest at all, for sleep consisted of sixty-four squares, a gigantic board in the middle of which, trembling and stark-

185

naked, Luzhin stood, the size of a pawn, and peered at the dim positions of huge pieces, megacephalous, with crowns or manes.

He woke up when his wife, already dressed, bent over him and kissed him on the glabella. 'Good morning, dear Luzhin,' she said. 'It's ten o'clock already. What shall we do today – the dentist or our visas?' Luzhin looked at her with bright, distracted eyes and immediately closed his lids again. 'And who forgot to wind up the clock for the night?' laughed his wife, fondly worrying the plump white flesh of his neck. 'That way you could sleep your whole life away.' She bent her head to one side, looking at her husband's profile surrounded by the bulges in the pillow, and noting that he had fallen asleep again, she smiled and left the room. In the study she stood before the window and looked at the greenish-blue sky, wintry and cloudless, thinking it would probably be cold today and Luzhin should wear his cardigan. The telephone rang on the desk, that was evidently her mother wanting to know if they would be dining at her place. 'Hello?' said Mrs. Luzhin, perching on the edge of a chair. 'Hello, hello,' shouted an unfamiliar voice into the telephone excitedly and crossly. 'Yes, yes, I'm here,' said Mrs. Luzhin and moved to an armchair. 'Who's there?' asked a displeased voice in German with a Russian accent. 'And who's speaking?' inquired Mrs. Luzhin. 'Is Mr. Luzhin at home?' asked the voice in Russian. '*Kto govorit*, who's speaking?' repeated Mrs. Luzhin with a smile. Silence. The voice seemed to be debating with itself the question of whether to come out into the open or not. 'I want to talk to Mr. Luzhin,' he began again, reverting to German. 'A very urgent and important matter.' 'One moment,' said Mrs. Luzhin and walked up and down the room a time or two. No, it was not worth waking Luzhin. She returned to the telephone. 'He's still sleeping,' she said. 'But if you want to leave a message . . .' 'Oh, this is very annoying,' said the voice, adopting Russian finally. 'This is the second time I've called. I left my telephone number last time. The matter is extremely important to him and permits of no delay.' 'I am his wife,' said Mrs. Luzhin. 'If you need

186

anything . . .' 'Very glad to make you acquaintance,' interrupted the voice briskly. 'My name is Valentinov. Your husband of course has told you about me. So this is what: tell him as soon as he wakes up to get straight into a taxi and come over to me. Kinokonzern "Veritas," Rabenstrasse 82. It's a very urgent matter and very important to him,' continued the voice, switching to German again, either because of the importance of the matter or simply because the German address had drawn him into the corresponding language. Mrs. Luzhin pretended to be writing down the address and then said: 'Perhaps you will still tell me first what the matter is about.' The voice grew unpleasantly agitated: 'I'm an old friend of your husband. Every second is·precious. I'll expect him today at exactly twelve o'clock. Please tell him. Every second . . .' 'All right,' said Mrs. Luzhin. 'I'll tell him, only I don't know – perhaps today will be inconvenient for him.' 'Just whisper in his ear: "Valentinov's expecting you",' said the voice with a laugh, sang out a German 'good-bye' and vanished behind the click of its trapdoor. For several moments Mrs. Luzhin sat there thinking and then called herself a fool. She should have explained first of all that Luzhin no longer played chess. Valentinov . . . Only now did she remember the visiting card she had found in the opera hat. Valentinov, of course, was acquainted with Luzhin through chess. Luzhin had no other acquaintance. He had never mentioned a single old friend. This man's tone was completely impossible. She should have demanded that he explain his business. She was a fool. What should be done now? Ask Luzhin? No. Who was Valentinov? An old friend. Graalski said he had been asked . . . Aha, very simple. She went into the bedroom, assured herself that Luzhin was still sleeping – he usually slept amazingly soundly in the mornings – and went back to the telephone. Luckily the actor turned out to be at home and immediately launched into a long account of all the frivolous and mean actions committed at one time or another by the lady he had been talking to at the party. Mrs. Luzhin heard him out impatiently and then asked who Valentinov was. The actor said 'Oh yes!' and continued: 'You see how forgetful I am, life is impossible without a prompter;' and finally, after giving a detailed account of his relations with Valentinov, he mentioned in passing that, according to him, he, Valentinov, had been Luzhin's chess father, so to speak, and had made a great player out of him. Then the actor returned to the actress of the night before and after mentioning one last meanness of hers began to take voluble leave of Mrs. Luzhin, his last words being: 'I kiss the palm of your little hand.'

'So that's how it it,' said Mrs. Luzhin, hanging up the receiver. 'All right.' At this point she recollected that she had mentioned Valentino's name once or twice in the conversation and that her husband might have chanced to hear it if he had come out of the bedroom into the hall. Her heart missed a beat and she ran to check if he was still sleeping. He had wakened and was smoking in bed. 'We won't go anywhere this morning,' she said. 'Anyway it's too late. And we'll dine at Mamma's. Stay in bed a while longer, it's good for you, you're fat.' Closing the bedroom door firmly and then the door of the study, she hastily looked up the "Veritas" number in the telephone book, listened to see if Luzhin was near and then rang up. It turned out to be not so easy to get hold of Valentinov. Three different people came to the telephone in turn and replied they would get him immediately, and then the operator cut her off and she had to start all over again. At the same time she was trying to speak as low as possible and it was necessary to repeat things, which was very unpleasant. Finally a yellowy, worn little voice informed her dejectedly that Valentinov was not there but would definitely be back by twelve thirty. She asked that he be informed that Luzhin was unable to come since he was ill, would continue to be ill for a long time and begged earnestly not to be bothered any more. Replacing the receiver on its hook she listened again, and hearing only the beating of her own heart she then sighed and said 'ouf!' with boundless relief. Valentinov had been dealt with. Thank goodness she had been alone at the telephone. Now it was over. And soon they would depart. She still had to call her mother and the dentist. But Valentinov had been dealt with. What a cloying name. And for a minute she became thoughtful, accomplishing during that one minute, as sometimes happens, a long leisurely journey: she set off into Luzhin's past, dragging Valentinov with her, visualizing him, from his voice, in horn-rimmed spectacles and long-legged, and as she journeyed through the mist she looked for a spot where she could dump the slippery, repulsively wriggling Valentinov, but she could not find one because she knew almost nothing about Luzhin's youth. Fighting her way still farther back, into the depths, she passed through the semi-spectral spa with its semispectral hotel, where the fourteen-year-old prodigy had lived, and found herself in Luzhin's childhood, where the air was somehow brighter – but she was unable to fit Valentinov in here either. Then she returned with her progressively more detestable burden, and here and there in the mist of Luzhin's youth were islands: his going abroad to play chess, his buying picture postcards in Palermo, his holding a visiting card with a mysterious name on it. . . . She was forced to go back home with the puffing, triumphant Valentinov and return him to the firm of 'Veritas,' like a registered package that has been dispatched to an undiscovered address. So let him remain there, unknown but undoubtedly harmful, with his terrible sobriquet; chess father.

On the way to her parents, walking arm in arm with Luzhin along the sunny, frost-touched street, she said that within a week at the outside they should be on their way, and before this they should definitely pay a visit to the forlorn grave. Then she outlined their schedule for the week – passports, dentist, shopping, a farewell party, and – on Friday – a trip to the cemetery. It was cold in her mother's apartment, not like it had been a month ago, but nonetheless cold, and her mother kept wrapping herself in a remarkable shawl with pictures of peonies amid verdure on it, twitching her shoulders with a shiver as she did so. Her father arrived during dinner and asked for some vodka and rubbed his hands with a dry rustling sound. And for the first time Mrs. Luzhin noticed how sad and empty it was in these echoing rooms, and she noticed that her father's jollity was just as forced as her mother's smile, and that both of them were already old and very lonely and did not like poor Luzhin and were trying not to refer to the Luzhins' impending departure. She recalled all the horrible things that had been said about her fiancé, the sinister warnings, and her mother's cry: 'He'll cut you up into pieces, he'll burn you in the stove . . .' And the net result had been something very peaceful and melancholy, and all smiled with dead smiles – the falsely swaggering peasant women in the pictures, the oval mirrors, the Berlin samovar, the four people at table.

A lull, thought Luzhin that day. A lull, but with hidden preparations. It wants to take me unawares. Attention, attention, concentrate and keep watch.

All his thoughts lately had been of a chess nature but he was still holding on – he had forbidden himself to think again of the interrupted game with Turati and did not open the cherished numbers of the newspaper – and even so he was able to think only in chess images and his mind worked as if he were sitting at a chessboard. Sometimes in his dreams he swore to the doctor with the agate eyes that he was not playing chess – he had merely set out the pieces once on a pocket board and glanced at two or three games printed in the newspapers – simply for lack of something to do. And even these lapses had not been his fault, but represented a series of moves in the general combination that was skillfully repeating an enigmatic theme. It was difficult, extremely difficult, to foresee the next repetition in advance, but just a little more and everything would become clear and perhaps a defense could be found. . . .

But the next move was prepared very slowly. The lull continued for two or three days; Luzhin was photographed for his passport, and the photographer took him by the chin, turned his face slightly to one side, asked him to open his mouth wide and drilled his tooth with a tense buzzing. The buzzing ceased, the dentist looked for something on a glass shelf, found it, rubber-stamped Luzhin's passport and wrote with lightning-quick movements of the pen. 'There,' he said, handing over a document on which two rows of teeth were drawn, and two teeth bore inked-in little crosses. There was nothing suspicious in all this and the cunning lull continued until Thursday. And on Thursday, Luzhin understood everything.

Already the day before he had thought of an interesting device, a device with which he could, perhaps, foil the designs of his mysterious opponent. The device consisted in voluntarily committing some absurd unexpected act that would be outside the systematic order of life, thus confusing the sequence of moves planned by his opponent. It was an experimental defense, a defense, so to say, at random – but Luzhin, crazed with terror before the inevitability of the next move, was able to find nothing better. So on Thursay afternoon, while accompanying his wife and mother-in-law round the stores, he suddenly stopped and exclaimed: 'The dentist. I forgot the dentist.' 'Nonsense, Luzhin,' said his wife. 'Why, yesterday he said that everything was done.' 'Uncomfortable,' said Luzhin and raised a finger. 'If the filling feels uncomfortable ... It was said that if it feels uncomfortable I should come punctually at four. It feels uncomfortable. It is ten minutes to four.' 'You've got something wrong,' smiled his wife, 'but of course you must go if it hurts. And then go home. I'll come around six.' 'Have supper with us,' said her mother with an entreaty in her voice. 'No, we have guests this evening,' said Mrs. Luzhin, 'guests whom you don't like.' Luzhin waved his cane in sign of farewell and climbed into a taxi, bending his back roundly. 'A small maneuver,' he chuckled, and feeling hot, unbuttoned his overcoat. After the very very first turn he stopped the taxi, paid, and set off home at a leisurely pace. And here it suddenly seemed to him that he he had done all this once before and he was so frightened that he turned into the first available store, deciding to outsmart his opponent with a new surprise. The store turned out to be a hairdresser's, and a ladies' one at that. Luzhin, looking around him, came to a halt, and a smiling woman asked him what he wanted. 'To buy ...' said Luzhin, continuing to look around. At this point he caught sight of a wax bust and pointed to it with his cane (an unexpected

191

move, a magnificent move). 'That's not for sale,' said the woman. 'Twenty marks,' said Luzhin and took out his pocketbook. 'You want to buy that dummy?' asked the woman unbelievingly, and somebody else came up. 'Yes,' said Luzhin and began to examine the waxen face. 'Careful,' he whispered to himself, 'I may be tumbling into a trap!' The wax lady's look, her pink nostrils – this also had happened before. 'A joke,' said Luzhin and hastily left the hairdresser's. He felt disgustingly uncomfortable and quickened his step, although there was nowhere to hurry. 'Home, home,' he muttered, 'there I'll combine everything properly.' As he approached the house he noticed a large, glossy-black limousine that had stopped by the entrance. A gentleman in a bowler was asking the janitor something. The janitor, seeing Luzhin, suddenly pointed and cried: 'There he is!' The gentleman turned around.

A bit swarthier, which brought out the white of his eyes, as smartly dressed as ever, wearing an overcoat with a black fur collar and a large, white silk scarf, Valentinov strode toward Luzhin with an enchanting smile, illuminating Luzhin with this searchlight, and in the light that played on Luzhin he saw Luzhin's pale, fat face and the blinking eyelids, and at the next instant this pale face lost all expression and the hand that Valetinov pressed in both of his was completely limp. 'My dear boy,' said radiant Valentinov, 'I'm happy to see you. They told me you were in bed, ill, dear boy. But that was some kind of slipup ...' and in stressing the 'pup' Valentinov pursed his wet, red lips and tenderly narrowed his eyes. 'However, we'll postpone the compliments till later,' he said, interrupting himself, and put on his bowler with a thump. 'Let's go. It's a matter of exceptional importance and delay would be ... fatal,' he concluded, throwing open the door of the car; after which he put his arm around Luzhin's back and seemed to lift him from the ground and carry him off and plant him down, falling down next to him onto the low, soft seat. On the jump seat facing them a sharp-nosed yellow-faced little man sat sideways, with his overcoat collar turned up. As soon as Valentinov had settled and crossed his legs, he resumed his conversa-

tion with this little man, a conversation that had been interrupted at a comma and now gathered speed in time with the
accelerating automobile. Caustically and exhaustively he
continued to bawl him out, paying no attention to Luzhin,
who was sitting like a statue that had been carefully leaned
against something. He had completely frozen up and heard
remote, muffled Valentinov's rumbling as if through a heavy
curtain. For the fellow with the sharp nose it was not a rumbling, but a torrent of extremely biting and insulting words;
force, however, was on Valentinov's side and the one being
insulted merely sighed, and looked miserable, and picked at
a grease spot on his skimpy black overcoat; and now and
then, at some especially trenchant word, he would raise his
eyebrows and look at Valentinov, but the latter's flashing
gaze was too much for him and he immediately shut his
eyes tight and gently shook his head. The bawling out continued to the very end of the journey and when Valentinov
softly nudged Luzhin out of the car and got out himself
slamming the door behind him, the crushed little man continued to sit inside and the automobile immediately carried
him on, and although there was lots of room now he remained dejectedly hunched up on the little hump seat.
Luzhin meanwhile fixed his motionless and expressionless
gaze on an eggshell-white plaque with a black inscription,
VERITAS, but Valentinov immediately swept him farther and
lowered him into an armchair of the club variety that was
even more tenacious and quaggy than the car seat. At this
moment someone called Valentinov in an agitated voice,
and after pushing an open box of cigars into Luzhin's
limited field of vision he excused himself and disappeared.
His voice remained vibrating in the room and for Luzhin,
who was slowly emerging from his stupefaction, it gradually
and surreptitiously began to be transformed into a bewitching image. To the sound of this voice, to the music of the
chess boards's evil lure, Luzhin recalled, with the exquisite,
moist melancholy peculiar to recollections of love, a thousand games that he had played in the past. He did not know
which of them to choose so as to drink, sobbing, his fill of
it: everything enticed and caressed his fancy, and he flew

from one game to another, instantly running over this or that heart-rending combination. There were combinations, pure and harmonious, where thought ascended marble stairs to victory; there were tender stirrings in one corner of the board, and a passionate explosion, and the fanfare of the Queen going to its sacrificial doom. . . . Everything was wonderful, all the shades of love, all the convolutions and mysterious paths it had chosen. And this love was fatal.

The key was found. The aim of the attack was plain. By an implacable repetition of moves it was leading once more to that same passion which would destroy the dream of life. Devastation, horror, madness.

'Ah, don't!' said Luzhin loudly and tried to get up. But he was weak and stout, and the clinging armchair would not release him. And, anyway, what could he attempt now? His defense had proved erroneous. This error had been fore-seen by his opponent, and the implacable move, prepared long ago, had now been made. Luzhin groaned and cleared his throat, looking about him distractedly. In front of him was a round table bearing albums, magazines, separate sheets of paper, and photographs of frightened women and ferociously squinting men. And on one there was a white-faced man with lifeless features and big American glasses, hanging by his hands from the ledge of a skyscraper – just about to fall off into the abyss. And again came the sound of that unbearably familiar voice: in order to lose no time, Valentinov had begun talking to Luzhin while still on the other side of the door, and when the door opened he continued the sentence he had begun: '. . . shoot a new film. I wrote the script. Imagine, dear boy, a young girl, beautiful and passionate, in the compartment of an express train. At one of the stations a young man gets in. From a good family. Night descends on the train. She falls asleep and in her sleep spreads her limbs. A glorious young creature. The young man – you know that type, bursting with sap but absolutely chaste – begins literally to lose his head. In a kind of trance he hurls himself upon her.' (And Valentinov, jumping up, pretending to be breathing heavily and hurling himself.) 'He feels her perfume, her lace underwear, her glorious young

194

body . . . She wakes up, throws him off, calls out' (Valentinov pressed his fist to his mouth and protruded his eyes), 'the conductor and some passengers run in. He is tried, he is condemned to penal servitude. His aged mother comes to the young girl to beg her to save her son. The drama of the girl. The point is that from the very first moment – there, in the express – she has fallen in love with him, is seething with passion, and he, because of her – you see, that's where the conflict is – because of her he is being condemned to hard labor.' Valentinov took a deep breath and continued more calmly: 'Then comes his escape. His adventures. He changes his name and becomes a famous chess player, and it's precisely here, my dear boy, that I need your assistance. I have had a brilliant idea. I want to film a kind of real tournament, where real chess players would play with my hero. Turati has already agreed, so has Moser. Now we need Grandmaster Luzhin. . . .'

'I presume,' continued Valentinov after a slight pause, during which he looked at Luzhin's completely impassive face, 'I presume that he will agree. He is greatly indebted to me. He will receive a certain sum for his brief appearance. He will recall at the same time that when his father left him to the mercy of fate, I was generous in shelling out. I thought then that it didn't matter – that we were friends and would settle later. I continue to think so.'

At this moment the door opened with a rush and a coat-less, curly-haired gentleman shouted in German, with an anxious plea in his voice: 'Oh, please, Dr. Valentinov, just one minute!' 'Excuse me, dear boy,' said Valentinov and went to the door, but before reaching it he turned sharply around, rummaged in his billfold and threw a slip of paper on the table before Luzhin. 'Recently composed it,' he said. 'You can solve it while you are waiting. I'll be back in ten minutes.'

He disappeared. Luzhin cautiously raised his eyelids Mechanically he took the slip. A cutting from a chess magazine, the diagram of a problem. Mate in three moves. Composed by Dr. Valentinov. The problem was cold and cunning, and knowing Valentinov, Luzhin instantly found

195

the key. In this subtle problem he saw clearly all the perfidy of its author. From the dark words just spoken by Valentinov in such abundance, he understood one thing: there was no movie, the movie was just a pretext . . . a trap, a trap . . . he would be inveigled into playing chess and then the next move was clear. But this move would not be made.

Luzhin made an abrupt effort and baring his teeth painfully, got out of the armchair. He was overwhelmed by an urge to move. Playing with his cane and snapping the fingers of his free hand, he went out into the corridor and began to walk at random, ending up in a courtyard and thence making his way to the street. A streetcar with a familiar number stopped in front of him. He boarded it and sat down, but immediately got up again, and moving his shoulders exaggeratedly, clutching at the leather straps, moved to another window seat. The car was empty. He gave the conductor a mark and vigorously shook his head, refusing the change. It was impossible to sit still. He jumped up again, almost falling as the streetcar swerved, and sat closer to the door. But here too he could not keep his seat – and when suddenly the car filled up with a horde of schoolboys, a dozen old ladies and fifty fat men, Luzhin continued to move about, treading on people's feet, and finally pushing his way onto the platform. Catching sight of his house, he left the car on the move; the asphalt swept by beneath his left heel, then turned and struck him in the back, and his cane, after getting tangled in his legs, suddenly leapt out like a released spring, flew through the air and landed beside him. Two women came running toward him and helped him to rise. He began to knock the dust from his coat with his palm, donned his hat, and without looking back walked toward the house. The elevator proved to be out of order but Luzhin made no complaint. His thirst for movement was not yet slaked. He began to climb the stairs and since he lived a very long way up his ascent continued for some time; he seemed to be climbing a skyscraper. Finally he reached the last landing, took a deep breath, crunched the key in the lock and stepped into the entrance hall. His wife came from the study to meet him. She was very red and her eyes glistened. 'Luzhin,' she said, 'where have you been?' He took off his overcoat, hung it up, transferred it to another hook, and wanted to fiddle about some more; but his wife came up close to him, and moving in an arc around her he went into the study, she following. 'I want you to tell me where you've been. Why are your hands in such a state? Luzhin!' He strode around the study, cleared his throat, and walked through the entrance hall into the bedroom, where he commenced to wash his hands carefully in a large green and white bowl entwined with porcelain ivy. 'Luzhin,' cried his wife distractedly, 'I know you weren't at the dentist's. I just called him. Well, say something.' Wiping his hands on a towel he walked around the bedroom, looking woodenly in front of him just as before, and returned to the study. She grasped him by the shoulder but instead of stopping, he went up to the window, drew the curtain aside, saw the many lights gliding by in the blue abyss of the evening, made a munching motion with his lips, and moved off again. And now began a strange promenade – Luzhin walking back and forth through the three adjoining rooms, as if with a definite objective, and his wife now walking beside him, now sitting down somewhere and looking at him distractedly, and occasionally Luzhin would go into the corridor, look into the rooms whose windows faced onto the yard, and again reappear in the study. For whole minutes it seemed to her that perhaps this was one of Luzhin's ponderous little jokes, but his face bore an expression she had never seen before, an expression . . . solemn, perhaps? . . . it was difficult to define in words, but as she gazed at his face she felt a rush of inexplicable terror. And clearing his throat, and catching his breath with difficulty, he still continued to walk about the rooms with his even gait. 'For God's sake sit down, Luzhin,' she said softly, not taking her eyes off him. 'Come, let's talk about something. Luzhin! I bought you a toilet case. Oh, sit down, please! You'll die if you walk so much! Tomorrow we'll go to the cemetery. We still have a lot to do tomorrow. A toilet case made of crocodile leather. Luzhin, please!'

But he did not halt and only slowed his step from time to

time by the windows, raising his hand, thinking a moment and then going on. The table in the dining room was laid for eight people. She remembered that it was just time for the guests to arrive – it was too late to call them off – and here ... this horror. 'Luzhin,' she cried, 'people will be here any minute. I don't know what to do. ... Say something to me. Perhaps you've had an accident, perhaps you met an unpleasant acquaintance? Tell me. I beg you, I can't beg any more ...'

And suddenly Luzhin stopped. It was as if the whole world had stopped. It happened in the drawing room, by the phonograph.

'Full stop,' she said softly and burst into tears. Luzhin began to take things out of his pockets – first a fountain pen, then a crumpled handkerchief, then another handkerchief, neatly folded, when she had given him that morning; after this he took out a cigarette case with a troika on the lid (a present from his mother-in-law), then an empty, red cigarette pack and two separate cigarettes, slightly damaged; his wallet and a gold watch (a present from his father-in-law) were removed with particular care. Besides all this there turned up a large peach stone. All these objects were placed on the phonograph cabinet and he checked if there were anything he had forgotten.

'That's all, I think,' he said, and buttoned his jacket over his stomach. His wife lifted her tearstained face and stared in amazement at the little collection of things laid out by Luzhin.

He went up to his wife and made a slight bow.

She transferred her gaze to his face, vaguely hoping she would see that familiar, crooked half-smile – and so she did: Luzhin was smiling.

'The only way out,' he said. 'I have to drop out of the game.'

'Game? Are we going to play?' she asked tenderly, and thought simultaneously that she had to powder her face, the guests would be here any minute.

Luzhin held out his hand. She dropped her handkerchief into her lap and hastily gave him her fingers.

'It was nice,' said Luzhin and kissed one hand and then the other, the way she had taught him.

'What is it, Luzhin? You seem to be saying goodbye.'

'Yes, yes,' he said, feigning absentmindedness. Then he turned and went into the corridor. At that moment a bell sounded in the entrance hall – the ingenuous ring of a punctual guest. She caught her husband in the corridor and grasped his sleeve. Luzhin turned and not knowing what to say, looked at her legs. The maid ran out from the far end and since the corridor was fairly narrow, a minor, hasty collision took place: Luzhin stepped back slightly and then stepped forward, his wife also moved back and forth, unconsciously smoothing her hair, and the maid, muttering something and bending her head, tried to find a loophole where she could slip through. When she had managed it and vanished behind the portiere that divided the corridor from the entrance hall, Luzhin bowed as before and quickly opened the door by which he was standing. His wife seized the handle of the door, which he was already shutting behind him; Luzhin pushed and she grasped it tighter, laughing convulsively and endeavoring to thrust her knee into the still fairly wide opening – but at at this point Luzhin leaned with all his weight and the door closed; the bolt clicked and the key was turned twice in the lock. Meanwhile there were voices in the entrance hall, someone was puffing and someone was greeting someone else.

The first thing Luzhin did after locking the door was to turn on the light. Gleaming whitely, an enameled bathtub came into view by the left wall. On the right wall hung a pencil drawing: a cube casting a shadow. At the far end, by the window, stood a small chest. The lower part of the window was of frosted glass, sparkly-blue, opaque. In the upper part, a black rectangle of night was sheened mirror-like. Luzhin tugged at the handle of the lower frame, but something had got stuck or had caught, it did not want to open. He thought for a moment, then took hold of the back of a chair standing by the tub and looked from the sturdy white chair to the solid forest of the window. Making up his mind finally, he lifted the chair by the legs and struck, using

199

its edge as a battering ram. Something cracked, he swung again, and suddenly a black, star-shaped hole appeared in the frosted glass. There was a moment of expectant silence. Then, far below, something tinkled tenderly and disintegrated. Trying to widen the hole, he struck again, and a wedge of glass smashed at his feet. There were voices behind the door. Somebody knocked. Somebody called him loudly by his name and patronymic. Then there was silence and his wife's voice said with absolute clarity: 'Dear Luzhin, open, please.' Restraining his heavy breathing, Luzhin lowered the chair to the floor and tried to thrust himself through the window. Large wedges and corners still stuck out of the frame. Something stung his neck and he quickly drew his head in again – no, he could not get through. A fist slammed against the door. Two men's voices were quarreling and his wife's whisper wriggled through the uproar. Luzhin decided not to smash any more glass, it made too much noise. He raised his eyes. The upper window. But how to reach it ? Trying not to make a noise or break anything, he began to take things off the chest; a mirror, a bottle of some sort, a glass. He did everything slowly and thoroughly, it was useless for the rumbling behind the door to hurry him like that. Removing the doily too he attempted to climb up on the chest; it reached to his waist, and he was unable to make it at first. He felt hot and he peeled off his jacket, and here he noticed that his hands were bloodied and that there were red spots on the front of his shirt. Finally he found himself on the chest, which creaked under his weight. He quickly reached up to the upper frame, now feeling that the thumping and the voices were urging him on and that he could not help but hurry. Raising a hand he jerked at the frame and it swung open. Black sky. Thence, out of this cold darkness, came the voice of his wife, saying softly: 'Luzhin, Luzhin.' He remembered that farther to the left was the bedroom window: it was from there this whisper had emerged. Meanwhile the voices and the crashing behind the door had grown in volume, there must have been around twenty people out there – Valentinov, Turati, the old gentleman with the bunch of flowers . . . They were sniffing and grunting, and more of them came, and all together they were beating with something against the shuddering door. The rectangular night, however, was still too high. Bending one knee, Luzhin hauled the chair onto the chest. The chair was unstable, it was difficult to balance, but still Luzhin climbed up. Now he could easily lean his elbows on the lower edge of the black night. He was breathing so loudly that he deafened himself, and now the cries behind the door were far, far away, but on the other hand the voice from the bedroom window was clearer, was bursting out with piercing force. After many efforts he found himself in a strange and mortifying position: one leg hung outside, and he did not know where the other one was, while his body would in no wise be squeezed through. His shirt had torn at the shoulder, his face was wet. Clutching with one hand at something overhead, he got through the window sideways. Now both legs were hanging outside and he had only to let go of what he was holding on to – and he was saved. Before letting go he looked down. Some kind of hasty preparations were under way there: the window reflections gathered together and leveled themselves out, the whole chasm was seen to divide into dark and pale squares, and at the instant when Luzhin unclenched his hand, at the instant when icy air gushed into his mouth, he saw exactly what kind of eternity was obligingly and inexorably spread out before him.

The door was burst in, 'Aleksandr Ivanovich, Aleksandr Ivanovich,' roared several voices.

But there was no Aleksandr Ivanovich.